Praise for
Sisters of the Sari

"This compelling debut novel is a cross-cultural story of unlikely friendships, forbidden love, and families lost and found. *Sisters of the Sari* is armchair traveling at its best. It's a story I'll always remember."

—Laura Fitzgerald, national bestselling author of *Veil of Roses* and *Dreaming in English*

"A vivid portrayal of a woman's personal journey to redefine herself and make a difference in the complex, foreign culture of urban south India."

—Anjali Banerjee, author of *Haunting Jasmine*

"A captivating tale of one woman's quest to improve the life of another . . . and discovering herself along the way. A delightful debut that's a colorful portrait of southern India, painted with both touching emotion and wry humor."

—Shobhan Bantwal, author of *The Unexpected Son*

"An absorbing read . . . an often funny, genuinely touching account of life in Chennai and the uncommon bond formed by two exceptional women."

—*Booklist*

"This is one of those books that I just can't recommend enough. It's funny, touching, and has lots of drama that ties in nicely together . . . five stars."

—Book Babe

"The characters are so well-defined. . . . There is humor and tragedy all mixed together. . . . This book is a winner!" —Book Reviews R Us.com

"The book is filled with moments that touch your heart and wrench it at the same time . . . outstanding. . . . I couldn't put it down."

—Wanderlust and Lipstick

"Funny and poignant . . . the sisterhood created through all of the women in the book is one that is easily relatable, regardless of location or culture."

—Great Thoughts

Written by today's freshest new talents and selected by New American Library, NAL Accent novels touch on subjects close to a woman's heart, from friendship to family to finding our place in the world. The Conversation Guides included in each book are intended to enrich the individual reading experience, as well as encourage us to explore these topics together—because books, and life, are meant for sharing.

Visit us online at www.penguin.com.

Also by Brenda L. Baker

Sisters of the Sari

The ELUSIVE MR. McCOY

Brenda L. Baker

NAL Accent
Published by New American Library, a division of
Penguin Group (USA) Inc., 375 Hudson Street,
New York, New York 10014, USA
Penguin Group (Canada), 90 Eglinton Avenue East, Suite 700, Toronto,
Ontario M4P 2Y3, Canada (a division of Pearson Penguin Canada Inc.)
Penguin Books Ltd., 80 Strand, London WC2R 0RL, England
Penguin Ireland, 25 St. Stephen's Green, Dublin 2,
Ireland (a division of Penguin Books Ltd.)
Penguin Group (Australia), 250 Camberwell Road, Camberwell, Victoria 3124,
Australia (a division of Pearson Australia Group Pty. Ltd.)
Penguin Books India Pvt. Ltd., 11 Community Centre, Panchsheel Park,
New Delhi - 110 017, India
Penguin Group (NZ), 67 Apollo Drive, Rosedale, Auckland 0632,
New Zealand (a division of Pearson New Zealand Ltd.)
Penguin Books (South Africa) (Pty.) Ltd., 24 Sturdee Avenue,
Rosebank, Johannesburg 2196, South Africa

Penguin Books Ltd., Registered Offices:
80 Strand, London WC2R 0RL, England

First published by NAL Accent, an imprint of New American Library,
a division of Penguin Group (USA) Inc.

First Printing, July 2012
10 9 8 7 6 5 4 3 2 1

REGISTERED TRADEMARK—MARCA REGISTRADA

LIBRARY OF CONGRESS CATALOGING-IN-PUBLICATION DATA:

Baker, Brenda L.
The elusive Mr. McCoy/Brenda L. Baker.
p. cm.
ISBN 978-0-451-23689-0
I. Title.
PS3602.A5848E48 2012
813'.6—dc23 2011053172

Set in Garamond Pro
Designed by Ginger Legato

Printed in the United States of America

PUBLISHER'S NOTE

This is a work of fiction. Names, characters, places, and incidents either are the product of the author's imagination or are used fictitiously, and any resemblance to actual persons, living or dead, business establishments, events, or locales is entirely coincidental.

The publisher does not have any control over and does not assume any responsibility for author or third-party Web sites or their content.

My husband and I fell in love at first sight. . . . Maybe I should have taken a second look.

—*Crimes and Misdemeanors*

The ELUSIVE MR. McCOY

Man of Mystery

TO A CASUAL OBSERVER, THE man standing in line at the Well Roasted Bean is the visual equivalent of Teflon, so unremarkable he is almost invisible. He is shorter than some men, taller than others. His thinning hair, halfway between blond and brown, frames tidy, regular features that are too lined to be young but not lined enough to be old. Nothing about him receives a second glance from most of the other late-night latte addicts checking out the quality of fix available at the newly opened coffee shop.

But Jason Cheddick is not a casual observer, and from where he's sitting, on an uncomfortable wrought-iron chair at a tiny faux-marble table, this man is easily the most interesting person in the room. Jason is intrigued, not by the man's appearance but by his behavior. The man's alert brown eyes study the other customers with an intensity beyond casual curiosity. He shifts his stance slightly to mimic the posture of the person he is looking at and avoids looking directly at Jason in a way that indicates he knows he's being studied in return. As a former police officer,

Jason tends to view unusual behavior with suspicion. He sips his espresso and wonders if the man is a pickpocket looking for an easy score, or maybe a con artist scoping out a gullible mark.

The customer in front of the interesting man, a stocky East Indian woman with steely hair pulled into a severe bun, finishes interrogating the barista about every pastry in the glass case by the cash register and decides on a chocolate biscotti. As she picks up her snack and moves with heavy dignity to collect her drink at the end of the bar, the man steps up and places his hands on the counter, palms down. The barista gives him the same bland half smile she gave Jason a few minutes earlier. Most men would be unable to resist the attraction of the spiderweb tattoo adorning the exposed upper slope of the barista's impressive breasts, but this one keeps his eyes fixed on her face. He grins at her and says something Jason can't hear. Her polite mask fractures into animated amusement. She giggles and reaches out to touch the man's hand in an unconscious gesture of attraction.

Annoyed by this rapid conquest of a woman who hadn't given him a second glance, Jason unfolds his newspaper but is unable to concentrate on the front-page article about a high-profile divorce trial.

Jason is far from vain, but if he were, he'd have every right to be. By any standard, he is a good-looking man, having inherited the best genetic material from both sides of his family. He has the black curls and intensely blue eyes of his Welsh mother, along with the arrow-straight nose, angular cheekbones and blunt jaw of his father's Slavic forebears. Only his eyelashes are a complete mystery. No one else in the family has anything approaching their length and thickness. He has always thought his looks gave him an advantage when it came to women, but even his best opening lines have never produced a response as warm as the barista's. He wonders what the man said to make her laugh.

The chair across from Jason's scrapes across the floor. He glances up to see the interesting man place a coffee mug on the table.

"So, what did you decide?" the man asks, as though they are in the middle of a conversation.

Shocked by this bizarre approach, Jason replies without thinking. "About what?"

"About me. You've been watching me." The man slings his backpack off his shoulder and slides it under the table before sitting down. "I've been watching you too. I think you're a cop."

"Why do you think that?"

"The way you look at people. Like you're searching for clues. Are you a cop?"

"Not anymore."

"But you still have a professional opinion, right?"

Despite his annoyance, Jason finds himself responding to the man's friendly insistence. "The way you got the barista to laugh? Made me think con artist."

A lopsided grin punches a deep dimple into the reddish stubble on the man's left cheek. "Pretty close."

Intrigued, Jason folds his paper and drops it on the table. "How close is pretty close?"

"You mean is it legal?" The man picks up his coffee. "I'd be pretty stupid to approach a cop—"

The mug drops, splashing coffee in a wide arc as it hits the tabletop, sending a scalding Americano waterfall over the edge and into Jason's lap. He leaps up to pull his soaked slacks away from his thighs. His chair clatters to the floor. Conversation in the coffee shop dies as customers look over to see what caused the commotion.

The man's eyes squeeze shut. His lips press together. Then his face relaxes. Slowly, as though he's falling asleep, his body curls forward until his forehead comes to rest on the coffee-soaked newspaper with a wet thud.

Jason strides around the table. "You okay, buddy?" No response. He pulls the unconscious man to a sitting position and gently lowers him to the floor. "Hey!" he calls out to the barista. "Call 911. Tell them there's a medical emergency."

She stares back, her scarlet mouth a perfect O, then reaches beneath the counter for the phone.

The woman who ordered the biscotti drops to her knees on the opposite side of the unconscious man. "I'm a doctor. What happened?" She presses blunt fingertips on the carotid artery.

Jason squats back on his heels. "Nothing. He just passed out."

The doctor's lips move silently as she looks at her watch. She places a thumb on one eyelid and pulls it open. "Do you have a flashlight?"

"Not on me."

She checks the other eye. "Any strange behavior? Blinking? Choking? Shaking?"

"His face squeezed up for a second. Like he had a headache."

"Show me."

Feeling a little silly, Jason folds in his lips and scrunches up his eyes.

The doctor pulls up the man's gray sweatshirt, exposing well-defined abdominal muscles. Jason is suddenly aware of his belt buckle poking into the upholstery of his own, less-impressive torso. She leans down, pressing her ear to the hard curve of the deltoids. "No medical bracelet. Does he have a bag?"

"There. Under the table."

"Check it. See if he's carrying medication."

Jason pulls the black canvas backpack out from under the table. In the main compartment he finds three comic books, a bag of trail mix, and a bottle of water. A zippered pocket contains a cell phone, an electronic key for a Lexus, and a slim leather wallet. "No meds."

"Check his pockets. There might be an inhaler or pill bottle."

From the right front pocket of the well-worn jeans, Jason pulls a handful of change. The left pocket produces a rabbit's foot key chain. He slides his hands under the man's body to feel the back pockets and pulls out a shabby rawhide wallet. Keeping hold of it as he stands, Jason informs the doctor there is no medication.

"His pupils seem a bit sluggish, but there's no obvious trauma." She pulls the sweatshirt back down over the muscular chest. "He's breathing properly. Heartbeat is normal. No fever or congestion or abnormal posturing. I can't check his blood pressure, but he's in good shape, doesn't have any signs of hypertension." She extends her hand toward Jason like an empress giving an audience. "Help me up." As he complies, she makes a sound, very ladylike but definitely a grunt.

The barista comes over to report. "I called 911. There's a fire department over on Fifteenth. It shouldn't be long." She looks down at the unconscious man with wistful eyes. "I hope he's okay. He's a really nice man."

"You know him?" Jason asks.

"No, he just seemed nice when we spoke. I'd better get back to work."

Jason watches the sway of her red miniskirt as she walks back behind the counter. He considers asking her what the man said to make her laugh, then reconsiders when he remembers the soggy condition of his pants.

The paramedics from the fire department arrive. The Indian

woman introduces herself as Dr. Chandra and fills them in on the results of her examination while Jason looks through the two wallets for the man's identification.

The Oregon driver's license in the black leather wallet belongs to Eric McCoy, forty-two years old. He lives in an upscale apartment building in Portland. The rawhide wallet contains a Washington driver's license for David McCoy, also forty-two, a resident of Brockville. The ID photos seem to belong to two different people. Eric McCoy's hair is slicked back and looks dark. His eyes are narrowed, and his mouth is compressed into a straight line. David McCoy looks into the DMV camera wide-eyed from under a receding tangle of sun-bleached hair. A short beard obscures his jawline and makes his lips appear full. The picture is overexposed, hiding the shape of the nose. The birth dates on both driver's licenses are the same, but the signatures, like the photos, are completely different.

The ambulance and police cruiser arrive at the same time, turning the plate-glass window of the coffee shop into a blue, red, and orange light show. While the ambulance team takes over from the paramedics, Jude Connelly, the uniformed officer responding to the call, approaches Jason. He knows better than to hug his sister while she's in uniform, so he limits himself to a smile and a brotherly, "Hey, squirt."

Jude pulls her notebook out of her back pocket. "That's Officer Squirt to you, civilian. Were you here when this happened?"

"He was sitting at my table. We were talking when he collapsed." Jason describes the man's collapse in the concise phrases he once used to make his own notes. He hands her the two wallets.

She checks the driver's licenses. "The signatures aren't similar. Twins?"

"He was behaving strangely when he came in. Tense, paying

too much attention to the other customers. It's a long shot, but he could be a pickpocket who just happened to lift a wallet from a guy with the same birth date and last name."

One of the paramedics approaches. "Dr. Chandra says you have the guy's ID."

Jude passes the wallets to the paramedic. He glances at the photos on the driver's licenses, then at the unconscious man. "Jeez. Bad pictures. Which one is his?"

"The Oregon license looks more like him, but he was carrying the Washington license in his pocket," Jason offers.

Jude takes the wallets back from the paramedic. "I'd better check them both out before contacting anyone."

"We'll list him as a John Doe for now. We're taking him to West General. When you get a name, you can contact the ER there." The paramedic returns to help his partner pack up their equipment.

"Can you do me a favor?" Jude asks Jason. "Before I try to contact anyone, I want to take statements from the other customers, see if anyone recognized him, or if anyone named McCoy is missing a wallet. Can you ride along in the ambulance, just in case he wakes up and can tell you who he is? Unless you're on a case."

"Nothing that can't wait. But how will I get back to my car?"

"I'll give you a lift back here when I'm done."

Jason reaches into the pocket of his soggy slacks for his house keys. "Can you swing by my place on the way? Pick me up a pair of dry pants?"

The man does not regain consciousness in the ambulance. At the hospital, a hard-eyed nurse who reminds Jason of his army drill sergeant takes down all the information he can give her, then asks him to take a seat in the waiting room while the doctors examine the unconscious man. Jason evaluates the two available chairs and sits beside a wild-haired elderly woman with her hand wrapped in a tea towel. He spends the next fifteen minutes listening to a graphic description of her husband's struggle with prostate cancer and wishing he'd chosen the chair next to the hygienically challenged man with a bad cough.

When the nurse calls his name, he gets up gratefully. She buzzes him into the emergency room, where a harried young man who doesn't look much older than Jason's sixteen-year-old son introduces himself as Dr. Bennett and asks, "Are you a relative?"

"Just a bystander. There's a complication with finding next of kin. The police asked me to stay with him until it's sorted out, in case he wakes up."

"He's not waking up anytime soon. He has a cerebral aneurysm. We've sent him up to surgery to stop the bleeding into his brain."

Jason follows the doctor's directions to the surgical wing, where he checks in at the nurses' station, then takes a seat in a small alcove behind the elevators and calls Jude. He tells her about the aneurysm and asks how much longer she's going to be.

"I just left your place," she says. "I'll be there in ten minutes. We couldn't establish an identity, so I had to call both families. They're on their way in now. I'm going to have to stick around until he's identified. Sorry."

A pretty nurse in a flowered smock walks by the alcove. Her eyes focus briefly on Jason's crotch as she passes. He grabs a tattered copy of *National Geographic* off the low table in front of his chair and flips it open to cover his lap. "Just bring me my pants."

Not My Husband

AT ABOUT THE SAME TIME the unconscious man is being wheeled into surgery at West General Hospital, Kendra McCoy is behind the bar in the Shalimar ballroom packing up unopened bottles of white zinfandel to return to the supplier.

Most event planners believe their work is done when the last guest walks out the door. Kendra is not one of them. This is why her company, Perfectissimo, continues to grow while other, less-dedicated event planners are being forced out of business by a recession economy. She knows the real work, the work that gets repeat customers and word-of-mouth references, starts after the guests leave. So an hour after the last guest has carried her bag of designer goodies from the ballroom, Kendra is still on the job.

The flower arrangements have been sent to Golden Spires Retirement Home accompanied by a graceful note from the organizers of the banquet, because it never hurts to give the client credit. The catering team has packed up the leftover food and delivered it to the Harbor Light Shelter, garnering more favorable

PR for the organizers. Kendra has collected all the personal items left behind by the guests. Tomorrow she will return each item to its owner in a tasteful gray satin bag with her company name and logo discreetly embroidered on the outside. Now she's down to the slog jobs. Laundry count, breakage reports, insurance documentation, liquor inventory—everything gets her personal attention. She's been at the Shalimar since before noon and doesn't expect to be home until after midnight. She doesn't mind getting home late, though, because Eric is on assignment again. He'd planned to attend this dinner with her, and she's disappointed he couldn't make it, but she accepts the frequent and usually unscheduled travel required by her husband's new contract.

As Kendra places the last of the bottles into the box, Charise Pelter, the woman who hired Kendra to organize the event, comes into the ballroom. Charise has taken off her shoes and holds up the hem of her gown to avoid tripping over it. Watching her client approach, Kendra reflects that a woman with those hip measurements should avoid satin in any color, but especially turquoise.

"Kendra!" Charise is one of those people who speaks almost exclusively in exclamation points. "We've just finished adding up the proceeds from the silent auction. You'll never guess how much we made on your free event planning voucher!"

Kendra doesn't really care how much they made. She donated the voucher to get her company name in the auction catalog. While she hopes it benefited the National Breast Cancer Foundation, the important thing for her is that nearly every charity matron in Portland now has firsthand experience of a Perfectissimo event. Charise is not aware of this, of course, and nothing in Kendra's expression indicates anything other than curiosity and hopeful anticipation. "How much?" she asks.

"Four thousand dollars!"

Kendra is genuinely impressed. "Fantastic."

"People are so generous!"

"Well, it's a worthy cause."

"And you did such a good job for us!" Charise gushes. "Everyone just loved the all-pink menu you put together for the dinner!"

"So glad they enjoyed it." Having worked for Charise before, Kendra knows the older woman is perfectly capable of exclaiming all night. Fortunately, Callum is standing in the service doorway that leads to the kitchen, thick arms folded across his chest and bushy eyebrows lowered ominously. "I wish I could stay and talk, Charise, but the caterer is waiting to go home and I have to check in with him before he leaves. I'll be sure to tell him how successful his efforts were."

Charise wiggles chubby fingers at Callum, then pats Kendra's arm maternally. "Well, don't stay too late, dear," she says before waddling toward the ballroom's double doors.

Kendra allows her smile to drop, then pins it back on when Charise turns around. "Oh yes, and I wanted to tell you. I have a fantastic idea for next year's dinner!"

"What's that, Charise?"

"Ethnic costumes! I got the idea from your Chinese dress. It's so nice to see people who honor their heritage."

Kendra is no more Chinese than Charise is. Her features are inherited from her Vietnamese war-bride mother. Usually she resents this kind of tactless ethnic assumption, but tonight she is more disturbed by having her five-thousand-dollar Mandy Monk original mistaken for a cheap Hong Kong cheongsam. She punches up her smile and focuses on landing the job. "What a wonderful idea," she says, as she walks backward toward the service door.

In the kitchen, Callum is sliding empty trays into the slotted boxes he uses to transport hors d'oeuvres. He has removed the hairnet he wears when cooking and his black curls, damp with sweat, cluster around his ears. "We have a level two incident." He turns to point at an inverted glass on the counter.

Kendra started Perfectissimo the same year Callum opened his catering business, Moveable Feast. They work together frequently and have developed a classification system for the unforeseen glitches that inevitably crop up at every event. Level one covers things like drunk clowns and too few desserts. Level five is reserved for situations like citywide power outages.

"Where did you find it?" she asks as she walks to the counter and bends over to examine the occupant of the glass. The cockroach waves its feelers in a parody of greeting.

"It was just strolling across the countertop."

"Any other sightings?" She doesn't bother to ask if the insect could have come in with Callum's food. She's seen his working kitchen, a stainless-steel temple dedicated to the culinary arts, ruthlessly scrubbed down after every job.

"Nope, just Archie here."

Kendra begins opening cupboards, checking for other signs of infestation. "The food was a hit tonight. I think you're going to get a lot of new clients out of this one."

"Especially since our little friend didn't make an appearance in someone's gazpacho. So Eric couldn't make it tonight?"

"Something came up. He flew out this morning."

"He was only back for a few days. I don't know how you do it. I'd go crazy if Zanne was gone all the time."

Finding nothing in the cupboards, Kendra leans against the counter where Callum is working. "Sometimes I think I will. Eric hates being apart as much as I do, but he understands I can't just drop everything I've built here and start over again."

Callum slides the last tray into its slot and snaps the carrier closed. "You don't worry when he's away?"

"He's a consultant. The biggest danger he faces is a paper cut."

"I was thinking more about other women."

Kendra laughs. "That's the last thing I worry about. Oh, I've seen him looking. Hell, I look too. But neither of us would do more than look." She pushes herself upright. "I'd better get back to work."

"Since you're alone, come over tomorrow. You can keep Zanne company while I test recipes."

"Thanks, but I can't. My mother finally agreed to take tomorrow off and buy a dress. I really have to go with her. Otherwise I'll be sitting next to a paisley basketball at the wedding."

"Let her wear what she wants. Your brother's not going to care."

"I care. I'm the *only* one in my family who cares."

Back in the ballroom, the cleaning team has finished vacuuming and left an invoice on the bar. Kendra slides it into her briefcase and pulls out her new smartphone. As she's making a note to call the Shalimar's management and complain about the cockroach, the phone rings. The caller ID display reads, UNKNOWN. She considers ignoring the call, then answers on the off chance it's Eric.

"Hello?"

"This is Officer Connelly. I'm with the Portland police. Who am I speaking to?"

"Kendra McCoy. How can I help you, Officer?"

"Are you related to Eric McCoy?"

Her stomach tightens. Despite her assurances to Callum that Eric is never in danger, she has secretly worried about getting a call like this. "He's my husband. Has something happened to him?"

"We don't know, Mrs. McCoy. A man collapsed in a coffee shop this evening. We're looking for next of kin. He was carrying two wallets. One of them was your husband's."

The tension in Kendra's body releases so quickly she is forced to lean against the bar for support. "It can't be my husband."

"How do you know that, Mrs. McCoy?"

"Because he's not even in the country."

"Where is he?"

"I don't know exactly. My husband is a freelance political analyst. He specializes in Middle Eastern politics. His work is usually classified. When he's on assignment he can't always tell me where he's going, but he always tells me when he's going abroad so I won't call him in the middle of the night."

There's a long pause on the other end of the line. "Would you be willing to come to West General Hospital and verify this man is not your husband?"

"Yes, of course." She glances around the room and estimates she has another half hour's work at the Shalimar. She considers going to the hospital, then returning to finish up, but there's no way of knowing how long she will have to wait, so she tells the police officer, "I can be there in an hour."

As she goes back to work, she wonders about Eric's wallet turning up in Portland and decides the man in the hospital is most likely a thief who stole Eric's wallet at the airport.

Not My Husband Either

AS KENDRA RETURNS TO HER CHORES AT THE SHALIMAR, Lesley McCoy sits on the fuzzy pink toilet seat cover in her mother's upstairs bathroom reading the instructions for a pregnancy test.

When she bought the test this afternoon, Lesley intended to wait until Dave came home before taking it, to share this once-in-a-lifetime moment with the man she loves. But she doesn't have any practice at delaying gratification, and Dave will be in Idaho for another two weeks. Rationalizing that it would be cruel to raise his hopes and then get negative results, she has decided to take the test tonight. She justifies this change of plan by promising herself Dave will be the first person to know.

Ignoring the recommendation to collect morning urine, since the instructions clearly state a random sample works just as well, she looks around the bathroom for something to pee in. At the back of a drawer under the sink, behind a clutter of hotel toiletry bottles, she finds the drinking glass that once held her grandmother's false teeth. As she pulls down her pajama bottoms, she hears Aunt Cass coming up the stairs. She knows it's her aunt and not her mother because Cassandra Wilcox is a woman who stomps her way seismically through life, as though made of something more solid than normal flesh and blood. Lesley imagines she can feel the house tremble as her aunt arrives at the top of the stairs.

"Lesley, honey, are you awake?"

"I'm in the bathroom. I'll be out in a sec." Lesley pulls up her pajama bottoms and looks for a place to hide the unused test. The medicine chest is too obvious, and this may be one of the nights her mother takes a sleeping pill. The drawers in the vanity are likely to be opened as well. She pushes the test box deep into the basket of dusty plastic flowers adorning the lid of the toilet tank before opening the bathroom door. "What's up, Aunt Cass?"

"Can you come downstairs, honey? We just got a phone call. You and Trixie should hear this together."

"Sure." Lesley follows her aunt down the stairs. "Is it bad news?"

"It's not good." Cassandra leads the way into the blue and white cottage-style kitchen where Lesley's mother, Beatrice, is sitting at the table. The sisters have been playing gin rummy. Their cards lie facedown on the flowered plastic tablecloth beside half-empty coffee mugs. A cigarette smolders in the ashtray by Cassandra's cards. Her aunt's smoking never bothered Lesley before, but now she might be breathing for two.

"Someone's died, haven't they?" Never phlegmatic at the best of times, Beatrice has become something of a disaster junkie since her husband's death.

"Calm down, Trixie. No one's died yet." Cassandra walks around the table and points at an empty chair across from hers. "Sit down, honey," she says to Lesley.

"But they're going to, aren't they?" Beatrice insists.

Picking up her cigarette, Cassandra takes her seat. "I don't know. I just got a call from the Portland police. Dave's wallet turned up in the pocket of a man who collapsed in a Portland coffee shop."

"Oh, dear God," Beatrice whispers, pressing a plump left hand to her chest.

"But that doesn't make any sense, Aunt Cass." Lesley props her elbows on the table and leans on them. "Dave's not in Portland. He's in Idaho. How could his wallet be in Portland?"

"Maybe because that's where he is." Cassandra stubs out her cigarette.

"No, he can't be." Lesley shakes her head emphatically enough to dislodge a few strands of pale hair from behind her ears. "It must be someone else's wallet."

Cassandra reaches across the table and places her hand on Lesley's arm. "It's Dave's, honey. He called you here last night. They got this number by tracing the last call on his calling card."

A tendril of doubt invades Lesley's certainty. Could the sick man in Portland really be Dave? She tests the idea and decides it makes no sense. Dave hates the city. He's never gone there before. He doesn't even know anyone there. And even if he had a reason to be in the city, he'd have told her on the phone last night. She pulls away from her aunt's hand and folds her arms across her chest. "It might be Dave's calling card. It might even be his wallet. But it can't be Dave."

"Well, you could be right, honey," Cassandra says. "The man is in surgery at West General Hospital. The police have asked for someone to come to the hospital and help identify him."

"I can't drive at night," Beatrice says, disqualifying herself immediately. "I'm night-blind."

Cassandra ignores her sister. "You don't have to go, honey. I can go."

Lesley, although she is sure the poor man in the hospital cannot be her husband, feels the need to see for herself. In the end, they all go, Lesley because she must, Cassandra because she is worried about Lesley, and Beatrice because she hates being left alone in the house at night. It's a one-hour trip from Brockville to Portland. Cassandra drives. Beatrice sniffles in the seat beside her. Lesley sits in the back, unsuccessfully attempting to come up with an explanation for why Dave's calling card would be in Portland without Dave. Could he have given it to someone? It would be just like him. He's always helping people out.

By the time they pull onto the freeway, Cassandra has lost patience with her sister's lachrymose performance. "For God's sake, Trixie. If it is Dave, you should save some tears for when we get there."

"It's not Dave," Lesley insists from the backseat.

Beatrice pulls a fresh tissue out of the box on her lap and blows her nose. "You're right, Cass. I'll have to cry for both of us, after all."

"What's that supposed to mean?"

"Well, it's not like *you're* going to cry for him. You never liked him. You're probably delighted this happened."

"Oh, come on. Just because I don't like someone doesn't mean I want to see him suffer. Besides, I never said I didn't like him. I said there's something strange about him."

"How can you say that? He's such a nice man. Exactly like Lars was." The memory of her dead husband causes Beatrice to pull another tissue from the box. "You never liked *him* either."

Cassandra grips the wheel tighter and says nothing. The rest of the drive to Portland takes place in silence, punctuated by an occasional sniffle from the passenger seat.

Inside the hospital, a clerk at the information desk directs the three women to the surgery wing on the third floor. As they get off the elevator, they are met by a policewoman who introduces herself as Officer Connelly. She takes their names, then destroys Lesley's theory that Dave gave away his calling card by showing them Dave's wallet and asking them to identify it. Lesley is too shaken to speak, so it's Cassandra who replies, "Yes. That's Dave's."

After asking a few more questions about Dave, Officer Connelly takes them to a small waiting room with orange plastic chairs lining two walls and double glass doors on the far side leading into a brightly lit corridor. When they enter the room, a tiny woman wearing a long royal blue dress with a high collar and a cascade of iridescent beading down one side looks up from studying the pointed toes of her shoes. With her creamy skin and China-doll hairstyle, she looks like the poster for Singapore Airlines in the window of the Far Away Travel Agency on Main Street in Brockville.

The four women exchange sympathetic half smiles appropriate for a hospital waiting room; then the woman in the evening dress asks Officer Connelly, "How much longer is this going to take?"

"The man is still in surgery," the policewoman replies. "When he comes out, we're going to ask for your help to identify him."

Impatience sharpens the woman's voice. "Obviously, this man is a thief who stole my husband's wallet. I can't possibly identify him."

"Oh!" Lesley exclaims with relief. "That's it! Dave's wallet was stolen!"

Our Husband

WHEN JUDE RETURNS TO THE alcove beside the elevators, she sits beside Jason and yawns.

Twelve years separate Jason from his sister. For most of his life, she was little more than a ponytailed irritation at the edge of his awareness. It wasn't until she came back from the army and enrolled in the police academy that he realized what an unusual woman his baby sister had grown up to be. Tough and taciturn, needing no protection from her big brother or anyone else, she's moving up fast in the force. He's incredibly proud of her and envious of how easily she's making the milestones he gave up trying to achieve. A delayed case of sibling rivalry causes him to ruffle the short dark curls so like his own. "Long shift?"

"Double shift. Shorthanded tonight. That's why I'm riding alone."

"Nathan out sick?" Jason asks, referring to her partner.

"His wife went into labor this afternoon. Listen, I need another favor."

Her uniform looks as crisp and tidy as when she started her shift nine hours before, but the skin beneath her eyes is smudged by fatigue. Remembering what it was like to pull a double shift, Jason asks what she wants him to do.

"Four women showed up for the identification. I can't keep eyes on all of them, and you're better at reading people than I am. I want you around when we take them in to see him."

"No problem. I've got to wait for you anyway." He plucks at the denim of his jeans. "And I'm presentable now. What have you got so far?"

Jude leans to the side, pulls her notebook from her hip pocket, and flips it open. "We have Mrs. Kendra McCoy, thirty-nine, married to Eric McCoy five years and has known him for eight. She's positive he has no scars, tattoos, moles, or birthmarks. She has no idea where her husband is, but she's certain he is out of the country on some sort of government assignment.

"Then there's Mrs. Lesley McCoy, twenty-one, met David McCoy eighteen months ago and married him a couple of months ago. She's also sure her husband has no distinguishing marks and just as certain he's in Idaho, leading a wilderness adventure group.

"We also have Lesley McCoy's mother, Mrs. Beatrice Sorrenson, and her aunt, *Mizz*"—Jude gives the honorific an extended buzz—"Cassandra Wilcox. Whatever you do, don't call her Miss."

"What about other relatives?" Jason asks.

"That's another thing they agree on. He's an orphan."

"Any idea which one is the wife?"

Jude closes her notebook. "My guess is Lesley."

"How come?"

"Remember Emmeline?"

"Your Barbie doll?"

"Now imagine a real woman who looks like that."

A woman wearing blue scrubs and a polka-dot plastic shower cap pushes through one side of the double doors at the end of the hallway. Surgical magnifying glasses hang from a cord around her neck. A line of reddish brown drops curves in a graceful arc across the front of her tunic. Jude and Jason stand as she approaches.

She stops in front of them. "Are you Officer Connelly?" she asks Jude.

"Yes. And this is Jason Cheddick."

"I'm Dr. Strachan. I performed the surgery." The doctor's small, hard hand clasps Jason's briefly. "We managed to fix the ruptured artery, but the patient has not regained consciousness yet." In a gesture that radiates exhaustion, she closes her eyes and reaches up to massage the muscles at the side of her neck. The action raises the short sleeve of her top to expose an elaborate Celtic-design tattoo circling her bicep. "I'm told there's some confusion about his identity and you want to be there when I notify the family."

"Families," Jude replies. "He had two sets of ID under two different names. We contacted wives for both."

"Well, this should be interesting." The doctor pulls at the stained fabric of her tunic. "I'm going to change first. No point in making it any harder for his relatives than it already is. I'll be back in a couple of minutes."

She disappears through the double doors and returns a few minutes later in fresh scrubs and minus the shower cap. A thick swath of gray hair at each temple adds gravitas to delicate features and soft eyes fringed with plush lashes. She has what Jason thinks of as a marrying face, wholesome and quietly pretty.

She takes them back through the double doors, past two dark operating theaters and a third one where nurses are collecting blood-soaked swabs into medical waste bins and wiping down the steel surface of the operating table. Beyond the theaters, a row of glass-fronted recovery rooms lines the hallway. Dr. Strachan stops at the second one from the end, where the man lies in a steel-railed hospital bed. Jason expects bandages, but sees only wires attached to the man's head and chest. The wires connect to machines at the side of the bed. Unlike medical machines in movies, these are silent and the screens are small, dim rectangles.

The doctor sticks her head into the doorway. "We're bringing in next of kin now," she says to the nurse. "Elevate the bed, please."

The nurse nods and presses a button on the bed frame, raising the unconscious man to semi-sitting position.

Dr. Strachan leads them around a corner into another hallway, much shorter than the last, then through glass doors into a small waiting room. A tall young woman with lush curves and a waterfall of platinum hair stands when they enter.

Jason stops short halfway through the door, overcome by a sensation as real as walking into a wall. He knows his body is responding to an accident of contour and coloring, to her youth and health, but that doesn't make it any easier to pull his attention away from those compelling curves and up to her face, which, in terms of recovering his equilibrium, doesn't help much. This must be Lesley McCoy.

A wave of movement distracts him as the other three women in the room stand. He manages to rip his attention away from Lesley and focus it on a petite woman with catlike features who must be the other wife, Kendra McCoy. The tall, gaunt woman with the careless gray hair and belligerent jaw is obviously *Mizz* Cassandra Wilcox, which means the equally tall, plump woman with the improbably red curls is the mother, Beatrice Sorrenson.

Jude introduces Dr. Strachan, who stammers out, "We—

We—" She blushes, blinks twice and tries again. "We managed to . . ." She stops once more, her eyes fixed on Cassandra's face.

"He died," Cassandra says.

"Oh no! No. He's alive." Dr. Strachan catches her lower lip under her overbite, then recovers herself. "We've repaired the aneurysm and drained the excess fluid from his brain. He's still unconscious, and we can't establish if there is any neural damage until he wakes up. But we got him into surgery within an hour, and there's every reason to believe he'll make a full recovery."

Beatrice clasps her hands in front of her chest. "Oh, that poor man."

Kendra and Lesley look at the doctor with interest, but no sign of distress.

Jude takes over. "We still need to identify him. He's ready to be viewed now."

"I can do that." Cassandra touches Lesley's shoulder. "You stay out here, honey."

Lesley steps abruptly away from her aunt. "It's okay, Aunt Cass. I'd rather do it myself."

"The patient is just down the hall. This way, please." Dr. Strachan pulls open one of the glass doors.

Lesley and Kendra walk through the door first. The doctor steps after them. Cassandra hesitates for a moment, then follows the doctor. "Wait for me!" Beatrice squeaks and hurries past Jason.

"What happened there?" Jason whispers to Jude as they bring up the tail end of the procession. "Why are the wives so calm?"

"They both think he's a thief who stole their husbands' wallets," she whispers back. "The aunt doesn't seem so sure and the mother is just a drama queen. Don't know what's wrong with the doctor."

Dr. Strachan leads them to the recovery bay, where they cluster in front of the glass wall. Kendra and Lesley stand closest to the glass, Cassandra takes a position behind her niece's shoulder, and Beatrice hovers beside her sister.

During his fifteen years on the force, Jason delivered his share of bad news. He saw people respond to tragedy in all kinds of ways. Most of them just stared for a few frozen seconds while the mind learned to think the unthinkable. After that, anything could happen. Jason was shoved, slapped and even punched. He heard every kind of sound, from the lowest of groans to the most piercing of shrieks. He saw people faint, or literally rip out handfuls of hair. He'd been vomited on more times than he cared to remember. Some people accused him of lying; others simply nodded in acknowledgment, as though they'd expected this all along.

As he looks at the four women standing in front of the observation window, Jason pegs Beatrice as a screamer, Cassandra as a nodder, Lesley as a fainter and Kendra as a moaner. He is wrong on three counts.

Beatrice moans and falls back against Jude, who staggers under the weight of the much larger woman.

Cassandra nods and exclaims, "Hah!" in a satisfied tone.

Lesley spins around to land a creditable right hook on her aunt's left eye. "Are you happy now, Aunt Cass?" she shrieks. "My husband could be dying!" She flexes her elbow as though to take another swing at her aunt.

Jason grabs her arm and raises his free hand to ward off her left fist as she twists to aim it at his face. Dr. Strachan pries Cassandra's hand away to examine the injured eye. Jude continues to prop up Beatrice, who is now whimpering, "No, no, not Dave."

In all the confusion, no one pays any attention to Kendra. They don't see her head turn as she looks from the unconscious man to Lesley and back. They don't see her eyes narrow and her chin jut forward. So they are taken by surprise when she says, quite crisply, "Bullshit."

Lesley stops struggling in Jason's grip. Jude gives up and allows Beatrice to slide down to the floor. Cassandra pushes Dr. Strachan's hands away. They all focus on Kendra as she bends over and deposits a surrealistically pink puddle of vomit on the white tiles of the hallway. She straightens up and wipes her chin with the heel of her palm. "He can't be your husband. He's mine."

What's That Smell?

KENDRA WAKES UP BEHIND THE wheel of her minivan, still strapped in by the seat belt. She squints through the windshield at the letters PH2 painted in navy blue on the gray cement blocks of the wall in front of her. It takes her a few moments to work out she must be in the underground parking garage of her apartment building. She doesn't remember driving home.

As she fumbles for the seat belt release, she plays a movie of the previous evening in her head, trying to understand why she fell asleep in the car. . . . *Cancer Foundation fund-raiser . . . Callum's amazing salmon in aspic . . . How much did I drink last night?* She climbs out of the car. *No, it was white zinfandel. I couldn't have had more than half a glass of that crap. Then cleanup . . . that disgusting cockroach.* Sliding open the side door of the van, she sees five silvery satin bags. *Got to drop those off today.* She picks up her briefcase, closes the door and walks to the elevator. *Drove to the hospital . . . those Amazons in the waiting room . . . the policewoman . . . that cute quiet guy . . . and that bizarre doctor—what was she on?*

Kendra's world tilts. In strobelike flashes she relives the events in the hospital. Eric's pale face on the hospital bed . . . blond hair flying outward as the woman spins . . . Eric's pale face . . . the woman's mouth twisted with rage . . . Eric's face . . . blue eyes, wide with disbelief. The visions retreat as suddenly as they attacked. She finds herself standing in front of the elevator in a bubble of numb calm. Extending her arm to press the call button, she feels like a puppeteer pulling her own strings. She pulls the strings again to get on the elevator and press the button marked PH, and again to step off the elevator into the hallway, where her mother is leaning against the wall beside the apartment door, chunky arms folded across the front of her flowered blouse, fresh perm bristling like a steel-wool helmet.

Peony McAllister pushes herself off the wall. "I thought you wanted to get an early start? I've been waiting here since—" She stops abruptly when she sees her daughter's face. "What happened?"

Kendra manipulates the strings once more to open the apartment door, enter the foyer and drop her keys in the cloisonné bowl on the marble hall table. "Eric's been cheating on me."

Peony is a woman blessed with remarkable intelligence and practicality, the kind of woman who deals with problems by fixing them. She does not waste time uttering exclamations of sympathy or enfolding her strangely calm daughter in a mother's comforting embrace. "Come." She takes Kendra's hand and leads her to the mushroom suede sofa in the living room. "Sit. Tell me why you think he's having an affair."

"Because I met the other woman." Kendra releases the strings and collapses onto the sofa.

"Yesterday?"

"Last night."

"What makes you think she and Eric are having an affair?"

"Because she thinks so. Actually, she thinks he married her. She has an engagement ring, and a wedding ring, and her mother and her aunt think she's married to him. He must have arranged some kind of fake wedding ceremony. It seems so . . . elaborate." She stops and sniffs twice. "What's that smell?"

"That fishy smell? It's your dress."

Kendra looks down at the dried vomit staining the front of her dress. Flecks of half-digested salmon augment the iridescent beading around the hem and cling to the ivory satin toes of her shoes. "I remember. I threw up. I'd better take this to the cleaner's before the stain sets." She starts to rise.

Peony grabs her daughter's hands. "You can do that later. Right now you have to tell me what happened last night. From the beginning."

Obediently, Kendra recounts the events of her evening in the manner of a child reporting on her day in school. Like the patient and practical mother she is, Peony does not interrupt her daughter's disjointed narration. ". . . so then the blond girl punched her aunt and screamed, 'My husband is dying,' or something like that, so I said he couldn't be her husband because he was mine. Then the policewoman—"

"Wait!" Peony, who never raises her voice, almost shouts. "It was Eric?"

Kendra removes her diamond watch, a present from Eric, and places it on the coffee table. "Yes."

"And you left him there alone? Why didn't you call me?"

"Because . . ." Kendra tries to remember, but her mind keeps slipping back to that blond woman. "How could he do this to me?"

Leaning slightly forward, her concerned eyes bisected by the lines of the cheap bifocals she wears, Peony pulls the topic of conversation back to her son-in-law's condition. "Where is Eric now? How is he?"

"At West General. He was still unconscious when I left after the police finished interviewing me." Kendra feels suddenly and intensely uncomfortable. She pulls her hands free and stands. "I really have to do something about this dress. It's a Mandy Monk original. Why don't you make us some tea while I get changed?" But of course this ploy doesn't work any better than it did when Kendra was a teenager attempting to prevent her mother from finding the pack of Marlboros in her school backpack.

Peony follows her daughter into the bedroom. "Kendra, Eric is ill."

"I know that, Ma."

"How can you be so calm about this?"

"The doctor says he'll be fine."

"You should come home. Stay with us for a couple of days."

"I can't deal with Pops right now. Can you get my zipper?" Kendra turns her back and looks at the cream Berber carpeting to avoid meeting her mother's eyes in the dressing table mirror.

The zipper hisses down. "I'll call your father and tell him I'm staying here for a few days." Peony grabs the skirt of the dress to help Kendra pull it over her head.

"No." Kendra's refusal, even muffled by blue silk, is firm. She has no intention of letting her mother hover with endless cups of tea and bombard her with impossible-to-answer questions about how she feels. From a lifetime of experience, she knows tea and questions cannot be avoided, but they can be postponed by a liberal application of logic. After pulling off her dress, she places it carefully on the bed to ensure none of the fish gets on the Egyptian cotton duvet cover, then grasps Peony's shoulders. "I have to sort out the medical insurance and I have two big jobs coming up. Losing my customers isn't going to help Eric. And you know what will happen if you leave Pops and Paul alone in the restaurant."

Peony's sagging jowls tighten as her jaw shifts forward. From within their hooded nest of wrinkles, her eyes are dark lasers scanning Kendra's face. For a moment, Kendra thinks her mother won't be deflected. Then Peony's jaw relaxes and dips into the pad of fat beneath her chin as she nods. "You call me tonight."

"I promise."

After her mother leaves, Kendra strips off her underwear and goes into the bathroom to take a shower.

Kendra is proud of her appearance and works hard to maintain it with frequent exercise and sensible eating. She considers the money she spends on cosmetics a good investment. Her bathroom cabinets are filled with special cleansers and creams for every part of her body. She uses five different products for her hair alone. On a normal day, she would spend half an hour exfoliating, toning, and moisturizing her body, then blow-dry her hair into a silken frame for her perfectly made-up face.

Today is not a normal day. She steps out of the shower, wraps a towel around her torso and another around her head. Ignoring the bottles and jars lined up on the vanity, she flips on the battery of lights surrounding the triple mirror and leans over the sink to examine her face.

She traces the faint delta of lines splayed across her temples despite thousands of dollars spent on anti-wrinkle treatments. She taps the incipient pad of fat beneath her chin that cannot be eradicated despite ten minutes twice a day spent massaging it upward with firming cream. She studies the texture of the epicanthic folds over her eyes and pinches the skin at the base of her throat until it looks like crumpled tissue paper. The logical part of her mind, the part that takes after her mother, knows this is exactly the same face she always sees in the mirror, the same face Eric kissed good-bye yesterday morning. But now it looks suddenly old. She recalls the casual, almost absentminded kiss, given as she was rushing out the door to get to the Shalimar before the florist arrived, and wonders if Eric saw her the way she sees herself now.

Grapevine

NEWS TRAVELS FAST ALONG THE tree-lined streets of small-town America. With only the slightest assistance from Beatrice, in the form of a single telephone call to her lifelong friend and bingo buddy, Eunice Kazinski, word of Dave's condition has electrified the Brockville grapevine. By late morning on the day following his collapse, a steady stream of cookie- and casserole-bearing neighbors and friends have "just popped by," ostensibly to offer sympathy, but unable to hide their avid curiosity about what happened. Some of them are still sitting in Beatrice's chintz extravaganza of a living room, drinking coffee and eating their own cookies.

Lesley knows the part she is expected to play. She's been on more than a few casserole runs herself and has an excellent role model in her mother. So although she doesn't feel like a woman whose husband is in the hospital, she is trying very hard to act like one. She doesn't really know what it is she's feeling. Maybe a bit worried about Dave, but the doctor said he should be okay.

She's annoyed with her mother, who is holding court on the couch like the queen of tears, and wants to shout: *Go home! Leave me alone!* every time she opens the door to another long-faced neighbor holding out a covered dish like a holy offering. Instead, she forces herself to whisper, "Thank you so much" as she accepts more cabbage rolls or another Bundt cake. Even more irritating, her aunt's eye, which has assumed the hue and dimensions of a squashed overripe tomato, has upstaged Dave's illness. "Oh, my God! What happened to your eye?" everyone exclaims when they see Cassandra, temporarily forgetting why they came.

The situation is made worse by secrecy. No one wants to explain how Cassandra got her injury or divulge the unusual circumstances surrounding last night's events. Cassandra has exiled herself to the kitchen to avoid being asked. In the living room, Beatrice deflects curiosity with soggy paeans to her wonderful son-in-law and the tragedy of his being struck down in his prime. Lesley is running out of patience with her mother's exaggerations.

"Poor Cass." Eunice, who was the first to arrive, studies the plate of cookies Lesley holds toward her and selects one of her own snickerdoodles. "Has she seen a doctor?"

Relieved to be given a question she can answer, Lesley replies, "Oh yes. The doctor said it will be fine in a couple of weeks. Would you like another cup of coffee?"

"Well, I really should be getting on home, but I suppose I have enough time for one more. Thank you, dear."

Lesley picks up the empty carafe from the imitation French Provincial coffee table and retreats to the kitchen to make more coffee. The penetrating voice of Alice Wilson, their next-door neighbor, follows her down the hall. "So, Trixie, I thought you said Dave was in Utah or Wyoming?"

In the kitchen, Lesley snatches the empty pot from the coffeemaker. "I wish they'd all go home."

"If you stop giving them coffee, maybe they will." Cassandra moves away from the sink, where she is washing cups and plates, to allow Lesley to rinse out the coffeepot.

"It's not the coffee, Aunt Cass. It's your fault. They want to know what happened to your eye."

Cassandra thumbs a cigarette out of the pack on the counter. "It's not like I hit myself."

"You deserved it." Lesley knows this sounds sullen, but she's still mad at her aunt and doesn't care.

"Lesley, honey, I've been apologizing to you all day. I'm sorry about what I said at the hospital. It just came out. I'd take it back if I could."

"And you shouldn't be smoking in the house."

"I live here. I can smoke in my own house."

"It's Mom's house, not yours."

"Actually, it isn't." Cassandra lights up, takes a long drag on her cigarette and exhales through her nose. "It's mine now."

Lesley twists her neck to look over her shoulder at her aunt.

"Your father didn't have much insurance. There was almost nothing in the bank after his debts were paid off and most of it went for that ridiculous mahogany coffin. When Trixie couldn't make the mortgage payments, I sold my house in Seattle and bought this one so she could stay here."

"You never told me that. I always thought it was because you and . . ." Conditioned by a lifetime of not talking about her aunt's love life, Lesley leaves the statement hanging.

"I'm not saying it wasn't convenient for me. And Trixie didn't want people to know about Lars's money problems. Anyway, this is my house and I'll smoke in it if I want to. Why do you care? It never bothered you before."

Lesley suddenly remembers why she cares. She shuts off the tap and hands the coffeepot to her aunt. "You make the coffee. I have to go to the bathroom."

As she washes out her grandmother's tooth glass with shampoo, to make extra sure it's clean, Lesley wonders if the little woman in the blue evening dress—she cannot think of her as the "other" woman—has any children. She decides it's not possible. Dave loves children. If he had any, he'd carry their pictures in his wallet and want to have them over on weekends.

He should have told her he was married before. Not telling is like lying. A hot flush of anger rises in her chest at the thought of this deception, but subsides when she reminds herself Dave is sick.

After setting up the test, she waits through the five minutes it takes to produce results with tears prickling at the backs of her eyes. This was supposed to be a happy moment. As two thick red lines form in the display window of the test stick, a terrible, cold emptiness collapses her body. She wraps her arms around her stomach and leans over until her face is almost touching her knees. "This is all wrong," she whispers. "All wrong."

"Honey, are you okay?" Beatrice calls through the bathroom door.

Lesley stands up, pushes her hair behind her ears and opens the door.

"You were in there for so long, I was starting to worry. And Alice . . ." Beatrice's eyes shift to focus on the pregnancy test and widen until they are as round and blue as the saucers of her favorite Delft china. "Is that a . . . ? Are you . . . ?"

"I think so. I'll have to—"

"Oh, my God!" Beatrice flings her arms around Lesley. "How wonderful!"

As Lesley lifts her arms to return the hug, her mother pulls away and runs to the head of the staircase. "I'm going to be a grandmother!" she shouts as she trots down the stairs. "I'm going to be a grandmother!"

Cassandra comes out of the kitchen, wiping her hands on a tea towel. As she reaches the bottom of the staircase, someone knocks on the front door. Lesley sighs and pulls herself together, preparing to receive yet another offering of food and sympathy. But Cassandra opens the door to two strangers, a man and a woman wearing dark suits. The woman holds up an identification badge and says something Lesley can't hear over the excited exclamations coming from the living room. Cassandra steps outside and pulls the door shut behind her. A minute later, she reenters the house and climbs the stairs.

Keeping her voice low, although there is little chance she'll be heard by the women in the living room, who have already moved from congratulations to discussing knitting patterns for baby booties, Cassandra says, "There are two FBI agents here to talk to you."

"About what?"

"About Dave. I've told them we have company, so they're going round back to the kitchen door. I'll go let them in, then get rid of the crowd in the living room. You stay up here until everyone is gone."

"But what do they want to know about Dave?"

Cassandra shrugs. "We'll find out soon enough."

Leaning over the banister, gripping the railing so hard she can feel her nails dig into the wood, Lesley watches her aunt descend the stairs and finally starts to cry. But these are the wrong kind of tears. They are not the fat, wet tears pushed out with heaving sobs that she cried when her father was ill. These are stingy tears, collecting slowly under her eyelids, trickling like acid down her cheeks and into the corners of her lips, tears of self-pity. She doesn't recognize the feeling at first because she's never really felt sorry for herself before.

Joys of Fatherhood

JASON IS NOT HAPPY. HE slept late and had to scramble to get to the airport on time. Vague rumblings in his stomach make him wonder if the cold pizza he grabbed for breakfast on his way out the door may have spent too long at the back of the refrigerator. He wasted half the morning hanging around the arrivals gate because mechanical problems delayed his son's flight from San Francisco. Mostly, though, he is unhappy with the reason he had to be at the airport in the first place. Less than five weeks after leaving to spend the school year with his mother, Jason's son has returned, this time on a permanent basis.

Sixteen-year-old Fletcher has his mother's verbal talent but lacks her self-restraint. He's been talking nonstop since he pushed his overloaded trolley out of the baggage claim area, primarily about the shortcomings of his new stepfather. It's a topic his mother, Kathy, is tired of listening to, which is why she has sent Fletcher to live with Jason, who doesn't want to hear about it either, although for different reasons. Jason listens with only half his attention as he turns off the main road onto Potter's Trail where he lives.

"... and he thinks he's some kind of big shot because he's a vice president, but he's, like, the most clueless guy in the galaxy, Dad. I mean, he watches sports."

Jason attempts to add perspective as he slows to pull into his driveway. "I watch sports."

"Yeah, but Mom never did. Now she sits with him on the couch all weekend watching ESP ..." Fletcher breaks off mid-acronym and twists his torso around to look through the back window. "There's Nez." He's out the passenger door and halfway down the driveway before the car comes to a full stop. "Hey, Nez! I'm back!"

Across the street, Inez Lopez glances over a bare shoulder. "Hey, Fletch," she says, as though she just saw him ten minutes ago instead of five weeks ago, then goes back to soaping the lime green, secondhand Kia she just bought with earnings from her summer job.

Three years is a long time in the life of a teenager. When Kathy took Fletcher to live with her in San Francisco, Inez was a shy girl with a mouthful of braces, who followed an embarrassed Fletcher around like an adoring puppy. Now she's an assured and attractive young woman in a well-filled halter top and cutoff shorts, while the object of her youthful affections has grown into a gawky beanpole with oversized feet, incipient acne, and an acute case of unrequited lust.

Jason watches his son attempt to impress an apparently indifferent Inez by helping her wash her car, and remembers his own youth with a blend of nostalgia and relief. Middle age may not be as intense as adolescence, but it's much less embarrassing. He pops the trunk and starts unloading Fletcher's baggage. Two suitcases, a backpack, a duffel bag, a snowboard and a surfboard later, Fletcher comes bounding back across the street as Jason is wrestling a bass drum out of the backseat.

"Dad, did you know that's her car?"

"Yeah. Her mom asked me to look it over before she bought it. Where'd you get the drums?"

"Norris got them for me. He asked what I wanted for my birthday. I said drums, just to mess with him, you know? But then I started lessons and it turns out I'm pretty good. I'll show you tonight, okay? Nez is taking me to the mall."

"I thought we'd spend the day together, Fletch. Catch up."

Fletcher executes the exasperated eye roll he perfected fifteen minutes after the onset of puberty. "Dad, I'm living here now. We'll have tons of time to talk."

Perversely, now that he has been released from the obligation of listening to his son trash his ex-wife's new husband, Jason is slightly put out by this rejection. "Ditching your old man for a hot chick?"

"No contest." Fletcher gives his father a no-hard-feelings grin and reaches into the backseat for a snare drum.

"You need money?" Jason asks as they carry the drums up onto the wide porch of the house.

"Nah. Norris gave me lots. He thought it would make me like him. What a jerk."

"Okay, then. Be home by six. We're going to Jude and Travis's for dinner tonight."

"Got it. See you later, Dad." Fletcher drops the drum beside the rest of his luggage on the porch and races back across the street.

Fletcher's relationship with his new stepfather creates mixed feelings in Jason. A part of him is proud to know his son's affections can't be bought with drums and a handful of cash. Another part is concerned by the casual cruelty in the way the boy is using

Kathy's new husband. A third, and by far the largest part, is delighted by the thought of Norris getting shafted. Jason, although he would never admit this to his son, dislikes Norris intensely.

It isn't that Norris took Kathy away. The marriage was over long before Jason and his partner pulled into the parking lot of the Whispering Pines Motel to meet an informant just as Kathy came out of room seventeen with her new boss. Then, he'd felt only relieved he wouldn't have to go to marriage counseling anymore.

It isn't the way Norris sat beside Kathy at the custody hearing, establishing possession with hand pats and supportive hugs and quick, triumphant glances over to the table where Jason sat beside his lawyer. If Norris thinks Kathy is some kind of trophy, he's in for a big surprise.

What Jason dislikes is Norris himself—the good-ol'-boy attitude, the aggressive handshake, the patronizing tone he uses when talking to anyone who isn't the vice president of a Fortune 500 company. As he shifts luggage from the porch to Fletcher's bedroom, Jason can't help feeling a smirking satisfaction at the way his son has managed to reject Norris and take the guy for a ride at the same time.

With Fletcher gone for the day, Jason decides to catch up on his bookkeeping, the aspect of self-employment he finds least appealing. For the most part, he likes being a private investigator much better than he liked being a cop. It gives him an outlet for what he prefers to think of as natural curiosity and what Jude calls nosiness, without the hassle of force politics. He works his own hours, takes only cases he likes, and meets a nicer class of people than the criminals and drug addicts who formed his clientele back when he wore the uniform. He was never comfortable wearing a gun, and although he still has one, and a permit to carry it, the only time it comes out of the safe is when he takes it to the shooting range to stay in practice.

On the way to the den, which has been converted into an office, Jason passes through the bedroom without seeing the unmade bed and thick layer of dust on the dresser. As he walks downstairs, his eyes come level with the cobwebs garnishing the front hall chandelier, but he doesn't spot them either. He manages to cross the living room without noticing the newspapers stacked by the sofa, or the gargantuan dust bunnies that have colonized the fireplace and spawned the baby fluff balls clinging to the baseboards. Housekeeping is not Jason's strong suit.

In his office, he shifts a stack of case files from his chair to the floor and sits down at his desk to tackle the shoe box where he tosses his receipts. He's about halfway through matching expenses to cases when escape comes in the form of a phone call.

"Cheddick Investigations."

"Hello, Mr. Cheddick. My name is Kendra McCoy. We met at the hospital last night. I got your number from Officer Connelly." Her words are businesslike, but her low-pitched voice and round vowels make them sound sexy.

"How can I help you, Mrs. McCoy?"

"I want you to investigate my husband."

"He had two sets of identification, Mrs. McCoy. I'm sure the police are already investigating him."

"Actually, it's the FBI. My husband speaks Arabic, so they think he could be a terrorist, and apparently that makes me a suspected terrorist. I'm not, of course, but as long as I'm under suspicion, they won't tell me anything. Which is why I want to hire you to find out about his relationship with that . . . that other woman." Her hesitation and tone of voice give Jason the impression she wants to say something much cruder.

They make an appointment to meet at her apartment in an hour; then Jason calls Jude to find out what the police have already learned about the man's dual identities.

The Man Who Wasn't There

THE BUILDING AT 1715 PARKLAND Avenue is an ornate red-brick cube in the exclusive and very expensive district of Riverside. Erected in the late 1890s, the building was originally a warehouse. A remnant of the old loading dock is still visible as the entrance to an underground parking garage. The rest of the structure has been encrusted with wrought-iron balconies and decorated with fake Doric columns in an attempt to hide its humble beginnings under the facade of a supersized antebellum mansion. Inside the stained-glass door of the entrance, the plantation theme continues into the lobby, with dark wooden floors and waist-high wainscoting. A well-built young man in a bottle green uniform sits behind an antique desk flanked by two aggressively healthy potted ferns. On a perch behind one of the ferns, a blue and gold parrot nibbles at the feathers under an outstretched wing.

The young man looks up from the comic book he is reading when Jason enters. "Can I help you, sir?"

"My name is Jason Cheddick. I have an appointment with Mrs. Kendra McCoy."

The young man nods. "One moment, please." He lifts the receiver of the telephone on the desk and punches in a four-digit number, then fastens his gaze at a point just over Jason's right shoulder while waiting for a response. Jason studies the lurid drawings on thc open pages of the comic. They appear to depict a wrestling match between a well-endowed woman wearing a very small dress and a muscular creature with a head similar to the parrot's.

"Hi, Mrs. McCoy. This is Michael at the desk. Mr. Cheddick is here. Shall I send him up? . . . No problem . . . Jack's fine. . . . All right, then. Thank you." Michael replaces the receiver. "Mrs. McCoy asked if you'd take Cracker Jack up with you."

"Cracker Jack?"

The parrot bobs his head and squawks, "Give us a kiss," in a ripe British accent.

Michael retrieves the perch from behind the palm. "Cracker Jack is the McCoys' parrot. He gets lonely, so we keep him down here when they're away for a long time. Mrs. McCoy forgot to pick him up last night."

"Blimey!" the parrot squawks, flapping his wings to maintain balance as Michael hands the perch to Jason. "Blimey!"

"Don't let him near your clothes," Michael warns. "He likes buttons. The elevators are just through that door and on your left. The McCoys are on the top floor, apartment two."

Holding the pole of the perch well in front of his body, Jason goes through the door. The parrot, spying the buttons on the sleeve of Jason's suit jacket, flops forward until he's hanging from the crossbar and stretches his neck out toward Jason's wrist. Jason shifts his grip farther down the pole, placing his buttons beyond the bird's reach. Cracker Jack sidles to the center of the crossbar and climbs down the pole, forcing Jason to shift his grip lower until the bird's progress is halted by the short chain fastened around one leg. The parrot twists his neck and glares at Jason with one pale yellow eye, then climbs back up to the crossbar and hangs upside down. He swings back and forth over Jason's head, squawking, "Blimey!" every few seconds. They ride the elevator this way to the penthouse floor.

When the elevator doors open, Jason's efforts to hold the perch upright prevent him from immediately recognizing the woman standing in the hallway as Kendra McCoy. Even without the sparkly dress and sophisticated makeup, she is still a remarkably attractive woman. With her hair tied back and her feet bare, she looks younger. The body revealed by her snug red T-shirt and white shorts is sleek and athletic.

Cracker Jack flaps his wings and swings wildly on the crossbar. "Hey, babe!" he shouts in a decent approximation of the voice Jason remembers from his short conversation with McCoy.

Kendra's lower lip sags open. Jason braces himself for tears. Instead, she takes a deep breath and reassembles her face into a polite smile of gratitude. She avoids eye contact, looking at the parrot instead. "Thank you for bringing Jack up, Mr. Cheddick. I completely forgot about him." She takes the perch from Jason and leads him along the hall to her apartment door.

"No problem," Jason lies, relieved his jacket has escaped the bird's button fetish.

Cracker Jack, still hanging upside down, sidles along the perch and opens his beak to touch Kendra's shoulder with a thick black tongue. "Mmmm. You smell fantastic."

She gently pushes the bird's head away. "Shut up, Jack."

"Shut up, Jack," the parrot agrees. Hooking his beak around the crossbar, he pulls himself upright and, miraculously, shuts up.

In the apartment, she carries Cracker Jack across the living room toward a cage constructed of steel bars that stretches over half the length of the window wall. "Just a minute while I put Jack back in his cage. Sorry about the mess."

"Mess" is an understatement. The living room is huge and sparsely furnished. A seating arrangement of angular, oversized furniture surrounds a deep red Persian carpet in the center of the room. The cushions from the sofa and chairs have been removed and tossed carelessly on the floor. Two ornate oriental cabinets, drawers and doors gaping, occupy one wall. On the opposite side of the room, bookshelves flank a marble fireplace. Most of the books have been pulled from the shelves and dropped on the floor. A huge picture of Kendra leans against another wall beneath the open door of a safe.

"Did you have a break-in?" Jason asks.

"I entertained a team of investigators from the FBI this morning." Kendra closes the door of the cage with enough force to make Cracker Jack exclaim, "Blimey!" then adds, "Can I get you something to drink? I just made coffee."

"Coffee would be great. How is your husband?" Jason follows her along the hallway that bisects the back half of the apartment. Through an open door he catches a glimpse of the master bedroom, where the floor and bed are covered in clothing.

"I called a while ago. He's still unconscious, but the doctor tells me all his vital signs are normal and she expects he'll be awake soon."

In the kitchen, cupboards and drawers hang open, and the floor beside the sink is littered with garbage from an overturned trash can. Unlike the living room, this room is small and narrow, with much of the available space taken up by a huge glass-fronted and very well-stocked wine storage unit. A fine layer of dust on the copper-bottom pans hanging from a rack over the cooktop gives Jason the impression that other than the wine unit, this room doesn't see much action.

Kendra takes two steel-banded glass mugs from a cupboard. The mugs look expensive and European, Swedish perhaps. "How long have you been a private investigator?" she asks.

Jason understands this question as the beginning of a job interview. "Two and half years. Before that I was a detective with the Portland police for five."

She pushes down the plunger on a French press. "And why did you leave the police?"

"My career options were limited."

"Officer Connelly said you do consulting work for the police. You must have been a good detective."

"I closed my share of cases. It was my political skills that were less than impressive."

Still avoiding eye contact, Kendra begins to pour coffee into the mugs. "What kind of cases do you usually work on?"

"Missing persons. Background checks. Hidden assets. I'm good at finding things."

She seems to like this answer. "Milk or sugar?" she asks.

"Black, thanks."

She hands Jason his coffee. On the surface, she is remarkably calm for a woman who has just learned her cheating husband is under investigation for terrorism, but Jason feels a tremor in her fingers as he takes the mug. She keeps her eyes focused on her hands, as though not looking at him maintains a barrier between them. "Are you usually successful?"

"Sometimes it's difficult to define success. My clients are generally satisfied."

She nods, signaling the end of the interview, and suggests they talk in the living room. As they return along the hallway, she walks ahead of him with the brittle, sharp-shouldered posture of a woman maintaining tight control.

While Kendra replaces cushions on the chairs and sofa, Jason crosses the room to look at the picture under the wall safe. What appeared from a distance to be a photograph is actually an oil painting. In firm brushstrokes, the artist captured a younger Kendra, seated on a driftwood log against a background of sky and water. Her head is tipped slightly back and her hands are linked around one upraised knee. Long, dark hair floats to the side, suggesting a breeze. Her face glows with an ethereal radiance, as though lit by a focused ray of sunlight. In the lower left-hand corner, the artist signed the work in rough, spiky letters: *McCOY.*

"Is your husband an artist?" Jason asks.

"Not professionally. He could be, but he says there's no money in it." Kendra drops the last cushion on the sofa and sits down. "His equipment is still in the studio, but he hasn't done anything for over a year now. Not since he got that big contract with the Pentagon."

Jason knows nothing about painting, but he recognizes training when he sees it. There is both patience and passion in the technique. This is not the enthusiastic effort of a Sunday painter. It is the product of study and practice and real talent. "I thought it was a photograph."

"Actually, he painted it from memory after our first meeting." She gestures toward double French doors leading out to the roof terrace. "His studio is in the conservatory if you'd like to see some of his other work."

"Maybe later." Jason walks around the teak-and-hammered-copper coffee table to sit across from Kendra. "Right now we should talk about why you want to hire me."

"As I said on the phone, I want you to find out about that other woman."

From her behavior last night, Jason is fairly sure he already knows the answer to his next question, but it has to be asked before he can accept the case. "Are you divorced, Mrs. McCoy?"

"I was, yes. From my first husband."

"I mean from Eric McCoy."

Her eyes narrow as she processes the question. Jason is impressed by how quickly she works out what it means. A mottled flush creeps up her neck. "He really married her?"

"I did some research after you called this morning. A marriage between David McCoy and Lesley Sorrenson was registered in Cowlitz County, Washington, two months ago. But unless you and Eric McCoy are divorced, that marriage is invalid."

Kendra rises abruptly. "We're not divorced." She walks over to stand beside Cracker Jack's cage, where she pretends to look out the window. "I felt sorry for her last night, getting tricked by a fake marriage ceremony. It never occurred to me he really married her."

"Not legally."

She spins away from the window and makes solid eye contact for the first time. Her face is so flushed it seems to radiate heat and her voice rises and cracks as she spits out, "That's the point, Mr. Cheddick. He's a criminal." Again Jason braces himself for tears. Again she surprises him. "He's a bigamist," she says softly, then adds, "Perhaps I won't need your services after all."

"He's a bigamist in Washington State."

"What do you mean?"

"Bigamy falls under state jurisdiction. When Lesley McCoy files charges, he'll be prosecuted there."

She looks at him incredulously. "I don't have any legal rights?"

"You have all the rights, assuming you are his first wife."

Surprisingly, Kendra responds to the idea positively. "Actually, that's worth discussing." She crosses to the seating area and curls up in the corner of the sofa with the graceful flexibility of a cat. "At the hospital, while we were waiting for the doctor, that woman said she hadn't seen her husband for two weeks. On the day he collapsed, Eric had only been home for four days." She leans over to pick up her mug. "Maybe what I need you to find out is where he was the rest of the time."

"Are you sure about this?" Jason asks. "You understand I am obligated to tell the authorities if I find any evidence of criminal activity?"

The corners of Kendra's lips pull back, exposing small white teeth in an expression that bears no relationship to a smile. "Good. If he's done something else illegal, he deserves to be punished for that as well."

Hula Hips

Eight years previously

AS SOON AS SHE STEPPED between the elongated wooden heads framing the doorway of the Freaky Tiki, Kendra wanted to leave. She grabbed Zanne's elbow and pulled her friend back onto the street.

"Let's go somewhere else. This is a pickup bar."

"Right." Zanne grinned. "Maybe we'll get picked up."

"I'm married."

"I'm not."

"What about Callum?"

"What about him? We've had two dates."

"You said"—Kendra tugged at Zanne's arm, not very gently—"he might be the one."

"And if he is, this could be my last chance." Zanne freed her elbow and wrapped a slender arm around Kendra's shoulders. "Look, I did the waterfall hike and the native art gallery for you today. The least you could do is keep me company for a couple of hours while I check out the talent."

This was a valid point. Kendra had chosen every activity on their vacation so far. "You wouldn't go to the whaling museum," she reminded Zanne, but it was a feeble protest.

"Make you a deal. You stay with me until I hook up, then you can leave, and I promise to do the museum thing tomorrow."

"Okay. But just for a couple of hours. Then I'm going back to the guesthouse."

Zanne reached up to pull the clip out of her hair. "If I can't get a guy in an hour, I'll go back with you." Inside the bar, she pointed to an unoccupied table against the wall. "Over there. You can hide behind the plant."

Kendra followed Zanne across the room and sank into a wicker chair beside an enormous golden pothos. She adjusted its heart-shaped leaves until her face was completely hidden from the men lining the bar.

Zanne dumped her bag on the other chair and pulled out her wallet. "I'll get the first round. What do you want?"

"Club soda, thanks."

"That's it?"

"That's it."

Zanne made her way toward the bar, exaggerating the sway of her hips as she threaded her body between the tables. Every male in the room, even those chatting up other women, turned to watch.

In high school, Kendra had been the brave one when it came to boys. Zanne, strong-featured and embarrassingly flat-chested, had hugged the wall during school dances and rejected the few boys not deterred by the orthodontic hardware in her mouth. It wasn't until college that Zanne found her confidence, in an acting class. No one would ever call her pretty, but she had something better—the angular, aggressive sensuality of a runway model. Zanne turned heads, and she liked doing it.

Kendra envied the attention Zanne was getting. Annoyed she had let herself get talked into hiding in a dark corner behind a plant so her friend could sow a few more wild oats, she looked around the room to distract herself.

Beneath the bamboo and potted-palm decor that seemed to dominate Hawaiian interiors, the Freaky Tiki was just like every other singles bar. Clumps of women sat around small tables cluttered with umbrella drinks, fussing with their hair and casting surreptitious glances across the room to where the men, most of them wearing gaudy shirts over cargo shorts and all of them holding bottles of designer beer, leaned with their backs against the bar, surveying the room in more obvious assessment. The lighting was dim and directionless enough to flatter. A few couples had already hooked up and were circling the dance floor to a Hawaiianized cover of "Water Runs Dry," played by two young men with ukuleles. The lyrics reminded Kendra of Brian, and why she was on vacation with a friend instead of with her husband. She peered out between the leaves of the pothos and felt sorry for herself.

"This is a bust," Zanne announced when she returned with a glass of club soda and a hollow pineapple garnished with a shish kebab of maraschino cherries and two paper umbrellas.

"What are you talking about?" Kendra waved a hand toward the bar. "They're not all studs, but there's some pretty good-looking guys here. What about the Wall Street type in the blue hibiscus shirt?"

Zanne didn't bother to look up. Plucking a paper umbrella from the pineapple, she began shredding it. "Not interested. You were right. I miss Callum." She drooped over her drink and sipped it through the straw. "Yeach! What the hell is in this?" She shoved the pineapple across the table toward Kendra.

After tasting it, Kendra pushed the drink back. "Mostly pineapple juice. Rum. Grenadine. Too much sugar." She drank some soda to clear the taste from her mouth.

"So, do I still have to do the whaling museum tomorrow?" Zanne sounded hopeful.

"Deal's a deal. It's not my fault you're in love."

"I am, aren't I? I'm going to call him when we get back to the room." Zanne pulled a cherry off its stick and popped it into her mouth.

"Better go now. He'll be just getting home from work."

They picked up their bags and walked toward the door. When they reached it, a man stepped in front of them. Without introduction or apology he said, "I want you to have this." He held a sheet of thick, cream-colored paper toward Kendra, a pencil sketch of a woman peering out from between overlapping heart-shaped leaves.

"Kendra, it's you!" Zanne exclaimed. She took the paper from his hand. "This is amazing. Did you draw this? Are you an artist?"

He shrugged and smiled, creating a devastating dimple in one cheek. "It's just a hobby." Although he responded to Zanne, his eyes remained fixed on Kendra's face. "Do you like it?"

Kendra loved it. She loved the way it made her look mysterious and beautiful. She loved the way he'd blended her hair into the shadows under the leaves, and shaded the hollows under her cheekbones, and drawn her eyebrows as graceful as seagull wings. "Very much," she said. "I like it very much. I should pay you for this."

The man held up both hands, palms out. Graphite smudged the heel of his right hand. "No, that's not what I meant. I just want you to have it. Something to remember your vacation by."

"How do you know we're here on vacation?" Kendra asked.

"This is a tourist bar." He pointed to a half-empty pineapple on a nearby table. "Locals don't drink this stuff. It's watered down and overpriced. Locals drink at Queenie's, down the road."

"You're here," Kendra pointed out.

"I came here to meet someone." He looked at his watch. "But it looks like she stood me up. So I guess I'll collect up my things and go drown my sorrows at Queenie's. You ladies enjoy the rest of your vacation." The dimple flashed once more as the man stepped aside and gestured gallantly toward the door.

"This is really lovely. Thank you very much," Kendra said.

"You're very welcome."

"Would you do one of me?" Zanne asked. "I'd pay you."

While the man studied Zanne's face, Kendra studied him. He was young, probably in his early thirties. His hairline had started to recede, and without a smile his face seemed bland, the features too neat and even to be memorable. In the dim light of the bar, she couldn't make out the color of his eyes, but thought they might be light brown. The only remarkable thing about him was the way he was dressed. His plain white shirt and blue jeans stood out in a bar filled with shorts and Hawaiian prints.

"You have wonderful bones," he said finally. "Strong features. I'd like to draw you. But I can't take money. Come with me to Queenie's. You can buy me a drink while I draw you."

Zanne raised an eyebrow at Kendra.

"I thought you wanted to call Callum," Kendra said.

"This is better. This is a present for Callum."

"After two dates, you're going to give him your portrait?"

"Not immediately. I'll give it to him when he's ready for it."

"Well, then, I guess we're going to buy a drink for . . ." Kendra looked at the man.

"Eric."

"Hi, Eric. I'm Kendra, and this besotted woman is Zanne."

Zanne and Kendra waited on the sidewalk outside the Freaky Tiki while Eric paid his bill. He came out of the bar carrying a scuffed leather artist's portfolio. "Do you ladies have a car? If not, we can take a taxi. Or walk. It'll take about half an hour."

They decided to walk. Eric led them inland, away from the last remnants of a spectacular sunset, toward dark, steep-sided hills. Outside its historic center, Lahaina quickly devolved into dusty vacant lots interspersed with modest bungalows and banyan trees. Queenie's bar stood in the middle of a shabby little strip mall, squeezed between a dollar store and a dive shop. Inside, a plywood-and-Formica bar stretched along one wall. The linoleum flooring felt slightly sticky under the soles of Kendra's sandals as they wove their way around an eclectic selection of tables and chairs to a table at the back. They were the only customers in the bar.

A tattooed slab of a man wearing a stained gray muscle shirt and baggy shorts followed them to the table. "So which one of these lovely ladies is the famous Joyce?" he asked in a voice as smooth as milk chocolate. Bright spots from the ceiling lights danced across his shaved head as he wiped a damp, sour rag over the table.

"Neither. She stood me up." Eric set his portfolio down. "Kendra, Zanne, meet Crazy Eddie Ladoux, also known as Queenie. He likes you. You can tell because he's trying to wash the table."

Crazy Eddie flicked the cloth casually at Eric's head before turning to Zanne and Kendra. "What can I get you, ladies?" He gestured at a large glass-fronted refrigerator behind the bar. "We have beer, beer and beer."

Zanne grinned up at him. "Hmmm, tough choice. Guess I'll have a beer. Got any Miller?"

Crazy Eddie nodded and turned his attention to Kendra.

Unimpressed by her surroundings and overcome by the moldy smell rising up from the damp table, Kendra scanned the contents of the refrigerator and ordered the same in a weak voice.

"Okay, it's not the Ritz." Eric laid his portfolio on the table. "But the light is good, and it'll get more interesting in an hour or so when the dive crews get here." He took out an artist's pad and two pencils, one hard, one soft. "Meanwhile, I can do your drawing."

Out of curiosity, Kendra moved her chair closer to Eric's to watch him work. There was a time when she had hoped to become an artist herself. Six months into art school, she'd realized she was one of those people who had the eye but no talent. She switched to art history and found a job at the edges of the art world as a receptionist in a gallery.

Eric didn't pose Zanne. He asked her questions as he sketched in a drafting-style cityscape background, then watched her carefully as the beer and his interest animated her responses. Occasionally he broke away from drawing buildings with the hard pencil to trace a line of shoulder or the curve of a nostril with the soft one. Then suddenly, Zanne's face emerged from the negative space in the center of the page. He drew Zanne at her best, vital and vivid. Her eyes sparkled wickedly, her wide mouth smiled sensuously. He'd caught her prominent nose at just the right angle to make it seem aristocratic and glamorous. The geometry of the background softened her square jaw and sharp collarbones and gave extra bounce to her long curls.

Watching Eric work, Kendra didn't notice as empty bottles collected on their table and the bar filled up with customers. When he finished the drawing, she came out of her trance and discovered she was on the wrong side of sober. She put the bottle she was holding—her third, judging from the clutter of dead soldiers on the table—beside its empty comrades. "I don't even like beer," she muttered.

"Could have fooled me," Eric said as he put his pad and pencils back in the portfolio. "Actually, it's not my favorite either."

"So why do you come here?"

"The people—why else?"

Kendra found the idea of drinking cheap beer as the price for hanging out with friends somehow odd. A person's friends, in her opinion, were chosen because they had similar tastes. She looked around the room and wondered what anyone could possibly find interesting in this rowdy crowd.

Zanne, delighted with her portrait, left the table to show it to Crazy Eddie and ended up showing it to everyone in the room while Eric stayed with Kendra and chatted about Maui and art. Zanne joined a group of divers at the bar and pulled one of them, a surfer type with shaggy, sun-bleached hair, back to the table with her. She introduced him as Kenny and announced he would be taking them scuba diving the next day.

"Do you dive?" Kenny asked Kendra.

She shook her head.

Kenny turned to Zanne. "Can't do it, babe. I can only watch one of you. She needs her own babysitter."

"That's okay." Kendra tried not to sound disappointed. "You go. I'll check out the museum."

Eric and Kenny spoke in alarmed unison. "The whaling museum?"

"Can't let that happen," Eric said. "I'll come out with you."

Over the next few days, Eric and Kenny taught Kendra and Zanne how to scuba dive and surf. They took the women hiking through rain forests, dune buggy racing along the beach and, with the assistance of an amazing cocktail called a scorpion, encouraged them to try their hips at hula dancing. Zanne had what proved to be her last vacation romance with Kenny, while Kendra and Eric walked platonically along the beach and discovered they had a great deal more in common than just an interest in the fine arts.

It wasn't that Kendra didn't find Eric attractive. The more they talked, the more she felt drawn to him. He never offered anything other than friendship, though she was sure he would if she gave him an opportunity. To prevent herself from doing that, she told him about Brian one afternoon while they were lying on the beach.

". . . and he's a brilliant lawyer. He could be a partner in five years."

Beside her, Eric raised himself on one elbow. "And that bothers you." It was a statement, not a question.

"Why do you say that?"

"You made a fist when you said it."

Kendra thought about denying it. She hadn't told anyone else about the fights—not her parents, not even Zanne. Then it occurred to her that she'd never see Eric again. As an outsider, he might be able to see the situation more objectively.

"He wants to quit the firm. Open a private practice. Go into family law."

"And you don't want him to do this because . . . ?"

"The thing is, there's no money in it. I want to start my own business. The bank manager doesn't see any problem with the loan approval, but that's partly because of Brian's income."

"Have you talked to him about this?"

"I try, but it always turns into a discussion about the kids."

"How many do you have?"

"None. That's his point."

Eric turned out to be a gifted listener. He never took sides, the way Kendra's girlfriends would have. He never offered explanations, or opinions. He just asked questions and listened to her answers with respect. As she talked, it occurred to her Brian's obsession with having children might have more to do with repairing their fractured marriage than with a genuine urge to be a father. While Eric listened, she explored ideas on how to save her marriage without giving up her dreams.

She left Maui with Eric McCoy's e-mail address tucked into the side pocket of her purse and no intention of using it. Her resolve lasted less than three months.

Mr. Nice Guy

CARRYING A TRAY HOLDING TWO glasses of iced tea and a bag of frozen corn, Cassandra pushes open the kitchen door with her hip and steps out onto the deck, where Lesley is sitting on the stairs leading to the backyard. "That was Floyd on the phone." Lesley's uncle Floyd is the Brockville chief of police. When the FBI asked to search the cabin on Saddleback Ridge where Lesley and Dave live, Floyd went up there with them.

"Did they find anything?" Lesley asks without looking up.

Cassandra sits beside her niece and hands her one of the sweating glasses. "He doesn't think so. They didn't take anything away with them. He says they tore the place apart, though." She picks up the bag of corn and holds it to her eye.

Lesley leans sideways to press against her aunt's bony shoulder. Cassandra puts an arm around her niece and for a time they just sit together, staring across the grass at the tangle of rhododendron bushes that line the back of the property. The old swing set, built by Lesley's father when she was a toddler, still stands in a corner of the yard, its wooden seat dangling from the end of one frayed gray rope. All traces of the bright yellow paint that once covered the posts are long gone. The wood glows silvery bright in the late-afternoon sun.

"Dave once said when our kids came along, he'd fix the swing. He said it would be like a gift from Dad to his grandchildren." Lesley turns her head to look at her aunt. "You were right all along."

"If it makes you feel any better, I wish I wasn't."

"How did you know? What was it about him?"

"Nothing specific. I just couldn't figure him out. For one thing, he was twice your age and he never talked much about his life before he met you. He was like your father in that way; Lars never talked about himself much either. But there's a lot of living in forty years. I always wondered if he was hiding something."

Lesley shrugs off her aunt's arm. "He's not a terrorist," she insists.

"I don't think he is either. I was talking about his other wife."

"He should have told me." Lesley puts her glass down on the deck beside her hip with a *thunk*. "Lots of guys are divorced. I wouldn't have minded."

"Oh, dear."

"What?"

"I don't believe he is divorced, honey." Cassandra puts the bag down to place a cold hand on Lesley's forearm. "Think about what she said."

"She was lying, Aunt Cass. Dave could never do anything like that."

"I don't think she was lying."

Lesley forces herself to replay the events of the previous night in her head. She remembers the woman's certainty that her husband's wallet had been stolen, her lack of nervousness. An image of the woman's face rises up, eyes so dark the pupils are invisible, scarlet lips moving precisely, and Lesley hears the words clearly in her mind. *He can't be your husband. He's mine.* The anger she has been directing at her aunt and mother all day finally takes aim at its true target. Her fingers curl into fists. "How could he lie to me like that? How could I have believed him?"

"You were in love. When people are in love, they want to believe. They're blind."

"Was it like that with you and Norah? Were you blind?"

"As a bat. I thought she was a goddess." Cassandra reapplies the bag of corn to her eye. "Took me two years to fall out of love, see how selfish and stubborn she was."

"But you stayed with her."

"I still loved her. I just wasn't in love anymore. There's a lot of good in Norah. There's a lot of good in Dave too."

Lesley remembers her aunt's partner as a scary, larger-than-life woman. On the few occasions when the family drove to Seattle to visit, Norah spent most of her time in the bookstore she and Cassandra owned, refusing to "make nice" with Cassandra's "hick" relatives. That Norah's avoidance sprang from Lars and Beatrice's clumsy inability to cope with her militant lesbianism in no way justified her rudeness. Lesley can't imagine what sort of good there is in Norah.

Not like Dave. His goodness is obvious. Everyone admires his quiet kindness and gentle patience. Even crabby Uncle Dolph, who never says anything nice about anyone, told her, as he walked her up the aisle at the wedding, "He's a good man, Blondie. Your dad would have liked him." The more Lesley thinks about it, the stronger her belief grows that whatever Dave's reason for not telling her about being married, it must have been motivated by kindness. When Dave wakes up, he'll explain everything. Until then, she won't judge him.

At the sound of tires crunching on the gravel of the driveway, Lesley slumps forward and covers her face with her hands. "I can't see any more people. I just can't."

Cassandra drops the corn back onto the tray as she stands. "It's probably your cousin Marcy and one of her ghastly tofu chili pots. She's the only one I can think of who hasn't been here yet. I'll get rid of her." She clomps down the steps and disappears around the corner of the house.

Two minutes later she returns. "Remember the man who was at the hospital with Officer Connelly?"

"The one who stopped me from hitting you again?"

"He's here. Turns out he's a private investigator. He's been hired by the other wife to find out about Dave."

"She didn't look like she cared about him last night."

Cassandra shrugs. "She might not. Maybe she has other reasons. He says you don't have to talk to him if you don't want to."

"Do you think I should?" Lesley asks.

"I don't see how it could hurt. And you might learn something."

Lesley feels a bit guilty, as though she shouldn't be talking to the investigator behind her husband's back, but she desperately wants to know what kind of man she married. She walks around the house with her aunt. The investigator climbs out of his car when he sees them approach. He introduces himself as Jason Cheddick, thanks her for being willing to talk to him and apologizes for intruding. He looks formal and serious in his suit, but his voice is gentle when he assures her, "Please don't feel you have to answer any questions you don't want to. I know this isn't easy for you."

His disclaimer puts Lesley at ease. She is comforted by his understanding and by the understated sympathy of his last statement, acknowledging her feelings without the theatrical sympathy of the morning's visitors. Normally, she'd invite him to talk in the living room, but her mother is sleeping in the bedroom at the top of the hall stairway, so she takes him through the house to the kitchen instead and asks if he'd like something to drink.

"A glass of water would be great. Thanks." He hangs his jacket over the back of a kitchen chair.

Lesley turns on the tap and takes a glass from the cupboard over the sink. Cassandra starts ferrying casseroles and desserts from the kitchen table to the countertops.

"How's your eye?" the investigator asks as he helps Cassandra clear the table by handing her a plastic-wrapped plate of Rice Krispies squares.

"It feels about how it looks," Cassandra replies. "The doctor says there's no damage to the eye and the swelling should go down in a couple of days."

He holds out a tray of lasagna. "Looks like it's going to be what my dad would have called a beaut."

"My dad used to say that too." Lesley hands him a glass of water and finishes clearing away the platters and casseroles while Cassandra retrieves her bag of corn from the deck. As they take their seats, Lesley asks, "So, what do you want to know, Mr. Cheddick?"

"Kendra McCoy has asked me to look into her husband's whereabouts when he wasn't in Portland. She says you told her you hadn't seen your husband for two weeks."

"That's right. He left for Idaho just before Labor Day," Lesley confirms.

"We know he was in Portland last week, but we don't know where he was the week before that. Obviously the FBI is looking into these absences as well, but their investigation has a different focus from the one I've been hired to perform." He says this quietly, in a factual way that makes it seem almost normal. Lesley discovers she's quite interested in Dave's whereabouts as well.

Cassandra puts down the corn and pulls her cigarettes from her pocket. "So what is your focus?" She stares at the pack for a moment, then places it on the counter behind her.

"I'm checking into the possibility of other marriages, since it makes a difference for how my client will go about ending her marriage. If there are none, she intends to divorce him. However, if Eric McCoy has another previous wife, then she will have to prosecute him for bigamy to get her marriage annulled."

Lesley tenses and presses a hand to her stomach. "He can't go to jail."

Cassandra contributes her usual dose of common sense to the discussion. "Why don't we wait and see what Mr. Cheddick finds out before we start talking about jail?"

Happy to stop thinking about Dave as a criminal, Lesley smiles at her aunt in gratitude, then asks the investigator again, "What would you like to know about Dave, Mr. Cheddick?"

"Primarily, I'm interested in finding out what kind of person he is. It would be very helpful if you could describe him to me and perhaps let me look through his possessions."

"Sure. All Dave's stuff is in the cabin. The FBI went through there this morning, but Uncle Floyd went with them and he says they didn't take anything. We can drive over there now, if you like. It's just outside of town."

Cassandra says, "Tomorrow might be better, honey. You should get some sleep before we leave for the hospital tonight."

"I'm not tired, Aunt Cass. I want to see how bad the mess is at the cabin. And if I go with Mr. Cheddick, you can smoke without feeling guilty."

They take the investigator's car. Lesley fastens the passenger-side seat belt as they back down the driveway, relieved to be away from her mother's—no, she corrects herself—her aunt's house. She is still surprised by her father's financial situation. For all her life, Lesley saw her father as a good provider, a man who gave his wife and daughter everything they wanted and much more. She remembers family vacations at Disneyland, and the car with the big blue bow tied over the hood that appeared in the driveway on her sixteenth birthday, and her mother's delight at the diamond necklace she received on their twenty-fifth wedding anniversary. It never occurred to Lesley that her father spent more than was sensible for a man who made his living as a schoolteacher. Now it seems obvious. Maybe Dave's deception should have been obvious too.

"I guess you must think I'm pretty stupid, Mr. Cheddick, not suspecting anything about my husband."

"No more than I was, Mrs. McCoy. My wife and I were in marriage counseling for over a year before she left me, and I never saw it coming. How long have you known your husband?"

"I met him in April last year. He rescued me."

Maiden in Distress

Eighteen months previously

LESLEY'S FIRST AND LAST EXPERIENCE with horses was also her first and last date with Jimmy Brock.

Accepting Jimmy's invitation to a barbecue on his uncle's ranch had seemed like a good idea at the time. She didn't know much about him, other than his family was rich and he was incredibly good-looking, and going on a date with one of the Brock boys gave her a kind of celebrity status among her coworkers at the Wee Tots day-care center. But Jimmy had neglected to mention the barbecue would be preceded by horseback riding. The closest Lesley had ever been to a horse was watching old John Wayne movies with her father on Sunday afternoons. In real life, horses turned out to be very large and very smelly.

She stood just inside the barn door watching everyone else saddle up their mounts. Jimmy pointed to a reddish brown horse in the third stall from the door. "You'll be riding Jezebel. I'll get you a saddle from the tack room."

While Jimmy went to get the saddle, Lesley walked up to Jezebel's stall and extended her hand to pat the horse's nose. Jezebel stretched her neck out over the half door, tossed her head and bared gigantic yellow teeth. Lesley backed away so fast she knocked over a bucket.

"Jimmy?" she called out. "Maybe I'll just wait here until you get back."

He came out of the tack room carrying a saddle draped with a red and blue striped blanket. "What?"

"You didn't say anything about horses. I don't know how to ride a horse."

"Seriously?"

"It wasn't something I thought I'd ever have to do."

"Well, it's not difficult, but maybe you'd be better up on Moonie. He's the gentlest horse we've got and he never spooks."

Moonie turned out to be the biggest animal in the stable, a palomino whose mane and tail were the exact same color as Lesley's hair. The horse did not bare his teeth when she reached out to pat his nose. He didn't bob his head or even bother to look at her at all. He just kept chewing on a mouthful of hay, as though she weren't there. She found this somehow reassuring.

Out in the stable yard, Jimmy made a cradle with his hands to boost her up into the saddle. He handed her the reins and gave her instructions while he adjusted the stirrups. "Grip with your knees. Keep your heels out." He fitted her foot into a stirrup, shifting her heel to the correct angle. "Moonie knows the trail. He'll just follow the other horses. All you have to do is keep his head up and stay on. He's an easy ride."

Moonie stood motionless while everyone else mounted up. Lesley hesitantly patted his neck and regretted it when her hand came away smudged with greasy dust. Horses not only smelled bad, they were dirty. The other riders began to trot as soon as they cleared the gate. She gripped her knees tighter as they approached the opening, but Moonie ambled through and followed his stablemates at a sedate walk.

Ten minutes into the ride, Lesley's thigh muscles burned from the effort of keeping her knees in and her heels out. She relaxed her legs slightly. Moonie just kept walking. She let her legs hang over the sides of the saddle and began to enjoy herself. The trail wound through scrubby second-growth forest covering the hillside that had been clear-cut by Jimmy's great-grandfather, the origin of the Brock family fortune. The other riders pulled farther and farther ahead as she rocked gently in the saddle and thought about Jimmy, or at least about what other interesting things she might do while dating him. Sailing? Skiing?

Because she didn't know where she was going, Lesley didn't notice when Moonie got tired of plodding uphill and left the trail. It never occurred to her, as they crossed a meadow, that fifteen other horses would have left a visible path through the long grass. By the time Moonie shuffled into the overgrown apple orchard, warm sun and fresh air had conspired to make her feel sleepy. She was dozing when the horse dropped his head to snuffle through the grass for fallen apples. The forward tip of his shoulders happened to coincide with a sideways sway of her body. She slid off the saddle, landing on her backside with a thud. For a moment she lay on the ground beneath the horse's belly, then scrambled away from his hooves and stood up.

She had no idea how to get back in the saddle. Not that it would have mattered if she had, since she had no idea of which way to go or how to make Moonie go there. Her cell phone was in her purse, which was in the trunk of her car, which was parked behind the Brocks' barn, so her only option was to walk back, but this was complicated by the fact that her tailbone hurt. And she still didn't know which way to go.

Having read her fair share of historical romance novels, Lesley was familiar with the concept of the handsome young hero galloping up on his spirited black stallion to rescue the fair maiden in distress. So when she heard hoofbeats, she limped as fast as she could in the direction they came from, shouting, "Help! Help! Help!" The hoofbeats stopped abruptly, then started up again. A few minutes later a man came riding toward her through the apple trees.

As heroes went, he was a disappointment. He was old, almost her mother's age, and not handsome at all. His horse was disappointing too, brown and white with gangly legs and a scrubby tail. Even so, she felt a warm wash of relief as the rider pulled his horse to a halt in front of her and slid off. He looked around as though confused, then asked, "Was that you calling for help?"

"I fell off the horse."

Moonie raised his head, apple-flecked saliva dripping from his mouth. He made a derisive noise by flapping his lips, then dropped his head back down and continued looking for fallen apples. The pinto tried to do the same, but the man jerked firmly up on the reins.

"So what's the problem?" he asked.

"I can't get back up." Aware this made her sound mentally subnormal, Lesley wished she had shouted out "Hello" instead of calling for help.

The man grinned. One side of his mouth lifted a bit higher than the other, creating a deep dimple in his cheek. "How did you get up the first time?"

"Jimmy helped me up." This sounded even dumber than her last statement, so she expanded her explanation. "I've never been on a horse before. Jimmy said Moonie was easy to ride and he would follow the other horses along the trail. But he didn't, and now I don't know where I am." She rubbed her tailbone, which had begun to throb painfully.

"Are you hurt?" he asked.

"I bruised my back when I fell off."

"Maybe I can help you find your friends. Where were they going?"

"I don't know, but we're supposed to be having a barbecue at the Brocks' ranch after the ride. That's off Highway Sixteen, about ten miles north of Brockville."

"How long have you been riding?"

"I don't know. I sort of fell asleep. Why?"

"The ranch is across the valley on the other side of Stony Ridge." He looked at his watch. "Assuming you don't get lost again, you won't get back until after dark. If you like, you can come with me to the stable where I keep Patches, leave Moonie there, and I'll drive you over."

Lesley knew better than to accept rides from strangers. She also knew that without someone's help, she'd be sitting in the orchard with Moonie all night. Besides, if the man turned out to be a serial killer or a rapist, they'd probably never get back to the riding stable anyway and there wasn't much she could do about it out here in the middle of nowhere. She accepted his offer. "Thanks. I'm Lesley Sorrenson, and I really appreciate your help."

"Dave McCoy." He shook her hand. "How badly are you hurt? Can you ride?"

"Do I have a choice?"

"No point in hurting if you don't have to." He removed Moonie's high-pommeled saddle. Placing his hands on either side of Lesley's waist, he lifted her up until she was high enough to get her leg over the horse's back. His hands were hard and warm and the action reminded her of the way her father used to lift her up onto his shoulders when she was little. It also impressed her, since she was just two inches shy of six feet and had weighed a hundred and fifty-four pounds the last time she stepped on the scale.

"Lean forward; lie along the neck. That way you won't bounce around and hurt your back more," Dave instructed her.

Lesley knew her best sweater was being ruined by horse gunk, but at this point she hardly cared. "What do I hold on to?"

"The mane." He picked up the saddle and gathered up Moonie's reins. Moonie, recognizing the tug of authority when he felt it, abandoned the apples and amiably followed Dave over to where Patches was sneaking a few apples of her own. Still holding Moonie's saddle and reins, Dave grabbed the pommel of Patches' saddle with his other hand and swung himself smoothly up onto the horse's back.

The journey back to the riding stable was slow but relatively painless. Dave turned out to be a good listener and she found herself telling him about her job at the day-care center.

"Sounds like you really like kids," he said as he dropped Moonie's saddle onto the ground of the stable yard and swung down from Patches' back.

"I love them. I'm an only child. Someday I want to have a really big family of my own."

He reached up to help her off her horse. "How big?"

"Really big. Six kids, maybe more." She put her hands on his shoulders and felt his muscles flex beneath the brown and green plaid flannel of his shirt as he lifted her down.

The riding stable owner let her use his house phone to call Jimmy, who sounded relieved to hear she was okay. She couldn't tell if it was because he'd been worried or because he and everyone else could stop looking for her and get on with the party. He offered to come pick her up, but her back hurt, her sweater and jeans were nasty with horse grunge, and she was annoyed with him for letting her get lost in the first place. So she asked Dave if he'd mind driving her home instead of to the Brocks' ranch.

When they got to Lesley's house, her mother invited Dave in for coffee. Somehow, he ended up staying for dinner. He praised Beatrice's pot roast, saying how much he loved home cooking and how rarely he got to eat it. He told them he had a place he was fixing up on Saddleback Ridge. After dinner, he helped with the dishes; then they played Rummoli. By the time the game ended, it was after eleven. Beatrice insisted he stay in the guest bedroom. The next morning, he replaced the leaky washer in the kitchen faucet before he left.

"What a lovely man," Beatrice said to her daughter as Dave's truck pulled out of the driveway. "He reminds me so much of your father."

Lesley remembered the feel of his hands on her waist, how easily he'd lifted her onto the horse, the way his eyes lit up when she mentioned wanting a large family, and felt a bit sad she would never see him again.

Two weeks later, Beatrice came home from shopping and announced, "You'll never guess who I ran into in the checkout line." Peering over her mother's shoulder, Lesley saw Dave retrieving grocery bags from the trunk of the car. A tiny shiver of happiness ran up her spine.

Ulterior Motives

AS JASON AND FLETCHER NEGOTIATE the last turn on the ramp leading up to the porch of the Connellys' house, the front door is thrown open by Travis, his square features split by a huge grin. It's an expression Jason hasn't seen since Travis's spine was crushed in a rock-climbing accident. Even more unusual is the cause of this expression. The top of Travis's head is once again six feet and four inches off the ground.

"I just got it working today. What do you think?" Travis asks.

"It's wicked, Uncle Trav!" Fletcher bounds up the last dogleg of the ramp to inspect his uncle's latest invention.

Jason, although he wouldn't use those exact words, has to agree as he grasps Travis's hand at normal height for the first time in more than a year.

Of all the difficulties associated with living in a wheelchair, Travis is bothered most by what he calls "life at crotch level." Jude, who is five foot seven, thinks her husband's complaint is frivolous compared to the logistical problems presented by tasks such as bathing and using the toilet. Jason, at just over six feet himself, understands perfectly. Travis has a big man's subconscious sense of superiority. He isn't patronizing or pompous like Norris, but he is accustomed to receiving the automatic respect given a tall, athletic male. For Travis, the indignity of being literally looked down on by far exceeds the physical inconveniences of maintaining personal hygiene.

Travis is also a born tinkerer, the kind of guy who fixes lawn mowers and rebuilds old muscle cars in his spare time. He has combined this natural talent with his army training as an aircraft mechanic to invent all sorts of devices to solve the problems of his disability. But nothing produced to date is half as impressive as the contraption he is strapped into now. What must have started out as an electric wheelchair has been modified beyond recognition. The chair's rear legs are elongated, the armrests collapsed downward. Thickly padded straps attached to the front legs, the forward-tilted seat and the back support hold Travis's body in an almost upright position, similar to leaning his shoulders against a wall.

"I'm calling it the Extensitter. Watch this." Travis swivels a tiny joystick on the inside of one armrest. With a high-pitched whine, the chair reconfigures itself. The back legs shorten, the seat and armrests rise to horizontal positions, and in seconds, he is seated in a nearly ordinary-looking wheelchair. He swivels the joystick again to return to an upright position, then uses a joystick on the opposite armrest to spin around in the doorway and scoot across the front hall. "Come on in. Dinner's almost ready."

"How does it corner?" Jason asks as he follows Fletcher into the house.

Travis rolls ahead of them into the living room. "Like you'd expect, given the center of gravity. It's better to stop and swivel."

Despite rustic furniture and an eclectic selection of throw pillows, the Connellys' living room exhibits a neatness bordering on pathological. Precision placement of ornaments on the mantel, pictures hung at regular intervals on the walls, books arranged by height on the shelves, all testify to the military background of the homeowners. The coffee table, with two magazines aligned at right angles to the edge, has been pushed against the wall under the front window. A pattern of tire tracks crisscrossing the carpet indicates Travis has been giving his latest invention a thorough test.

In the kitchen, which is equally well-ordered and organized, Fletcher and Jude hug with enthusiasm. "How's my favorite nephew?" she asks.

Fletcher, her only nephew, groans in honor of this old joke between them and pulls open the door of the refrigerator. "Can I have a beer, Dad?"

Unlike Fletcher's mother, Jason believes his son should learn about alcohol at home and under supervision. He's seen too many kids pulled from the twisted wreckage of smashed cars after drinking irresponsibly. "Just one, so make it last. Get me one while you're in there." He hugs his sister. "That's some invention Trav has there. How's it feel to be married to a genius?"

"He didn't look all that intelligent this morning when he was ramming into walls."

Travis glides up to the island in the center of the kitchen and continues to work on the salad he's building. "Minor problem with the front wheel assembly. Took ten minutes to fix."

They talk about the Extensitter while Travis and Jude finish cooking, then move out to the patio to eat. Fletcher manages to consume two helpings of everything except salad while entertaining them with a hilarious description of his mother's attempts to learn how to cook by watching Jamie Oliver reruns on PBS.

"By now, the outside of the chicken is totally black, and the inside is still raw, so she decides to nuke it. But it's still got those little tinfoil mittens on the tips of the wings, so it's like the Fourth of July in a microwave, and I yelled"—he pauses to heighten the suspense—" 'Alive! It's alive!' "

Jason and Travis laugh. Jude just looks at Fletcher.

"From the movie? *Young Frankenstein*," Fletcher explains, then shrugs. "Mom didn't get it either."

"It's a guy thing," Travis consoles his nephew.

Jason, remembering years of Hamburger Helper and canned soup, appreciates the irony of Fletcher's anecdote as well as the slightly bitter delivery. Kathy never made the kind of effort for her son and former husband that she is making for her new husband. Jude sees it as well and shifts the conversation by asking Jason if he's heard from Kendra McCoy. Travis knows about McCoy, but this is the first Fletcher has heard of him. He is so intrigued by the story he forgets to eat.

"So he's a bigamist *and* a terrorist?" Fletcher asks, holding out his plate to Jude for a third helping of mashed potatoes.

She plops a spoonful of potatoes on the plate. "Well, for sure he's a bigamist. I talked to our FBI liaison before I left work, and he gave me the impression the bureau is drawing a blank on the terrorist investigation so far. There's nothing in the system on this guy and they didn't find anything when they searched his residences."

"That's so cool," Fletcher says. "Two women love him."

Jason eyes the pork roast and considers a second helping, but decides against it. "After today's interviews, I'm not sure about that."

"They don't love him?" Jude forks up the last of her green bean casserole.

"Well, they certainly loved someone. I'm just not sure who

that someone is." Jason intercepts Fletcher's hand on its approach to the meat platter. "Finish your salad first."

While Fletcher slides green pepper slices and carrot slivers to the side of his plate with the precision of a munitions expert disarming a bomb, Jason tells them about his interviews with Kendra and Lesley McCoy. He describes the tailored suits, the Italian shoes, and the glass-walled art studio built out onto the roof terrace of Kendra's apartment.

"And McCoy Two is some kind of Grizzly Adams tree hugger." Jason picks up a green pepper slice from Fletcher's plate. "He lives in this DIY log cabin just outside Brockville in Washington. Brews his own beer, grows his own vegetables, even generates his own electricity with solar panels and a windmill. There's nothing hanging in his closet except his wedding suit and some plaid flannel shirts. About the only thing he's got in common with McCoy One is his shoe size. So, yeah, both wives love him, but they obviously don't love the same guy."

Travis takes a pull on his beer. "Split personality?"

Jason thinks about this for a moment, then shakes his head. "I'm not a psychologist, but I've never heard of anyone who could control it like that. Think about it. He's got two wives who think he's a completely different person, and he's maintaining a third life neither of them knows about. Seems pretty well planned to me. But I can't imagine a terrorist would complicate his life like that."

"Is the second wife filing a complaint?" Jude asks.

"No. I think she actually expects McCoy to divorce his first wife."

Fletcher doesn't believe this. "After what he did to her?"

"She's not happy that he lied to her, but from her viewpoint she's the one he really loves." Jason watches his son's face shut down and realizes his mistake. He tries to repair it. "It's not the same, Fletch. Your mother loves you. She just needs some time alone with her new husband."

Fletcher shoves his salad plate away. "Whatever."

Jude gives her nephew a sharp look, but lets the comment pass. She begins stacking plates and asks Jason, "So, you think you'll find another wife?"

Grateful for his sister's restraint in ignoring Fletcher's rudeness, Jason replies, "I'll be happy to find McCoy's medical insurance. If I don't, I probably won't get paid."

Jude and Travis have recent firsthand experience of how fast hospital bills mount up, so Jason is surprised when his sister abruptly hands him the plates she's stacked, snatches up two serving bowls and says, "Trav, why don't you give Fletch that ride in the Extensitter you promised him? Jason and I can clean up."

Travis rolls away from the table. "C'mon, Fletch. Your aunt has something to say, and she doesn't want us to hear it."

Jason is confused. "About what?"

"Beats me. But I've seen that look, and I'm glad it's not aimed at me this time. Fletch and I are going to take cover in my workshop."

Travis glides toward the garage. Fletcher gives his father a sympathetic look before following his uncle. Jason enters the kitchen with trepidation.

Jude scowls down at the mashed potatoes she's scraping into a storage container. "What the hell are you thinking? Fletch has just been rejected by his mother. He needs you."

"And I'm here for him. What's this about?"

"It's about you bringing another woman into Fletch's life right now."

Jason dumps the plates on the counter over the dishwasher. "What other woman?"

"Oh, come on, Jason. You're doing the white knight thing

again. This is how all your relationships start. You're planning on rescuing one of those women, aren't you?"

"No. I just feel sorry for them. Especially the first wife. It's not like I can't sympathize."

"Enough to investigate on your own dime?" Jude takes a roll of tinfoil out of a drawer. "There's no ulterior motive here?"

Jason trusts his sister's radar, so he thinks about her words carefully as he ferries the rest of the dishes from the patio into the house. Kendra is a good-looking woman and Lesley is a knockout, but given the extremities of McCoy's schizophrenic living arrangements, it's unlikely either of them would find his average-guy lifestyle attractive. And even if one of them did, he'd have to be a monster to hit on a woman who was happily married less than twenty-four hours ago. Jason is pretty sure he's not a monster. He remembers watching McCoy talking with the barista and realizes his ulterior motive, if he has one, is probably much simpler.

"When I first saw him," he tells his sister as they load the dishwasher together, "I thought he was a con man. Then the way he approached me was so bizarre. I'm curious about what he was up to. And maybe a little pissed off at him too. I think he was trying to con me."

Girls' Night Out

LESLEY SITS ON THE BOTTOM step of the staircase in the front hall to put on her sneakers. "So what movie are you seeing tonight, Mom?"

"Well, I don't know. It's Eunice's turn to pick one." Beatrice firmly suppresses the urge to check her watch. Lesley and Cassandra should have been halfway to Portland by this time.

Cassandra, looking uncharacteristically tidy in tailored slacks and a blue button-down shirt, searches in her purse for her car keys. "Then it's probably going to be something with lots of explosions. Don't bother cooking tonight. Dr. Strachan wants to talk to us after we see Dave, so we'll pick up something to eat on the way home from the hospital."

Beatrice's concern evaporates when she hears this. There will be plenty of time. "Maybe I'll ask Eunice if she wants to go out for a bite after the show."

"Debbie at work says the new gourmet burger place is good."

Lesley follows her aunt out the door. "See you later, Mom. Stay out of trouble."

"What kind of trouble could I possibly get into at the movies?" Beatrice mutters as she waves good-bye to her sister and daughter. She waits until Cassandra is backing down the driveway, then scurries into the living room to peep between curtains and watch them drive away.

People are always telling Beatrice she lives a charmed life. On the whole, she agrees with them. As the youngest of five children, born to a nurturing mother and a doting father, pampered by her much older sister, and guarded by three overprotective brothers, she grew up in an era that demanded nothing more of women than attractiveness and domestic accomplishment, two qualities Beatrice had in abundance. When she left home at eighteen, it was only to move, with her adoring new husband, into this house, located three blocks from her childhood home and purchased with the help of a down payment received from her father as a wedding present. She has never held a job and, until recently, never had a moment's worry over her equally domestic and even prettier daughter.

A price must be paid for such good fortune. All her family relationships are social contracts, agreements of role and hierarchy. Now that Lars has passed and Lesley is married, Beatrice plays a supporting role in the lives of her relatives—the one who maintains bonds by organizing the many birthday parties and reunions that glue her large family together, the go-to girl in times of trouble who handles the mundane tasks of daily living when illness or misfortune strikes her less lucky relations. She honors these obligations and enjoys doing them. But deep inside, she knows she's more than just a social coordinator and fill-in cookie baker.

As soon as the taillights of Cassandra's car disappear around the corner, Beatrice hurries to her bedroom, unbuttoning her blouse as she climbs the stairs. Her "partner in crime," as she thinks of Eunice, will be here in less than an hour, barely enough time for makeup and hairstyling. Thank goodness she got home from shopping in time to do a manicure. A firm believer in first impressions, because these are the only kind she forms herself, Beatrice wants to look her very best tonight.

An hour and a half later, as Eunice parks in the closest spot she can find to the entrance of the Howling Wolf Casino, Beatrice flips down the passenger-side sun visor to freshen her lipstick. In the driver's seat, Eunice checks her own makeup and says, "I've got around a hundred. How about you?"

Beatrice opens her purse and extracts an envelope full of cash. "Just over two hundred, but I'm going to save half for next time." She pulls out five twenty-dollar bills before putting the rest of the money in the glove compartment.

The two women exchange excited, here-goes smiles and get out of the car. Inside the casino, they walk quickly past the slot machines, a solitary form of gambling and therefore of no interest to them. On the gaming floor, they hug briefly before going their separate ways. Eunice, with her earthier personality, likes the rough-and-tumble at the craps table, while Beatrice feels she meets a better class of player at the roulette wheel.

Eunice and Beatrice are not here to gamble, although the rare occasions when they win are certainly exciting. They are here to meet men. In the confined social world of Brockville, they are just so-and-so's aunt Eunie or cousin Trixie, as familiar as a favorite sweater, invisible as wallpaper in an upstairs bedroom. At the Howling Wolf, they are women again, individuals in their own right. They aren't looking for boyfriends, or even casual sex, just hoping to flirt with a man they haven't known since high school.

Before Eunice discovered the casino, they did their flirting at singles dances and mixers. This was unsatisfactory for a number of reasons, chief among them the distance they had to travel to be unrecognized by other attendees and the appalling male-to-female ratio. Women invariably outnumbered men at mixers two to one. The Howling Wolf has solved both problems. It's less than forty miles from Brockville. Most of the clientele are male and, as a bonus, slightly inebriated, making them much more willing to strike up conversations. The dim lighting helps as well.

As she approaches the roulette table, Beatrice is delighted to see Andrew, in his soft tweed suit and quaint bow tie, placing his single-chip bet on red. She's talked to Andrew before. He is courtly and charming, generous with compliments and almost handsome in a chubby, double-chinned way. Being plump herself, Beatrice enjoys sharing acidic observations with him about the casino's popsicle-stick waitresses. He has never stepped across the bounds of gentlemanly behavior. She sometimes wonders if he is gay, but isn't bothered by the possibility.

He looks up and bows slightly when he sees her. She smiles back and edges in beside him at the table.

"Dear lady," he exclaims, "I was hoping to see you today!" His eyes shift down to the neckline of her dress. "And wearing such a flattering outfit too."

"This old thing?" she replies and decides he's not gay after all.

Collision of Opposites

UNDER NORMAL CIRCUMSTANCES, KENDRA WOULD be delighted that the voucher she donated to the Breast Cancer Foundation auction was bought by Charlotte Prescott. The Prescott fortune is as old as money gets in Portland, and Charlotte sits on half the charity committees in the city.

But circumstances have been far from normal since Eric's collapse. Kendra sits in a rattan armchair on the Prescotts' spectacular garden terrace, nibbling on figs stuffed with walnuts and listening to Charlotte outline her ideas for her in-laws' sixtieth wedding anniversary party. As she nods and smiles and types into her laptop, Kendra wonders sourly if the senior Prescotts' marriage has always been as idyllic as their daughter-in-law describes it. Four days ago, secure in her own happy marriage, this suspicion would never have crossed Kendra's mind. Now all her thoughts are tainted by Eric's betrayal.

When Charlotte runs out of suggestions for party favors and flower arrangements, Kendra finishes off the interview with the less glamorous, but far more important topics of allergies and physical disabilities. No Perfectissimo party will ever be destroyed by a guest having to be rushed to a hospital. She takes leave of her hostess with the assurance this will be a party to remember.

The Prescotts' house, more accurately described as a mansion, is located on the northeastern edge of Forest Park—five thousand acres of hilly woodlands that separate the city proper from its western suburbs. As a city girl, at home in the art galleries, expensive restaurants and chic boutiques of northwest Portland, Kendra has no appreciation of nature. To her, it's all bugs and dirt. When she has to drive through the forest, she prefers to take the highway, but her GPS navigation system indicates Cornell Road will be faster.

Normally, she would ignore the scenery as she drives through the park. Today, she remembers what the investigator told her after he visited the cabin in Washington. She tries to visualize Eric living on an isolated farm surrounded by trees like the Douglas firs climbing the hillsides on either side of the road, but the idea is completely ridiculous, as is the image of her sophisticated husband wearing plaid shirts and leading wilderness hikes.

Her first appointment at the hospital is with an accountant, to pick up a statement of expenses incurred for Eric's treatment so far. The amount shocks her. In the elevator on her way to talk to Dr. Strachan, she slumps against the cold metal of the wall, unable to imagine how to pay the hospital bills if the assets she knows Eric must have are not found soon. As the elevator doors slide open, she straightens her spine and tugs down the hem of her suit jacket before stepping briskly out into the neurology department.

This is the first time she has returned to the hospital in the four days since Eric's operation. An extremely healthy person herself, she feels uncomfortable around illness. Besides, there's no point in visiting Eric while he is unconscious, and certainly no point in risking an encounter with his other family. This is what she calls Lesley now: "Eric's other family." It's an easier phrase to say, even in her head, than "Eric's other wife."

The crisp clicks of her high heels echo along the corridor as she approaches the nursing station. One of the three nurses on duty, a dumpy woman with dyed black hair whose broad, pale forehead is made even broader by the quarter inch of silver roots framing it, looks up from her computer screen. "Can I help you?"

"I'm Kendra McCoy. I have an appointment with Dr. Strachan."

The woman's eyes widen. Three yellow pills tumble out of a paper medication cup held by one of the other nurses and clatter to the floor. Kendra cringes internally at this indication Eric's marital situation is a topic of hospital gossip. She keeps her eyes fixed straight ahead and her own features expressionless.

"Dr. Strachan was called to ER on a consult," the nurse says.

"Will she be long?"

"I can call down and find out. In the meantime, Mr. McCoy is in room 417 if you'd like to visit him."

"Is he conscious?"

"No. I'm sorry. He's still . . ."

"Then I'd prefer to wait in the doctor's office."

Kendra ignores the susurration of whispering from the nursing station as she walks to the doctor's office. Inside, she puts her briefcase on one of the tweedy gray visitor's chairs and pulls out her laptop to organize her notes on the Prescotts' anniversary party. She tries to focus on music preferences and favorite foods, but her thoughts keep sliding to the spreadsheet she's been working on for the past two days. She clicks it open and stares at the columns, taking comfort in the way they reduce her life with

Eric to numbers. Right now, numbers are easier to cope with than the wreckage of what she once thought was a perfect partnership.

In the assets column, she has listed the antiques, the high-season luxury time-share in Sun Valley, Eric's Lexus (although she still has no idea where it is), the better-quality jewelry, the vintage wine collection, the balance in their joint checking account and even Cracker Jack, although she has listed him as "talking macaw" and has not entered a value. Being a firm believer that the best investment in her future is an investment in herself, Kendra has no mutual funds or personal savings to enter in the assets column, and no idea if Eric does or not, since they never pooled their resources. Even so, the total at the bottom is comfortably higher than the total in the liabilities column, which contains only two outstanding credit card balances.

The income and expenditures columns are in much worse shape. Here, the profit she expects to receive for upcoming jobs is nowhere near enough to cover next month's budget for things like lease payments on her van, rent, utilities, gym membership fees and insurance. She has had to guess at things like food and entertainment, since Eric always paid when they went out, and they rarely ate at home. Kendra always knew her husband contributed more to their joint account than she did. She never gave it much thought. He'd insisted there was no need for financial equality until her business became more profitable, and they were never short of money.

She types "medical bills" into the liabilities column and the amount she has just been given by the accountant. The total now exceeds her assets. Unaware she is returning to a habit she broke herself of twenty years before, she chews at the skin beside her right thumbnail while she tries to decide if she should liquidate these assets to pay Eric's hospital bills, or whether it would be better to keep paying the private investigator in the hope he turns up something useful. When Dr. Strachan arrives, Kendra shuts down the computer, grateful for a reprieve from the numbers, which are now depressing.

Well rested and wearing gray slacks and a red turtleneck sweater under her white coat, the doctor looks more like a suburban housewife than the exhausted surgeon Kendra met four days ago. "I'm so sorry to keep you waiting, Mrs. McCoy."

"No problem." Kendra tucks the laptop back into her briefcase and stands to shake the doctor's hand. "I know you're busy. What did you want to see me about?"

Dr. Strachan closes the office door and takes her seat behind the cluttered desk. "It's time we talked about your husband's condition. I understand you are Mr. McCoy's legal wife and decisions about his continuing care will be made by you."

"What kind of decisions?"

"Well, there's just no way to know at present. The patient's condition is stable. He doesn't need life support, and as far as we can tell, there is nothing preventing him from regaining consciousness. However, a coma of this duration indicates a serious underlying issue."

Up until this moment, Kendra has thought of Eric's condition as a temporary inconvenience, like a broken bone or a concussion. For the first time, she realizes her husband is seriously ill. "Is he in danger?"

"Not immediately. If he remains in a comatose state much longer, then he's at risk for pneumonia due to immobility. There are some other, less common conditions related to coma that can cause death. The real concern is his level of impairment when he regains consciousness."

"What kind of impairment are we talking about?"

"Almost certainly some loss of memory. Because he's been

unconscious for so long, you should also be prepared for paralysis, loss of speech and reduction in cognitive function."

A chilling vision of spending the rest of her life paying for the hospitalization of a vegetable flits through Kendra's mind. Over the past few days, she has come to think of Eric as almost a stranger, but she is certain he would hate being trapped in a crippled mind and body for the rest of his life. Both she and Eric would be better off if he were on life support; then at least he could be taken off it. She does not say this, of course. Instead she asks about treatment options, which turn out to be both expensive and questionably effective. After thirty minutes of listening to her future being sucked into a medical black hole, Kendra can barely muster the strength to stand and say, "Thank you, Doctor. I appreciate your candor."

"You're welcome." Dr. Strachan walks around her desk to open the door. "One more thing you might find helpful: West General has a charity fund to assist financially disadvantaged patients. Of course, you would have to exhaust your own resources first, but there's no need to worry about your husband's continuing care."

Hiding her annoyance at this tactless reference to her impending poverty, Kendra picks up her briefcase. She thanks the doctor once more as she steps out of the office. Because she is looking back over her shoulder, she doesn't see the tall woman approaching along the hallway until they collide, and Kendra's shoulder sinks into the soft valley between the woman's breasts.

"Oh! I'm so sorry!" The woman places a steadying hand on Kendra's arm. "I didn't see you."

Embarrassed, Kendra dredges up the last of her self-control to take her share of the blame. "Well, I wasn't looking either, so it's just as . . ." Her voice trails off as she looks up into Lesley's concerned face. Horrified by this much-too-close encounter with the breasts that enticed Eric away from her, Kendra jerks her arm free and takes a step back. The tip of one stiletto heel lands at an awkward angle and snaps off. Pain shoots up her leg as her ankle buckles. She struggles for balance, then topples sideways, ending up sprawled facedown at Lesley's feet.

The festering knot in her chest, controlled by willpower alone for the past four days, cracks open and boils out in a sobbing tide of anguish. She covers her face with her hands and, in the small corner of her mind not overwhelmed by humiliation, wishes she could die.

WITH REFLEXES honed over a lifetime of dealing with her emotionally flamboyant mother, Lesley is the first person to respond to Kendra's collapse. She falls to her knees beside the sobbing woman. "Oh, I'm sorry!" she apologizes again. "That must have been such a shock for you." She slides an arm under Kendra's body and attempts to lift her. Unfortunately, she is also the last person Kendra can accept sympathy from. With a choked howl, Kendra rolls away and draws her knees up into the fetal position.

Dr. Strachan crouches down and attempts to turn Kendra over on her back. Now hyperventilating, Kendra wraps her arms around her head and begins making a high-pitched pulsating sound halfway between a gasp and a shriek.

In the end, Cassandra's solution produces the most favorable response. She hooks her hands under Kendra's armpits and half drags, half carries the distraught woman into the doctor's office, where she lays her down on the carpet. Kendra's legs relax away from her chest and she reverts to sobbing. Lesley attempts to follow them into the office, but Cassandra pushes her niece back into the hallway. "You'll just set her off again. You go sit with Dave. I'll go to the cafeteria and get us some coffee."

But Lesley cannot just walk away. After her aunt leaves, she leans against the wall and listens to the muffled sobs coming from inside the doctor's office.

With four days to think about Dave's previous marriage, and no facts to get in her way, Lesley has constructed a romantic drama of a sensitive, affectionate man tied to a cold, calculating businesswoman, whose avarice has fueled a long and bitter divorce as the lawyers fight over division of assets. She likes this story very much. It allows her to believe Dave insisted on a six-month engagement because he believed he would be a free man by then. As their wedding day approached, and he realized he wouldn't be free after all, he said nothing to save her the embarrassment of having to call off the wedding.

She had no problem believing this comforting fantasy as long as her last memory of Dave's first wife was watching the tiny woman walk coolly away from her unconscious husband. After that spectacular meltdown in the corridor, Lesley isn't sure her fantasy bears much resemblance to reality. Kendra isn't crying from pain. She didn't fall all that hard, and her sobs came too quickly and much too violently to be caused by a twisted ankle or a bump on the head. Lesley closes her eyes and replays the expressions on Kendra's face just before she fell. Shock. Then fear. Then—was it shame? Shock seems normal. Who wouldn't be surprised to bump into an ex-husband's new wife like that? But fear and shame make no sense. As the sound of sobbing subsides, Lesley wonders if there's a different explanation for Dave's behavior, one that does not involve a delayed divorce, or any divorce at all for that matter.

Dr. Strachan comes out of her office and startles when she sees Lesley. "You're still here?"

"How is she?" Lesley asks.

"She sprained her ankle." The doctor bends down to pick up Kendra's shoe. The snapped heel dangles from the torn sole.

"Small wonder, considering the size of her foot and the height of this heel. There are no obvious broken bones, but I'm sending her to radiology to check for hairline fractures."

As Dr. Strachan walks toward the nursing station, Lesley hesitantly pushes open the office door, ready to run if sobbing or shrieking breaks out again.

Kendra is lying on her back. The right leg of her slacks is rolled up over her calf. Her foot is bare, the ankle swollen to the size of a small grapefruit. At the other end of her body, her eyes are black slits between puffed red lids. Smeared mascara coats her cheeks. She turns her head when she hears the door hinges squeak. Lesley tenses, but Kendra just closes her eyes and mutters, "Go away."

"Can I ask you something first?"

"What?"

"Are you and Dave getting divorced?"

Kendra opens her eyes as far as she can and stares at Lesley.

"What I mean is, Dave never said anything about you, and I was wondering if that's because he thought he'd be divorced by the time we got married."

Kendra lifts herself up on her elbows. Her eyes squeeze shut with pain, then open to fix on Lesley's face. "He never told you about me?"

Encouraged by the other woman's relatively calm response, Lesley edges farther into the room. "No. I would never have married Dave if I knew."

"Well, we're not divorcing. He lied to you about his name too. His name is Eric."

"It can't be. I've seen his driver's license."

"So have I."

Dr. Strachan returns with an orderly and a wheelchair. They lift Kendra into the chair and place her briefcase on her lap. As the orderly pushes the chair toward the door, Lesley holds out her hand, palm up, as though begging forgiveness. "I'm sorry," she apologizes again, this time for much more than the accident in the hall.

Kendra hesitates, then lightly touches Lesley's fingers, granting forgiveness as though it were a coin. "It's not your fault." She opens a side zipper on her briefcase, retrieves a business card and hands it to Lesley. "Call me. We should talk. You should know the truth."

Lessons in a Car

AFTER SIX FRUSTRATING DAYS OF investigating Eric/David McCoy, Jason reluctantly admits he has hit a wall. "It looks like Eric McCoy is the only name he used until a year ago," he tells Kendra over the phone. "The only connection between David and Eric McCoy is the ownership transfer of his Washington property."

"Even in his finances?" she asks.

"I talked to Agent Hauver at the FBI about that. He won't tell me much, but he did say it looks like David McCoy doesn't have any finances other than his joint account with Lesley McCoy. He must have paid for everything in cash. Actually, I've worked with Daniel Hauver before and it's a good sign that the case has been turned over to him. He's a forensic accountant. My guess is they drew a blank in the searches and background checks, so they've turned it over to Hauver to follow the money."

"Did they tell you how much money that is?"

"I asked, but that's not information they're releasing."

Kendra sighs. “And how long will it be before they do?”

“Financials take longer, and it depends on what they find, but it could be a while. I got the impression this isn’t a high priority for them at the moment. There’s no immediate threat, and they could be waiting for Mr. McCoy to wake up.”

“If the doctor is right, that won’t be much help to any of us.” Kendra tells Jason the grim prognosis for McCoy’s recovery, finishing her report with, “So the hospital bills are mounting up and I have no idea how I’m going to pay them. If I liquidate everything we own, even Jack, I can’t come close to enough.... Unless... Have the police found his cars?”

“Not yet, and when they do, the vehicles will go to impound.” Frustrated by being the bearer of so much bad news, Jason tries to offer hope. “Have you approached the other...” He stops himself from saying “wife” and substitutes, “family? They might be willing to help out.”

Kendra makes a noise that could be a choked-off laugh, or just a hiccup. “Actually, I ran into her at the hospital the other day. We’re getting together this afternoon. Is there anything else you can look into?”

“Not at the moment.”

“I appreciate your honesty. If you’ll send me your report and a bill, I’ll put a check in the mail.”

“I’ll send you my report, but there’s nothing useful in it. Why don’t we just suspend my investigation for now? Let’s wait and see what’s in the cars when they turn up. There might be something I can work with. I’ll stay in touch with the FBI as well.”

“What about your expenses?”

“There haven’t been any yet.” This isn’t entirely true, but Jason is willing to overlook compensation for his time, since he hasn’t turned up anything helpful to Kendra, and given her financial difficulties, it seems unjust to charge her for his failure.

She agrees to wait and Jason hangs up, feeling pleased to still be on the case. For a forty-two-year-old man, McCoy has left a remarkably small footprint in the bureaucratic sands, but a trail of driver's licenses through several states indicates he was something of a gypsy until he met Kendra. Jason can understand McCoy's decision to settle down. Beneath that ultra-feminine packaging, Kendra has a quick, analytical mind. It's an unusual combination Jason finds intriguing as well, one he'd be interested in exploring himself under different circumstances. He pushes the thought away and gets to work on his report.

AT FOUR thirty, when Jason pulls up to the school entrance, Fletcher breaks away from his latest, and obviously still unsuccessful, attempt to convince Inez to go out on a date. He walks backward toward the car, watching Inez's hips roll as she makes her way through the school parking lot.

Jason is fairly sure Inez hasn't outgrown her crush on Fletcher; she's just better at hiding it. As he follows the progress of his son's un-romance, Jason has become convinced the boy's intentions are not honorable. Because he was a teenage boy himself once, Jason has no expectation his son will remain a virgin until marriage and no real objections to teenage sex either, provided the boy is properly prepared. He'd be far more concerned if Fletcher didn't show any interest in sex. However, Jason has strong objections to sexually transmitted diseases and no intention of becoming a grandfather anytime in the near future. He has already had the safe-sex talk with his son three times, and has received Fletcher's solemn promise not to take any foolish risks, but there's no harm in having it again soon. It might be a good idea to steer the boy away from Inez at the same time. Mrs. Lopez is a formidable woman with a quick temper and Jason would prefer to remain on her good side.

When Fletcher sees his father already sitting in the passenger seat, he makes a roll-down-the-window gesture. "Can we do a parking lot today? I'm not ready for rush-hour traffic."

Fletcher's reluctance to drive baffles and irritates Jason. It baffles him because his son has always been a daredevil, and he can't understand this sudden timidity about something as innocuous as driving. It irritates him because he's not interested in a second career as Fletcher's chauffeur. "You can't get a license just for parking lots, Fletch."

"Sarcasm doesn't help, Dad. Can we at least wait until everyone else is gone?"

Looking at the crowded schoolyard, Jason decides his son is reluctant to embarrass himself in front of his new schoolmates. "Okay. Today we'll start out at the mall. But you're driving home."

En route to the mall, Fletcher keeps up a running commentary on the performance of other drivers on the road, making sure his father is aware of things like rolling stops, unsafe lane changes and cell phone usage. Jason would find this catalog of misdemeanors more amusing if he wasn't guilty of so many himself. He parks at the farthest end of the mall and they switch seats. Fletcher practices cruising up and down rows of parking slots, then, in what is clearly a stall technique, declares he needs practice backing into a parking space. Jason points to where a mud-spattered truck and a shiny blue-gray sedan are parked under a tree at the edge of the lot separated by one empty space. Fletcher cuts his first attempt too close to the front bumper of the truck.

"Don't just look out the back window," Jason instructs him. "Use your mirrors. Pull out and try it again."

Fletcher follows this advice and tucks the car neatly between the two vehicles on his second attempt.

Jason hikes up his hip to get his cell phone from his pocket. "Pull back out."

"Jeez, Dad! What was wrong with that one?"

"Nothing. I want to see something." Jason scrolls through his contacts list and selects a number while Fletcher shifts into drive and eases out of the space. Twisting his torso to look through the back window, Jason speaks into the phone. "Hey, Jude. Have you got your notes on McCoy handy? I think I just found both his cars."

Jude, who is just getting off shift, keeps him on the line while she goes back to her locker to get her notebook. They verify the license numbers of the truck and the car; then she asks Jason to wait with the vehicles while she contacts the FBI liaison for instructions.

While they wait, Fletcher peers through the windows of the Toyota. "Nothing in the truck except the seats," he reports and moves over to check the Lexus. "There's a plastic bag on the front seat of the car, but it looks empty. Wonder why he parked them here?"

Jason wonders the same thing. This end of the mall backs onto the side of a hill. A rustic wooden stairway leads up to what must be Seventeenth Street. It would come out just beside the Well Roasted Bean, which explains why Jason had no luck when he drove around the neighborhood earlier in the week searching for one of McCoy's cars.

Jude arrives in her own car and wearing street clothes. She looks tired and preoccupied. "The FBI is sending someone over. They asked you to stick around and give a statement."

"You okay?" Jason asks his sister.

"Fine. Just didn't get much sleep last night. Trav and I had another fight."

"Another fight?"

"I don't want to talk about it." She waves at an approaching black SUV. "The FBI is here."

Agent Daniel Hauver is an older man who looks like the accountant he was before joining the FBI. Jason has worked with him before on a fraud case, and he respects the agent's thorough and careful approach to investigation. Daniel Hauver does not make mistakes. He doesn't usually work on high-profile cases either, which is one of the reasons Jason thinks the FBI has back-burnered the McCoy case.

Agent Hauver takes statements from Jason and Fletcher separately, then enlists Jude's help in going through McCoy's vehicles.

The Lexus contains nothing useful. Everything in the glove compartment, which is only the owner's manual and insurance documentation, is issued to Eric McCoy and shows the Parkland Avenue address. In the trunk, a carry-on suitcase contains only clothing and toiletries. Jude searches under the seats and finds some change and a book titled *The Wine Lover's Guide to the Pacific Northwest.* The plastic bag on the front seat is empty.

The Toyota is equally disappointing. Along with insurance and an owner's manual, the glove compartment coughs up a plain gold wedding band and a key for the fiberglass tonneau covering the bed of the truck, where they find a saddle, a sleeping bag, and a one-man tent.

Agent Hauver shuts the tonneau and relocks it. "Not much here. I'll get a team to run prints, but I doubt we'll find anything."

"There's got to be something," Fletcher insists. "Maybe you can find out where he's been by analyzing the mud on the truck."

"Mud analysis?" Jude scoffs. "You watch way too much television, kid."

"I agree you probably won't find much," Jason says. "These

cars are like props or camouflage. Look at how he keeps everything totally separated. But I think we've got a better handle on the guy. He put a lot of thought and effort into his fake lives. He's logical. We can use that."

At the edge of the parking lot, Jude stands with her hands in the back pockets of her uniform, looking at the wooden stairway. "Logically, he'd park close to where he lives. You should canvass the neighborhood with his picture."

"Resources are tight right now and I've got a lot on my plate. We'll probably bounce that one back to you," the agent tells her.

Jason offers his services. "I've worked with the FBI before. I could do the canvassing. His wife is still my client, and I know a fair amount about the guy already, so I might catch something someone who's new to the case would miss."

Agent Hauver thinks about this for a minute, then agrees. "On the condition you report anything you find to me first." He gives Jason his card and asks Jude to arrange to have the vehicles towed to the impound lot before he leaves.

Fletcher wants to start canvassing immediately. "It's not like we have anything else to do tonight," he says, in a less than subtle attempt to end his driving lesson.

"I'll come with you." Jude walks over to lock her car.

"Not going home to cook dinner?" Jason asks.

Jude scowls. "Trav can get his own dinner tonight. Might smarten him up."

Dr. Jekyll and Mr. McCoy

LESLEY STANDS IN THE DOORWAY OF THE KITCHEN, watching her mother pipe salmon mousse onto poppy seed crackers in preparation for her weekly euchre club meeting. Beatrice hums happily to herself as she squeezes the piping bag with expertise developed over years of decorating the cupcakes and canapés that form the currency of her social life. She has recovered quickly from the shock of Dave's illness, falling back into her daily patterns as though everything were exactly the same.

But it's not the same. It's never going to be the same again, and Lesley is puzzled by her mother's lack of concern about Dave. In many ways, Beatrice is just like the children at Wee Tots, untouched by worry and responsibility. Is it because she has always had a caretaker—first her father, then her husband and now her sister—to solve her problems for her? A week ago, when she had her own protector, this thought would never have occurred to Lesley. Now every minute not spent worrying about Dave is devoted to worrying about how she will raise a child on minimum wage if Dave doesn't get better, which the doctor says gets more likely the longer he remains in a coma.

"I'm leaving now, Mom. Say hi to the ladies for me."

Beatrice swirls the last of the mousse onto a cracker. "Can you get me the olives out of the fridge?"

"Black or green or stuffed?"

"Oh, black. I always think they look so much prettier on salmon. Aren't you going to wait for Cass?"

"No. I'm going now." Lesley places the olive jar on the counter beside the platter of canapés.

"But you always go with her."

"Well, today I want to go alone."

"Oh, honey, you should wait. You shouldn't go alone."

"I think it's time I started doing stuff on my own, Mom. I'm not a child anymore."

"Well, I never said you were. I just think Cass is better at dealing with doctors and things like that."

"And I think I should learn to handle those things myself. I'm going to have a baby soon. It's a lot of responsibility."

"Dave's very responsible."

After running into Kendra at the hospital, Lesley has doubts about how responsible Dave will be even if he does recover. She doesn't try to explain this to her mother because she wants to leave before her aunt, who will be much harder to convince, gets home. "When Dave gets better, he'll still be working most of the time. I need to handle stuff myself." Lesley snags her car keys off the shelf beside the back door. "I'll get something to eat on the way home. See you."

It took Lesley two days to find the courage to call Kendra. At first she was afraid of the truth. Then yesterday, as she leaned against the wall of a bathroom stall at the day-care center recovering from her first bout of morning sickness, she understood that avoiding the truth wouldn't help the baby. She had to know if Dave would be a good father, a man worth fighting to keep, or if she should have the marriage annulled.

Kendra sounded surprisingly nice on the phone—supportive, almost kind, nothing like the cold, ruthless businesswoman of Lesley's imagination. She laughed at the awkwardness of calling each other Mrs. McCoy and suggested they use first names. It was this friendliness, more than anything else, that made Lesley decide to go alone. Aunt Cass had a way of putting people's backs up.

Now, as she steps off the elevator on the penthouse floor, Lesley wonders if she should have brought her aunt after all. This apartment building intimidates her. She feels she is walking through a movie set and can't imagine Dave, in his scuffed boots and well-worn jeans, ever entering those stained-glass doors in the lobby, or taking that smooth, silent ride in the wood-paneled elevator to this elegant hallway. She reminds herself the man who lives here is not Dave. She's here to learn about someone else's husband. Taking a deep breath, she knocks on the door just beneath the shiny brass 2.

Kendra cracks open the door and hops back on her crutches to let Lesley in. "Thanks for driving down. Come in."

"How's your ankle?" Lesley steps into the foyer.

Kendra scowls at her bandaged foot. "I'm living on ibuprofen. The doctor said it's going to be weeks before I can use it." She turns herself awkwardly around and crutch-hops toward the living room. "The real problem is not being able to drive. I've had to cancel four jobs so far."

"What do you do?"

"I own an event planning business. Mostly weddings and parties, but I'm starting to get into fund-raisers. What about you?"

"I work in a day-care center." Lesley stops when she enters the living room, overwhelmed by the decor. She gapes at the high, corniced ceilings, the paintings, the flowing gauze drapes framing a view of the city through the expanse of windows stretched along an entire wall. She cannot believe Dave lives his other life in a place like this. "It's beautiful! Just like in a magazine. Oh! Is that a parrot?"

"His name is Cracker Jack. He was an anniversary present. Say hello, Jack."

"Hello, Jack," the bird complies.

"He talks!" Lesley crosses to Jack's cage. "Hello, Jack."

"Hello, Jack." Cracker Jack sidles along his perch right up to the bars, lowers his head and fixes an eye on her chest. "Give us a kiss, luv."

"Is he looking at my breasts?"

Kendra chuckles. "It's the buttons on your dress. He's got a thing about buttons. Would you like something to drink? There's wine, tea and coffee, all kinds of liquor, if you'd rather have a mixed drink."

"Have you got any pop or iced tea?"

"No iced tea, but there's mixers from the party we had a few weeks ago. Come into the kitchen and let's see what's left."

"Oh, let me get it. You should be resting your foot. Can I get you something too?"

"A club soda. Thanks. It's impossible to carry anything when I'm on crutches." Kendra sinks onto the couch. "Down the hall, second door on the right."

The kitchen smells funny, like garlic and fish. Although it's a very nicely furnished room—Lesley particularly likes the black granite countertops—it's not very convenient. The wine storage juts out into the room, making it too narrow for more than one person to work at a time, and she has to step to one side to open the refrigerator door, releasing more of the funny smell, which seems to come from stacks of takeaway containers labeled LUCKY DRAGON. She takes out two cans of pop and searches through the cupboards for glasses while she ticks off two more boxes on the bad-Dave list she's begun keeping in her head. He never drank wine, and he didn't like eating in restaurants because he said the food never tasted as good as homemade. She adds another tick when she remembers what Kendra said about having a party. Dave always avoided parties.

Back in the living room, Kendra is sitting on the sofa with her foot propped up on the cushions. She takes the glass of soda and waves it toward a chair. "Thanks. Have a seat. I guess the best way to start is by telling each other what we know about him. How did you meet?"

Lesley begins the story of her adventure on Moonie, but stops when Kendra, sipping her drink, begins to cough violently. Soda fizzes out her nose and down the front of her sweater. She heaves herself up to a sitting position and chokes out, "He has a horse?"

AN HOUR later, Kendra puts her laptop on the coffee table and turns the screen toward Lesley. "It's like Dr. Jekyll and Mr. McCoy."

Lesley pulls the laptop toward her to study the lists Kendra has made. In two columns, under the headings *Eric* and *Dave*, Kendra has entered everything the women can think of about their husband. Very few items in the *Eric* column match those in the *Dave* column. Jobs, hobbies, clothing, music, even favorite movies—almost everything is different.

"Do you really think he's crazy?" Lesley asks.

"No. Do you?"

"Aunt Cass always says he's one of the most sensible people she ever met."

Kendra picks up the laptop and types "sensible" in the *Dave* column and "adventurous" in the *Eric* column.

This is not what she expected. She suggested this meeting with the intention of discovering what it was, aside from the obvious, Eric found attractive in the other woman, to understand why he'd gone as far as bigamy. He must have had a compelling reason, one that would allow Kendra to graciously offer to divorce him, one that would permit her to walk away with dignity from the responsibility of rehabilitating the husband who humiliated her. Instead, she has met a woman as deluded as herself, betrayed by a man neither of them ever really met, a man who planned and plotted his deceptions right down to his preference in underwear. Worse yet, Lesley has no idea where his money comes from either.

Kendra pinches at the bridge of her nose. "This is a nightmare."

"It's way worse than that." Lesley folds her arms under her breasts as she leans back in her chair. Her usually limpid eyes are narrowed, brilliant blue irises glittering with something feral, primitive as a wolf's. "You can wake up from a nightmare. This is real, and I have to figure out how to deal with it."

"What do you mean? I'm the one that's legally responsible for the bastard."

"And I'm the one carrying his baby."

"Oh, dear God! He got you pregnant?"

"We got me pregnant. It's why we got married, to start a family."

"He wanted children?"

"Lots."

Kendra types another entry into the spreadsheet before flopping back against the arm of the sofa. "He told me he didn't want any."

Rose Petals

Five years previously

KENDRA FELT THE MUSCLES OF Eric's back stretch under her hands as he bent his head to lay a soft path of kisses along the side of her neck. He nipped the lobe of her ear gently and murmured, "Welcome to the mile-high club, babe."

She tightened her still-trembling thighs around his hips. "I thought this was an urban legend," she whispered back. "These washrooms always seemed too small."

"We haven't got to the difficult part yet."

"What's that?"

"Getting your panties back on."

She pressed her face into his chest to muffle her laughter.

Eric was right. Getting decent in such a small space turned out to be much harder than getting indecent. In the end, she kicked off her panties and he put them in his pocket. When Eric pulled open the door, a babble of exclamations erupted from the line of passengers waiting to use the facility.

"Way to go, guy!" from a chubby man in a wrinkled suit.

"Well, really!" from an elderly woman in a rose twinset.

"Awesome!" from a perforated teenager, his face studded with tiny steel balls.

"I can't pee in there!" The last comment was delivered in a Texas accent by a woman in a leopard print shirt, whose teased puff of brassy hair had been flattened on one side by sleeping in her seat. Long turquoise and silver earrings chimed as she spun around and marched toward the washrooms at the rear of the plane.

"Sorry, folks," Eric apologized. "We're trying to get pregnant and it was either this or a washroom stall at JFK." He leaned over and stage-whispered, "Next time, check the chart before we leave home."

When they got back to their seats in business class, she punched his arm. "You are totally evil."

Eric gave her the dimple. "And you, madam, are totally wanton."

"Only with you. I wish I'd met you ten years ago."

"You might not have liked me ten years ago."

"Why? What were you like back then?"

"Kind of like way-to-go guy outside the washroom. Envying other people. Wishing, but never making it happen."

"And now?"

Eric reached over and ran his fingers lightly from elbow to wrist along the sensitive skin on the inside of her forearm. "Now it happens." He lifted her hand and kissed her fingertips. "We'll be landing soon. You want another glass of champagne?"

"If I have much more to drink, you'll have to carry me off the plane."

"Then you're definitely getting more to drink."

While Eric leaned into the aisle to catch the flight attendant's attention, Kendra relaxed into her seat and tried to remember if she'd ever felt so happy. When she'd told Eric about her decision to leave her husband, she'd worried that without the stimulation of clandestine encounters to make their illicit romance exciting, sex would soon devolve into a stale, mechanical routine, the way it had with Brian. She'd never been more wrong about anything in her life. Eric had a vast and imaginative arsenal of ideas to keep sex interesting, the most recent being today's initiation into the mile-high club.

Still, when he left Hawaii, rented the apartment on Parkland, and asked her to move in with him, she refused. Six years of struggling through the endless compromises of marriage had left her wary of tying her life and her dreams to another person. Now Eric's exuberance and passion filled every corner of her life. She couldn't imagine going back to the bland existence she'd had before she met him. Looking down on the patchwork of New England fields and woodlands far below, she decided the next time he brought up the subject of living together, she would say yes.

There was more champagne in the stretch limousine Eric had hired to pick them up at JFK, and still more in the antique-filled suite of the boutique hotel just off Times Square where the limousine dropped them off.

"Eric! Come see this Jacuzzi. It's almost a swimming pool."

He finished tipping the bellboy and joined her in the pale pink marble temple of the bathroom. "Ah. This must be why it's called the Spa Suite."

"You think? Look at that shower. Eight nozzles." From the

velvet-covered chaise longue—Kendra had never been in a bathroom large enough to contain real furniture before—she picked up a leather-bound book to scan the services offered on its pages. "Pedicure, facial, four kinds of massage . . . Oh! Listen to this. They even have rose petals for the bath. Red, white and tea rose."

Coming up behind her, Eric took her by the shoulders and pulled her against his chest. "How many pounds should we order?"

"Don't be silly. Look at what they cost."

"You're right. The shower will be much cheaper." He slid his hands down her body to pull her hips closer. "Want to try it out before dinner?"

Giving the shower a proper "tryout" took so long they missed their reservation at Blue Bistro and ended up ordering room service.

As the trip was to celebrate the finalization of Kendra's divorce, Eric insisted she choose all their activities. Over the next three days they saw an exhibition of Gossart portraits at the Metropolitan Museum of Art; caught two plays, one on and one off Broadway; checked out the shopping on Fifth Avenue; and, on the recommendation of the concierge, fell in love with a fabulous little Mexican restaurant called Quetzalcoatl's Pantry just around the corner from the hotel. They also "tried out" a dressing room at Saks and, very late one night, a patch of lawn in a postage-stamp park, screened from the street by heavenly smelling lilac bushes.

On the night before their flight home, Eric decided he couldn't leave without at least one soak in the Jacuzzi. Kendra listened to the water running into the tub as she packed her suitcase. When it stopped, Eric called out from the bathroom, "Can you come help me with something?"

She pushed open the bathroom door. "What do you . . . Oh,

Eric!" In the soft light flickering from dozens of candles, the rose petals floating in the tub became a mysterious, crimson sea, hiding all of Eric's body except his head and shoulders. "It's so beautiful! And the scent is incredible."

Eric lifted a petal-covered arm out of the water. "They feel even better. Like butterfly kisses. Come in and try it."

She wriggled out of her clothes, tucked her hair up in a clip and stepped into the tub. But when she tried to kiss him, he pushed her away. "Not yet. I have something I want to talk about."

"You filled a giant bathtub with exorbitantly expensive rose petals to have a discussion?"

"A very important discussion." He slid around the tub until he could place his arm around her shoulders. "I can't do this anymore."

Kendra laid her head on his chest. "Do what?"

"Live apart. I'm away so often. When we're together, we should be really together. All the time. This your-place-or-mine routine is driving me crazy."

"You're right. It's time I moved in with you."

"I'd like that. But what I mean is we should get married."

"Marriage?" She lifted her head to look at his face. "Why?"

"Why does anyone get married? Because we're in love. I'm in love. Aren't you?"

"Yes, of course. But I just got divorced."

"So?"

"So why complicate things?"

"I'm trying to simplify things."

"Living together will do that. Marriage is about more. It's about commitment, making a home, having children."

"What's wrong with commitment? What's wrong with making a home?"

Kendra held her breath, waiting for him destroy everything by asking the next question. When he said nothing, she placed her hand on his chest and rose to her knees in the water to look directly into his eyes. "You didn't ask what's wrong with having children."

Eric's bellow of laughter echoed around the marble walls. "You should see your face." He dropped his arm to the small of her back and pulled her onto his lap. "Haven't you heard? Children interfere with your sex life."

Big Break

JUDE SPREADS THE MAP ACROSS the hood of her car. "We're here." She points to an intersection. "This is where the staircase comes out on Seventeenth. We've canvassed every street three blocks each way."

Jason checks his watch and leans over the map. "We've got an hour. Let's start at Meadow"—he points to a street and traces a zigzag route—"then along Grove and Paddock, and finish up on Millpond."

This is their third night of looking for McCoy's other residence. So far no one has recognized the picture Jude had enlarged from Eric McCoy's driver's license, the one that looks most like him. While Jason appreciates Jude's help, he is also concerned she is using the search as an excuse to avoid going home. "Are you and Trav still fighting?" he asks as they walk to the first house.

She scowls and shoves her hands into the pockets of her sweatshirt. "Yes."

"Do you want to talk about it?"

"Not right now." She steps onto the front walk of the first house on Meadow Lane.

By the time they reach Millpond Road, six blocks from the stairway to the mall parking lot, they are ready to abandon the search. Jude's theory about McCoy parking close to his other residence seems to be wrong, although this leaves them with no explanation for why he left his cars at the mall.

Their luck changes when Jude's knock on the door of 18 Millpond Road is answered by an elderly woman carrying a white Persian cat with runny eyes. The cat hisses at them asthmatically.

"Stop that, Peabody." The woman, whose fluffy white hair and pug nose give her an uncanny resemblance to her pet, scratches Peabody lightly between his furry ears. "He doesn't like strangers. Can I help you?"

"I'm Jason Cheddick and this is Judith Connelly. We're canvassing the neighborhood looking for information about this man." Jason holds up McCoy's picture. "Have you seen him?"

The woman squints at the photo. "I need my reading glasses. Would you mind coming in so I can close the door? Peabody isn't allowed out."

Jude and Jason squeeze into the tiny vestibule. Jason closes the door. The woman drops Peabody, who scurries up the staircase and hisses at them from the upper landing. In the cluttered living room, every chair is coated with cat hair. A strong suggestion of Peabody's litter box hangs in the air. The woman introduces herself as Margaret Waterston while she searches for her glasses, finally finding them folded inside a knitting magazine. She hooks them over her ears and stretches out her hand for the picture.

"Yes, of course I know him. This is Eric McCoy."

"Eric McCoy? You're sure about that?" Jason asks.

"I've spoken to him several times. Is he in some kind of trouble? I warned Rita about this, but she wouldn't listen. Although I have to say, he seemed like such a lovely man. And so polite."

To avoid answering her question, Jason asks one himself. "Who is Rita?"

"Rita Gardener. Her yard backs onto mine. Eric is house-sitting for her. I told her she was taking a terrible risk leaving Jack with a stranger."

"And Jack is?"

"Cracker Jack. Her parrot. Well, technically, I suppose he's a macaw." Margaret slides her glasses down her nose to peer at Jason. "Is something wrong?"

"Sorry. I just remembered something. Please continue."

"Well, you see, Rita got transferred back to England—she's a director at that big sports company in Beaverton—oh, must be almost a year ago now, and she didn't want to take Jack because quarantine is so long and she's only going to be there for two years. Parrots need so much attention. They're very social birds, you know. Rita just knew he'd be completely traumatized by being left alone in quarantine. I offered to take Jack myself, but she felt he might be too much for me, what with Peabody and my arthritis. I was just going to make some hot chocolate before *Jeopardy!* comes on. Would you like some?"

Jason has no desire to drink hot chocolate in Margaret's ammonia-scented house. "We really haven't got enough time. But thank you for offering. If you could just tell us Mrs. Gardener's address?"

"It's on Grove Street, number twelve."

"That poor parrot is probably dead by now," Jude says as they return to the sidewalk.

"Actually, the bird is fine." While they walk around the

block, Jason tells Jude about meeting Cracker Jack at Kendra McCoy's apartment.

"Did she say how much the bird is worth?" Jude asks.

"No. Why?"

"Because it's felony theft if it's worth more than a thousand."

"I'd say that's the least of his problems."

The home at 12 Grove Street is a ranch-style house surrounded by a tidy lawn, which is in turn surrounded by a neatly clipped, waist-high hedge. No light glows through the drapes pulled across the front windows. Jude rings the bell and, when no one answers, knocks loudly on the door. After another minute, she says, "No one's home. You check out the carport; I'll check out the backyard. Then I guess we can call it a night."

The carport contains nothing but some old oil stains and a battered metal garbage can with a warped lid. As Jason is returning to the front walkway, the living room lights come on. A moment later, Jude opens the front door. "The back door was unlocked. You should see this place."

Rita Gardener's taste in decor is decidedly horticultural. In the living room, rose-covered wallpaper clashes with the poppy-covered drapes and jungle-print cushions on the rattan couch and side chairs. Cabinets and tables painted with leafy vines are topped by silk flower arrangements in ornate vases. Even the pile of the carpet is sculpted in a fern-shaped pattern. A curlicued wrought-iron birdcage, less than a quarter of the real estate Jack currently occupies, stands by the front window. The hothouse theme continues through the dining room into the kitchen and reaches its zenith in the two bedrooms, where the addition of lace curtains and ruffled bed skirts adds a Victorian atmosphere.

Aside from some toiletries in the bathroom and clothes in one of the bedrooms, McCoy has dumped his possessions in the dining room like a squatter. One wall is stacked high with boxes and cardboard tubes. He has pushed the dining table against another wall to make room for a professional-looking drafting table and a metal cabinet on casters. The paper clamped to the drafting table contains sketches of a sleek sailing ship with oddly configured rigging. On the dining table, a snarl of wires connects a laptop computer to a flat-screen television, a keyboard, a printer, a joystick and four gaming consoles.

Jason pulls open one of the boxes, which turns out to be filled with comic books.

Jude flips open a binder beside the computer. "Listen to this: *I knew we were closing in on Vortor. I could smell him on the wind, hear his laughter taunting me across the waves.*"

"What is it?"

"Some kind of story?" She turns back to the first page. "*Starima's Revenge.*"

Jason laughs and picks up the first book in the box. "It's a comic. There's one here called *Starima and the Ruby Sword.*" He holds it up so Jude can see the cover illustration.

In the foreground, an extremely well-endowed redhead clad in skimpy leather armor and holding a red sword is obviously Starima. Behind her, an old woman leans on a staff, and a man wearing elaborate robes and a featureless gold mask stares off into the distance.

As Jason drops the comic back in the box, a piece of paper sticking out from under the flap of a neighboring box catches his eye. He lifts the flap and says, "Jude, come see this." She crosses the room and they stand together for a silent moment, looking down into the box full of cash. The bills have been tossed in loosely and seem to be mostly new and mostly twenties.

"Well, this will make Agent Hauver's day," Jude says. "We'd better not touch anything else until the FBI goes through here."

After Jason leaves a message for the agent, they leave the

house and walk back to Jude's car. On the drive back to Jason's, she asks, "Can I stay at your place for a few days?"

"Sure. Can Trav manage on his own?"

"He's got the Extensitter now and the house is rigged up like a giant jungle gym. He's safer in the bathtub than I am in the shower."

"Well, you're welcome to stay. But why?"

"Travis and I need a time-out. Actually, Travis is the same as always. I'm the one who needs to get away." Her cyes are fixed on the road, her hands at ten and two on the steering wheel. "You know we've been fighting a lot lately. Well, it's got to the point where I can't even look at him anymore without yelling at him." Jude is a practical, even-tempered woman. Whatever this argument is about, it must be something serious to make her so angry.

"Are you ready to talk about it now?"

"Yes, but not while I'm driving." She turns into the entrance of a strip mall and parks the car in front of a bar. "And I could use a drink."

When they are seated in a booth at the back of the bar, and Jude has knocked back a shot of bourbon and started on her beer chaser, Jason says, "Tell me what you're fighting about. Maybe I can talk to Trav."

Jude takes a long swallow from her bottle. "It's about our kids."

"You don't have any kids."

"And he says he doesn't think we should." She signals the waitress. "You're the designated driver tonight."

The waitress takes Jude's order for another boilermaker. Jason pushes his beer to the side and orders coffee.

"He says it's not fair to me," Jude continues as the waitress walks away, "because his disability would prevent him from helping out much. He says I'd be sacrificing too much."

"What kind of sacrifices?"

"For starters, I'd have to give up on becoming a detective and move to a desk job, something safer, with regular hours. But that's not the point. The point is, it's my decision to make."

"Is that his only reason?"

"It's the only one he's given me." Jude runs a frustrated hand through her hair. "But it's so stupid, I think there has to be another one. He told me this story once, about when he was four years old and locked himself in an upstairs bathroom. His dad climbed a ladder to the bathroom window and broke in to rescue him. Maybe he's reluctant because he couldn't do something like that for his own kids."

"Have you asked him about it?"

"Yes, but you know Trav. Mr. Strong-and-Silent. He'd never admit to anything like that." She finishes the last of her beer in one long swallow. "I feel like he's forcing me to choose between staying with him and having a family. That's just so unfair to me."

While it's true Travis never complains, not even about his disability, Jason thinks his sister is the one being unfair to her husband. Travis has his pride, but not so much that he'd lie about something this important. Jason doesn't voice this opinion, though. Right now, Jude is too upset to hear it. Instead, he asks, "So what are you going to do?"

The waitress arrives with their drinks. Jude picks up her bourbon. "I have no idea. But I'll tell you what I'm not going to do." She downs the shot. "I *know* Trav. He wants kids as much as I do, and I'm not giving up without a fight."

Love of Wind and Rock

FROM HER PLACE BEHIND THE CASH REGISTER, Peony watches her husband stacking clean mugs on the shelves beneath the coffeemakers. His ponytail, much thinner without the hair that once grew on top of his head, hangs down his back in a sleek white snake. Over the stringy muscles and ropy veins of his arms, her memory superimposes the firm, round strength that held her safe when she came from Vietnam to join him in America knowing only a handful of English words. A warmth of affection blossoms through her chest.

As though sensing this, Sam looks up from where he is squatting behind the counter and smiles. "She should be here by now."

"She's always late. She tries to do too many things at once."

"Now, who does that remind me of?"

"I'm never late."

Sam grasps the countertop to pull himself upright. "That's because you've got me to hustle you up." He looks at the wall clock. "I should help Paul with the vegetables."

Before going into the kitchen, he crosses over to the cash desk. Seated on the high stool, Peony is taller than when she is standing, which allows Sam to wrap his arms around her from behind and press his chin into her gray curls. "You worry too much. It'll be fine. I promise."

"You won't fight?"

"Not unless she starts it."

Peony's hope of a happy homecoming dies. She turns her head and kisses her husband's wattled neck. "Go help your son. It's almost eleven."

They still open every morning at eleven. When Peony and Sam took over the Lucky Dragon from Mr. Fong, they took over his menu as well. For thirty-five years they have served sanitized chop suey stir-fries supplemented with American favorites like hamburgers and chili. The formula worked well until recently. Now they are losing business to the upscale restaurants that have sprung up around the neighborhood to service the white-collar invasion of what was once a working-class community. The new residents want designer interiors and cuisines, items the increasingly shabby Lucky Dragon does not provide. Kendra has tried to convince her parents to refurbish the decor and the menu, but Peony is not convinced the resulting increase in business would offset the cost. The income from take-out orders is still good when augmented by the savings on staff. It's been two years since their last waitress left, and they haven't needed to hire another.

As Peony finishes preparing the till by breaking rolls of change into the coin slots, she also prepares herself for her daughter's arrival and the end it will bring to peace and harmony in the McAllister home. Sam loves his daughter and Kendra loves her father, but it is the love of wind and rock. Sam is a negotiator; in his world there are no absolutes—everything can be accomplished by discussion and eventual agreement. Kendra has no talent for compromise, unshakable conviction in her own opinions, and ruthless tenacity when it comes to getting her own way. Like all Buddhists, Peony believes suffering is created by the mind, but she finds this philosophy less than helpful when the mind creating the suffering belongs to someone else.

Love does not blind Peony to her daughter's faults. It would be an exaggeration to describe Kendra as selfish, but she is too goal-oriented to pay much attention to anything that does not directly affect her, and perhaps she is too invested in her image. For the past few years, Kendra has spent more time building her business than she has with her husband, and although Eric has never complained, the relationship has become one-sided, with Eric making accommodations for his wife's happiness but Kendra making none for her husband's in return. So Peony is not really surprised by Eric's infidelity. What man deprived of his wife's attentions could resist being seduced by a woman Kendra describes as a blond goddess? Marrying the woman was wrong, of course, and so was hiding his real profession.

Peony's last task before opening is to replenish the packets of plum sauce and soy sauce in the bowls on the cash desk. As she heaves herself off the stool, she sees Kendra's silver van pull up to the curb and calls out to her husband and son, "She's here," as she crosses the restaurant to unlock the door.

Kendra slides open the van's side door, hops out and stands on one foot to retrieve her crutches. Her friend Zanne gets out of the passenger seat. Zanne's boyfriend, Callum, walks from the driver's side to the back of the van and begins piling Kendra's possessions on the sidewalk.

Perhaps it is the way the crutches push Kendra's shoulders up that gives her an air of despair as she watches Callum pile all she is keeping from her previous life, six suitcases and a few boxes, on the pavement. Although she has only begun liquidating assets to pay for Eric's medical bills, Kendra has decided to move back in with her family today, claiming the building management company is bringing prospective new tenants through the apartment all the time. Sam has tried to talk her into waiting until Eric wakes up, with predictable results.

Peony understands Kendra's impatience to leave the apartment as an attempt to pre-divorce Eric, close the door on their marriage and get on with her life. This won't work, of course. In many ways, it was a good marriage. At some point, Kendra will have to grieve her loss. If she thought it would do any good, Peony would try to help the process along, but interference will just make Kendra more resistant to grief than she already is. With a sigh, Peony slides back the dead bolts and opens the door.

Kendra pauses to kiss her mother's cheek before entering the restaurant to stand beside the tarnished brass statue of a laughing Buddha, its belly rubbed bright by departing customers who pat it for luck. She looks around the dining room—at the faded dragon tapestry hanging over the cash desk, the frayed edges of the tablecloths, the worn spots in the dingy carpet—as though confused by these familiar surroundings.

Zanne, bending almost double, gives Peony a hug as she follows Kendra inside. "How are you, Peony?"

"I'm fine, dear." Peony reaches up to hug Zanne in return. "It's good you could help Kendra today."

Callum pushes Zanne gently in the back with the box he is carrying to move her along. "Some help. I'm the one doing all the heavy lifting."

Zanne defends her empty arms. "I did all the packing. I'm here for moral support now."

"Well, stop blocking the doorway and go support." Callum

turns to Peony. "Good to see you, gorgeous. When we get this stuff upstairs, can I talk to you about those little shrimp and rice dumplings you made for Sam's birthday? Have you got a recipe?"

"Not really. But I can show you."

Wiping his hands on a tea towel, Sam comes out of the kitchen, followed by his son.

Whereas Kendra takes entirely after her mother, Paul is a perfect blend of East and West. He is tall, broad-shouldered and lean-featured like his father, but has his mother's dark, heavy-lidded eyes and straight black hair. In temperament, he is exactly like Sam, an optimistic and generous idealist. Peony often wishes her beautiful son had inherited some of her pragmatism and hopes his levelheaded fiancée will provide the common sense he lacks.

When the flurry of hugging and handshaking subsides, Paul helps Callum ferry Kendra's possessions up to her old room. Zanne and Kendra take seats opposite each other at one of the tables. Sam goes to the service counter to get tea. Peony sits beside her daughter and asks, "Where is the bird?"

The corners of Kendra's lips droop momentarily, but she forces them back up. "His new owner picked him up yesterday."

Sam places a blue and white china teapot, inherited from Mr. Fong along with everything else in the restaurant, on the table. "You sold Eric's bird?"

The reproof in his tone is mild, but Kendra bristles defensively. "Jack was mine, Pops. Eric gave him to me. Besides, according to the doctor, he may not be able to take care of himself, let alone a parrot."

As he unstacks tea bowls, Sam asks if his son-in-law's condition has improved. Kendra says it hasn't. "The doctor says he's a seven on the coma scale, and statistically most of those people die. But she thinks he has a much better chance because they relieved the pressure on his brain so quickly. Actually, she expected him to be conscious by now."

"Thanks." Zanne accepts a bowl of green tea from Sam. "And when he does wake up?"

"It's like a stroke. It all depends on what areas of the brain were injured. In Eric's case, there's no obvious injury, but Dr. Strachan says he'll almost certainly be disabled. Like I care."

Annoyance flashes across Sam's face. Peony, knowing her daughter's remark is motivated by anger and not cruelty, looks at him pleadingly. His jaw tightens, but he nods, sits beside Zanne and asks her what's new in her life.

Peony leans toward her daughter and whispers, "Don't provoke him like that. You know how much he likes Eric. This is a difficult time for everyone."

"He's not the one who got cheated on." Kendra doesn't bother to whisper her reply. "He's my father. He should be on my side."

Sam breaks off his conversation with Zanne to remonstrate with his daughter. "I am on your side. I just think you shouldn't flush away a good marriage without giving Eric a second chance. People make mistakes."

Kendra spits back, "Exactly what definition of good marriage includes bigamy?"

They are dancing between the legs of an elephant that fills the room. No one is going to remind Kendra of the yearlong affair she had with Eric while still living with her first husband, but everyone remembers it. They also remember the time, twenty years ago, when Peony found Sam across the street with a salesgirl in the changing room of Ellie's Fine Bridal Fashions.

Sam defends Eric. "Okay. He did a bad thing. I'm not saying he didn't, just that it may not be so black and white. Maybe she got pregnant."

"Well, as it happens, she *is* pregnant. They were *trying* to get pregnant. And unprotected sex is not really a plus point either."

Zanne, whose lifelong friendship with Kendra grants her the status of honorary family member, has seen this bickering many times before. She sips her tea and follows the exchange like an observer at a tennis match.

Paul, carrying two of Kendra's suitcases, passes behind Peony on his way to the stairway that leads to the family quarters. He bends down and whispers in her ear, "That didn't take long."

New Tricks

FOR THE THIRD TIME, Cassandra navigates through the menu of her new cell phone and attempts to type in a text message. For the third time, she accidentally presses END instead of * on the keypad and her message disappears. For the third time, she fights the urge to throw the damn thing against the side of the house.

When she bought this new cell phone, with its minuscule keyboard that should have made texting easier, she felt modern and adventurous. Now she feels archaic and foolish, an old dog trying to learn new tricks. Texting looks so easy when Robyn does it, her tapered thumbs dancing over the keys like a ballerina *en pointe*. Cassandra's blunt digits clump around the keypad in army boots.

The phone vibrates in her hand. Startled, she drops it between the planks of the back deck, where it makes a muffled buzzing in the dirt. She is tempted to leave it there, but the message can only be from Robyn, and now that Lesley no longer visits Dave, this phone is Cassandra's only link to her new love.

That first night in the hospital, she didn't recognize Dr. Strachan as the sweet-faced young medical student she'd met at a party almost a quarter century before. Their casual, uncomplicated flirtation had been a comfort to Cassandra, who was struggling with jealousy during Norah's affair with that slutty writer, and easily forgotten when Norah came to her senses and realized the writer was more interested in getting her book into the bookstore window than she was in Norah. Robyn had no problem recognizing Cassandra, though. While Lesley sat with Dave, Cassandra and Robyn had coffee in the hospital cafeteria every evening, reminiscing and catching up. But they soon discovered their ancient attraction hadn't entirely expired.

Dating Robyn has gifted Cassandra with something she never expected to experience again. It's not only the sex, uninhibited and so much more joyous than those last years with Norah; it's the acceptance and even approval Robyn offers. Five years of hiding her true self from the gossiping busybodies of Brockville have left Cassandra feeling alienated and aching for her own kind.

With a sigh, she walks down the steps, kneels on the grass and peers beneath the deck. Six feet out of reach, the phone buzzes mockingly. She flattens her body to the ground and wriggles under the planks, her fingers touching the plastic casing just as the noise stops. As she begins to back out, the back door opens and footsteps knock dust down on her head.

"Cass? Cass, are you out here?" Beatrice calls.

Cassandra swipes a cobweb off her mouth before answering. "I'm under the deck."

Beatrice kneels down to peer between the boards. "What are you doing under there?"

"Not having fun." Wriggling backward, Cassandra emerges and attempts to wipe the worst of the dirt off her T-shirt. "I dropped my phone." She wants desperately to check Robyn's message, but forces herself to put the phone in her jeans pocket. "What's up?"

Beatrice is so upset she actually wrings her hands. "Lesley is packing. She wants to leave."

"Did she say where she's going?"

"Back to the cabin. I told her she shouldn't be alone right now. I told her she needs her family at a time like this. She won't listen to me. You have to talk to her."

Cassandra doesn't understand why Beatrice is so upset. It's not like the girl is moving to another country. The cabin is just a few miles out of town. Beatrice is probably projecting her own dislike of being alone onto her daughter. Brushing the last of the loose dirt off her jeans, Cassandra follows her sister into the house and up the stairs to Lesley's bedroom.

Lesley looks up from folding a skirt. "What happened to you?"

"I dropped something under the deck," Cassandra replies. "Trixie says you want to go home."

"I am going home, Aunt Cass. You're not going to talk me out of it. I promised Kendra I'd make a list of Dave's assets, and I need time to think."

"About what?" Beatrice sits on the chair in front of the desk where Lesley once did her homework.

Lesley drops the skirt into her suitcase and sits on the end of the bed. "I have to make decisions. About Dave and the baby."

"We'll make them together," Cassandra says.

"No. They have to be my decisions. Not yours."

"Oh." Beatrice expels an exasperated breath. "That's just nonsense. You're pregnant. You're in no condition to make decisions. You should listen to your aunt."

"Pregnancy doesn't make me stupid, Mom."

"I didn't mean that. I mean you have hormones."

"Hormones don't make me stupid either." Lesley's hair becomes a curtain hiding her face as she drops her head. She scuffs the toe of her sandal across the lavender pile of the bedside rug her great-aunt Ellen hooked for her when she was eight. Beatrice opens her mouth to speak, but Cassandra holds up a grubby hand to silence her.

When Lesley finally looks up, her expression is wary but determined. "I love you, Mom. And I love you, Aunt Cass. But you can't take care of me forever. I have to learn to take care of myself."

Concerned for the first time, Cassandra folds her arms across her chest. "Immediately?"

"Will it be easier after the baby is born?"

"But Dave—" Beatrice begins.

Lesley cuts her mother off. "I can't count on Dave. What if he never wakes up? And what will he be like when he does? And even if he's fine, I don't know if I can trust him again. Maybe I should do what the investigator said. Get an annulment."

"This is what your mother means." Cassandra frees a hand from its containing elbow and extends it toward her niece. "It's too soon to make a decision like that. We have to think this through."

"What you mean, Aunt Cass, is that you have to think it through. In this house, if it's not your decision, it's never going to happen, is it?" Coming from Lesley, who has always been a mild, amiable girl, this defiance is shocking. She stands up and closes her suitcase. "Well, I'm going to make my own decisions. And if they're wrong, I'll learn from my mistakes." She turns her back on her mother as she presses the locks of the suitcase shut. "I can't be a child anymore. I'm having a child. I need to grow up."

Beatrice's features compress with confusion. "I don't understand why you keep saying that."

Cassandra looks at her sister and imagines being responsible for Lesley and the baby as well as for Beatrice. She uncrosses her arms and pushes her hand into her jeans pockets, closing her fingers around the cell phone and the hope it represents. "She's right, Trixie. It doesn't matter where she is. It matters that she learns to trust herself." She smiles at her niece. "You go home, honey. Make your decisions. No matter what you decide, we'll support you."

An hour later, when Lesley has left and Beatrice has reluctantly accepted that her daughter's departure is not the end of the world, Cassandra goes back out to the deck and takes the phone from her pocket. Robyn has sent a text message: *missing u. when can i see u? xox*

She holds the phone in her left hand and, with a careful baby finger, types back: *dinner saturday? xox*

LESLEY'S DEFIANT ATTITUDE DOESN'T SURVIVE her trip home.

She parks in front of the cabin and carries the box of groceries her mother insisted on giving her into the kitchen. Through the archway leading to the living room, she sees the rolls of insulation and remembers Dave promising to get them installed when he got back from Idaho. Squeezing her eyelids together to hold back tears, she puts the box on the counter by the sink. Crying won't help her now. She needs a plan, but a lifetime of following other people's plans has left her ill-equipped to make one of her own.

Lesley goes into the tiny room Dave used as an office, looking for paper and a pen to start working on the list for Kendra. The floor and the dented surface of the metal desk are still littered with papers the FBI left out after they went through the house. She picks up a notepad from the floor and is searching for a pen when her cell phone rings.

"Hello?"

"Hi, Lesley. It's Kendra."

"Hi, Kendra. How's your ankle?"

"Doesn't hurt as much. Listen, I just got a call from the FBI. They found McCoy's other place. He was house-sitting for a woman who's in England. They've finished going through it and taken what they want, so they said I can pick up everything else."

At first, Lesley is shocked by the way Kendra uses her husband's surname as though he were a stranger. Then she understands that's exactly what he is for both of them. "Does this mean McCoy has been cleared?" she asks, trying the name out for herself and experiencing a sense of release in the honesty of it.

"No, not yet. The FBI agent said they'd decided to suspend the investigation until McCoy wakes up, but when they went through the house, they found a big box of cash, so now it's an active investigation again."

"He's not a terrorist," Lesley insists.

"They don't think that anymore. Apparently he was an illustrator."

"An illustrator?"

"You sound surprised."

"I didn't know he could draw. What did he illustrate?"

"I don't know. I didn't ask. Anyway, a box of money is pretty suspicious, so now they're looking into things like forgery and blackmail. Meanwhile, I was wondering if you'd like to come help me go through McCoy's things on Saturday. You might recognize something I don't."

"Sure. I'd like to see what his other life was like. What time?"

"About two o'clock. Can you pick me up? I still can't drive."

Lesley agrees. After hanging up, she says, "McCoy," out loud, and has the sensation of taking a mental step back. "This is McCoy's desk." She thumps the metal surface in front of her and stands, physically mirroring the inner distance the word gives her. She spreads her arms wide. "This is McCoy's house."

She finds a pen on the floor behind the desk and prints *Mine* and *McCoy's* at the top of the first blank page in the notebook. Then she walks through the house, assigning ownership to everything she sees, feeling lighter and freer with every item she can list in the *McCoy's* column. For the first time since that terrible night in the hospital, Lesley remembers what it is like to feel normal. The feeling builds until she looks out the kitchen window and sees the old barn. She writes "barn" in the *McCoy's* column and underlines the word three times, scoring through the paper. Then she throws the notepad across the room, braces her arms against the counter and howls out her loss.

What Happened in the Barn

Nine months previously

DAVE TURNED HIS TRUCK OFF the highway onto a dirt driveway—nothing more than two tire tracks bisected by scrubby weeds, snaking up through the forest covering Saddleback Ridge. "It doesn't look like much now," he said. "But it's got real potential."

"Oh, Dave. It's so cute," Lesley exclaimed as the cabin came into view around a curve in the driveway. "I never knew these places still existed."

The cabin, constructed of weathered logs, sat in the center of a small meadow tucked into the side of the ridge. A deep, covered porch and two gables jutting out from the steep roof gave it a quirky kind of personality. Bare cornstalks poked up from the dark soil of a large vegetable garden. Beside the house, a wooden barn with a tin roof squatted in the shadow of a skeletal modern windmill.

"It's over a hundred years old." Dave parked the truck. "When the last owner died, his kids didn't want to spend the money to fix it up, so I got it cheap." Climbing down from the driver's seat, he walked around the front of the truck to open Lesley's door, a quaint and courtly gesture she adored. "I've been working on it for almost six years," he continued as they approached the house. "Installed the solar panels and the windmill last year. Dug a new well this year. I want to be as self-sufficient as possible here. Watch the second step. It's rotten." He unlocked the front door and pushed it open for her to precede him into the cabin.

The rooms were filled with stacks of renovation materials: wallboard and plywood, two-by-fours and plumbing pipes. Wires hung from ceilings and poked out from between bare studs on the walls. Wide oak planking, liberally coated with sawdust, covered every floor. In the kitchen, scarred pine cupboards, as solid as the day they were made, lined walls covered in peeling wallpaper.

"It's not as bad as it looks," Dave said when they'd completed the tour of the cabin. "The plumbing and wiring are almost done. Then it's just finishing."

"Where do you sleep?" Lesley asked.

"Weather's still good, so I'm sleeping in the barn. Come see."

Inside the barn, Dave had stacked straw bales to insulate a room-sized space and piled loose straw on the floor under his sleeping bag. Boxes laid on their sides gave temporary accommodation to his clothes, and an old arborite kitchen table with rust-speckled chrome legs held a paperback book and a radio.

"You want a beer?" Dave asked. "I've got a six-pack in the truck."

Lesley sat on a bale of straw. "Sure."

When Dave returned with the beer, he sat beside her, popped the tab on one of the cans and held it out. "I'm thinking about turning this place into a working farm."

"But you like being a guide," Lesley said as she took the beer.

"I'm tired of all the driving between jobs. And it's time I settled down. I talked to a guy in Seattle last week who has a stall at one of the farmers' markets. He said there's a big demand for organic produce and heirloom vegetables. I could put in a bigger garden here and sell to him. And I'm pretty handy. If I can pick up a few odd jobs in town over the winter, I think I could make a go of it here."

Lesley liked the idea of Dave settling down. Unlike the boys she'd dated in high school, Dave never tried to squeeze her backside while they kissed, never thrust his hand between her thighs while he drove her home from dinner or a movie. Sometimes, when she saw the way his eyes strayed to her breasts or felt the gentleness of his hand cupping her cheek as they kissed good night, she thought maybe he wanted more.

For her part, Lesley definitely wanted more. She imagined Dave's body beside hers in bed before she fell asleep. She dreamed about him and could almost feel his arms around her when she woke up. Every cell in her body was tuned to Dave. He was the one. She just knew it. She also knew, with some ancient, feminine instinct, that Dave held himself back because of the difference in their ages. For a physical relationship to happen, she had to make the first move. And that was a problem.

Like most voluptuous women raised during the age of anorexia, Lesley was timid about her sexuality, embarrassed by the small pads of subcutaneous fat that rounded her belly and hips, emphasizing the slenderness of her waist. In high school, potential beaux had interpreted her rejection of their exploratory hands as prudery, and this, coupled with the fact that her father taught physical education to every boy she dated, resulted in a number of first, second, and sometimes even third dates, but no steady boyfriend. She was still a virgin. She had no idea how to seduce a man.

When they finished the beers, Dave stood up. "We should go. Your mother will be wondering what I've done with you."

Lesley remained seated. She stared at the slight bulge in the crotch of Dave's jeans and remembered Sandy, one of her high school girlfriends, bragging about the size of her boyfriend's equipment. With no idea what equipment really looked like, Lesley had requested details, but found Sandy's description less than enlightening.

"Why do you keep dating me, Dave?" she asked.

He sat back down on the straw bale and hung his hands between his knees. "Because I can't stop."

"Why not?"

"Because you're kind and gentle and I feel good when I'm around you." He straightened his back and turned his head to look into her eyes. "And because you're the most beautiful woman I've ever seen. I like looking at you."

She reached out and lightly pressed her fingertips in the hollow beneath his Adam's apple. "Just looking?"

"Lesley, honey . . ."

Something in his voice gave her sudden courage. "Just looking, Dave?" She flattened her palm and dragged it down between the muscles of his chest. "Is that all you want to do?"

His response was hoarse, almost inaudible. "No."

Raw, heavy warmth flooded through her pelvis. She passed her hand down, across the ridges of his abdomen, and cupped it over the bulge that now pushed against the zipper of his jeans. He shuddered. In the tiny image of her face reflected in his eyes, Lesley saw something in herself she had never seen before. Power.

"Me neither," she whispered, and leaned forward to gently bite his lower lip.

Jason in the Middle

ON SATURDAY MORNING, WITH BOTH Fletcher and Jude to feed, Jason decides to make French toast. Because Jason's mother loved to cook, he never made anything more complex than a sandwich until he started college, when he added hot dogs and macaroni and cheese dinner to his culinary repertoire. Real cooking, what his mother would have called good plain cooking, he learned after marriage in self-defense. A man can endure only so many canned soup suppers. Starting in the traditional male arena of barbecuing, he has, over the years, acquired creditable skills in the kitchen. Breakfast is his specialty.

Fletcher slouches into the kitchen a little after nine, wearing saggy shorts and a graffiti-scribbled T-shirt that could easily accommodate a boy three times his size. "Morning, Dad."

"Morning. Breakfast's in the oven." Jason looks up from his newspaper. "What the hell are you wearing?"

"This is what they wear at school here. It's not like the academy." Fletcher pours himself a glass of orange juice from the pitcher on the table.

Jason knows his son isn't drawing a negative comparison between the exclusive school Norris paid for in San Francisco and the public high school that is all Jason can afford. The remark still stings, making his response sharper than he intends. "You look like a refugee."

"Yeah, but so does everyone else." Pulling open the oven door, Fletcher exclaims, "Awesome! French toast. Thanks, Dad." He loads his plate with six slices and soaks them liberally with syrup as he takes a seat across from his father at the kitchen table. "Where's Aunt Jude?"

"Out running."

"She's really in shape, isn't she? You should run, Dad."

The phone rings. "Is this your polite way of saying I'm out of shape?" Jason asks as he gets up to answer it. "Hello?"

"Jason? It's Kathy. Is Fletcher up?"

"I'll check." He covers the receiver with his hand. "It's your mother."

Fletcher shakes his head emphatically. "I don't want to talk to her."

"You're going to have to talk to her eventually."

Fletcher picks up his plate and stalks out of the kitchen.

"Kathy? He's in the shower. I'll tell him you called."

"Don't lie. I know he's not in the shower."

"Okay. He still doesn't want to talk to you."

"He's just like you."

"Hey. I'm talking to you."

"I mean you both sulk."

Unwilling to dignify the accusation with denial and get dragged into another discussion of his faults as a husband, Jason says nothing.

"Have you talked to him?" Kathy persists.

Jason takes refuge in technical truth. "I talk to him. He needs more time."

A frustrated expulsion of breath on the other end of the line evokes the memory of a younger Kathy's little-girl pout, an expression Jason initially adored and soon came to dread. "Well, tell him I love him and I'll call him in three weeks when Norris and I get back from Italy."

"Got it." Jason hangs up without saying good-bye and goes into the living room, where he finds his son sprawled across the sofa in front of the television. "Your mother says she loves you and she'll call you when she gets back from vacation."

Fletcher shoves a forkful of French toast into his mouth and keeps his eyes fixed on the screen.

Jason knows he should challenge this defiance, but there's nothing he can do to help Fletcher and Kathy repair the rift between them. They have to sort it out themselves. Kathy was wrong to send her son away. Fletcher is wrong to freeze his mother out. Caught in the middle, Jason takes abuse from both sides and resents the unfairness of inheriting a situation he had no part in creating. It's easier just to walk away, and that's exactly what he's doing when a line of dialogue from the television catches his attention.

"This is an omen, Starima. The Kav has chosen you."

Jason retrieves his half-eaten breakfast from the kitchen and returns to the living room. "Move over. What are you watching?"

"Cartoons." Fletcher swings his legs to the floor.

"I can see that." Jason sits beside his son. "What's the name of this one?"

"*Kav'erse.*"

When Jude returns from her run, she finds her brother and

nephew eating French toast and watching television together. Jason waves his fork at her. "Come see this."

"See what?" She enters the room far enough to see the screen. "Whoa! Is that . . ."

"Yep. It's Starima." Jason moves over to make room for his sister.

Instead of sitting on the sofa with her nephew and brother, Jude goes to the kitchen and returns with a bowl of soapy water. "So it's more than just comic books?" she asks as she starts cleaning the knickknacks on the mantel. She spends most of her time in the house tidying and cleaning. It annoys Jason, but he lets it pass since he knows organizing his home is helping her organize her thoughts.

"Way more." Fletcher fills her in around a mouthful of French toast. "There's this show, a bunch of video games, toys, all kinds of stuff. When the show's over, we're going to check it out on the Internet."

"Starima seems to be an industry," Jason adds. "This could add up to a lot of money for my client. As near as I can make out, Starima is a spy for someone called the Exiled Emperor. I think the old broad is the one we saw on the book cover. She's some kind of witch."

"She's a priestess of Kav," Fletcher corrects him.

Jude stops wiping at a pottery candlestick and squints at the screen. "What's that flashy stuff that keeps popping in the distance?"

Again Fletcher shares his expertise. "Bombing."

"Then what's the point of the sword?"

"It's like light sabers. You know. In *Star Wars*?"

With her military background and empirical mind-set, Jude is unable to appreciate this explanation. She snorts her derision and replaces the candlestick on the mantel. "They don't make any sense either."

When the show ends, Fletcher brings his laptop to the kitchen. Jude gets her own plate of French toast, Jason pours his third cup of coffee, and they stand behind Fletcher while he mans the keyboard.

Starima is the creation of the cryptically identified E. McCoy. Originally the heroine of a comic book, she has branched out into novels and a cartoon television series. PlayStation, Xbox and Nintendo all have games based on her character, which also graces several role-playing Web sites. Opportunities to buy Starima toys, books and novelties abound.

E. McCoy is harder to pin down. His Wikipedia article is little more than a bibliography. His name can be found on blogs, usually prefixed by the adjective "reclusive," but he does not appear to have a Web site of his own.

Fletcher is astonished by this. "How can he not have a Web site? Everyone has a Web site. I have a Web site."

It's Jason's turn to be astonished. "You do?"

"Well, sort of. I bought my domain name, FletcherCheddick.com. In case I get famous."

"For what?" Jude asks.

"I don't know. I'm only sixteen."

"What I want to know," Jason says, "is if this Starima is so famous, how come I've never heard of her?"

"'Cause you don't play video games, Dad. I didn't realize it started with a comic, though. Always thought it was just a game. Like Lara Croft."

After they finish checking out Starima, Fletcher retreats to the garage to practice on his drums, Jude showers and Jason returns to his newspaper. When the phone rings, he lets the call go to voice mail, then picks up when he hears Travis's voice.

"Hey, Trav. How're you doing?"

"Pretty good. I'm thinking of hiring a cleaning lady, though. Is Jude there?"

"She's in the shower. Can I take a message?"

"Is she really in the shower or she just doesn't want to talk to me?"

Now that he's telling the truth, Jason is offended by this question. "She's really in the shower. What do you want me to tell her?"

"Just ask her to call me. How is she?"

Jason decides Travis doesn't need to know about Jude's midnight tears. "Well, let's just say my house hasn't been this clean in years. Hang on—I think I heard the bathroom door open." He covers the mouthpiece with his palm and calls out, "Jude?"

She appears in the kitchen doorway wearing Jason's striped bathrobe and rubbing her damp curls with a towel. "What?"

"Trav is on the phone. He wants to—"

Jude grabs the receiver from Jason's hand before he can finish his sentence. "Has something happened? Are you okay?" A second later, she slumps against the kitchen counter in obvious relief. "Sorry. I forgot about that. I don't know if I'm ready yet. Can you call the restaurant and cancel?" Travis's reply must be the wrong one. Her eyes flash and her voice rises. "Two reasonable adults? What's that supposed to mean? I'm not the one who's being unreasonable here. . . ."

Jason grabs his newspaper off the kitchen table and retreats to his office.

Confused and Abused

DEPRESSED BY THIS MORNING'S PHONE fight with Travis, Jude slumps in the backseat of the car and tries to ignore her brother and nephew bickering in the front seats.

"Why'd you put your turn signal on?"

"Because I'm turning, Dad."

"Not for half a block."

"The guy behind me is tailgating. I'm giving him lots of warning."

Jason looks out the back window. "He's not tailgating. All you're doing is confusing him."

Fletcher slows as they approach the four-way stop and comes to a smooth halt as a silver van approaches the intersection from the left.

"You have right-of-way, Fletch. What are you waiting for?"

"I'm waiting to see if the van stops."

"It's stopped. Turn."

Fletcher eases forward, then slams on the brakes hard enough to rock the car.

Jason yells, "What the hell is wrong with you?" just as a boy on a bicycle whizzes by from the right, mere inches in front of the hood. "Oh, God." Jason scrubs his face with both hands.

Fletcher, much calmer than his father, turns sedately onto Grove Street. "It's okay, Dad. You didn't see him. What's the house number?"

"Twelve," Jude replies, relieved that the trip is over. "It's the driveway on the other side of the hedge."

Fletcher turns into the driveway and parks in the carport. Jude climbs out of the car just as the van they met at the four-way stop pulls in behind them.

Lesley McCoy emerges from the driver's seat. She walks around the front of the van to slide open the back door on the passenger side, revealing Kendra McCoy sitting with her legs extended along the backseat, her right foot wrapped in an elasticized bandage. Lesley takes a pair of crutches from the floor of the van and props them against the side. She turns to help Kendra out, but Jason is already there, holding out his hand.

"What happened?" he asks.

Kendra takes his offered hand and slides off the seat. "Just a sprained ankle. It's my own fault. I wasn't looking where I was going."

"I wasn't looking either, so it's my fault too." Lesley hands the crutches to Kendra. "Hello, Mr. Cheddick. It's nice to see you again."

"It's good to see you too, Mrs. McCoy."

"Given the number of Mrs. McCoys here," Kendra observes dryly, "first names are probably easier for everyone."

"Sounds good to me," Jason agrees. "I'm Jason. You've already met my sister, Jude. And this is my son, Fletcher. They've volunteered to help us pack things up."

"That was so amazing the way you stopped back there at the corner." Lesley extends her hand toward Fletcher. "That kid came out of nowhere. He's lucky you were driving."

Fletcher's cheeks flush. He shakes Lesley's hand and mumbles, "I just saw him in time," then develops an intense interest in his sneakers.

Since Jude saw them last, these women have changed.

Kendra's glossy self-assurance has vanished. Even allowing for the flat shoes and the hunched posture forced on her by the crutches, she seems to have shrunk. Dark circles beneath her eyes and three deep vertical lines between her eyebrows give her an exhausted, defensive expression. She hops forward tentatively, as though reluctant to participate in collecting McCoy's belongings.

The assurance that left Kendra has migrated to Lesley. The blue eyes Jude remembers as soft and vague are now focused and brilliant, scanning the house and garden in careful assessment. Lesley tosses her platinum hair out of her eyes, squares her shoulders and sets her jaw with the bravado of a warrior queen going into battle before following Jason and Kendra to the front door.

"She's like a movie star," Fletcher whispers to Jude.

As they enter the floral wilderness of the living room, Lesley says, "This is pretty."

Judging by Kendra's expression, this is an opinion she does not share. Her eyes lock onto the birdcage. "Why would he have a cage here? Jack was always at the apartment."

"Oh, sorry; I forgot to tell you," Jason apologizes. "According to the neighbor, babysitting the bird was the reason for the house-sitting agreement. Cracker Jack actually belongs to the owner of this house."

Lesley is shocked. "He gave you someone else's pet as an anniversary present? That's horrible."

"It gets worse." Kendra slumps over the armrests of her crutches. "I sold Jack already. Now I have to buy him back."

"That might not be a problem. We have some good news." Jason's voice is neutral, but Jude isn't fooled. She glances over at Fletcher, who is too preoccupied trying not to stare at Lesley to notice the warmth in his father's smile.

Jason shares the results of the morning's research into Kav'erse and its creator. Judging by the surprise and confusion on both women's faces, neither of them has ever heard of Kav'erse or any of the characters that populate it. Jude tries to imagine Travis hiding something that huge and dismisses the idea as ridiculous. McCoy must be one hell of an actor. Maybe he found it easy to fool a naive woman like Lesley who hadn't known him very long. But the amount of effort required to deceive a sharp-witted woman like Kendra over five years of marriage borders on sociopathic.

The FBI search team have been through the house thoroughly, leaving behind floors littered with the contents of drawers, cupboards and boxes. The laptop is gone, along with several boxes, including the one filled with cash. From their previous visit to the house, Jason and Jude know McCoy's possessions were stored in the dining room, so Kendra decides that is the only room they will pack up.

Fletcher begins by collecting the comic books. He makes slow progress with the task, since his efforts primarily center around reading them and periodically exclaiming, "Awesome!"

Lesley and Kendra make equally slow progress. They sit together on the floor beside a pile of photograph albums containing pictures of foster families from McCoy's childhood. The women examine each album before packing it, commenting on his expression and attempting to guess his age, as though looking for the Rosetta Stone that will translate these images of McCoy into a version they recognize. Jude listens to them and realizes neither woman knows anything about the many families he must have lived with as a child. She finds this incredible and somehow sad.

When Jude and Travis were dating, she knew they would marry as soon as they started talking about their childhoods, as though words could make up for all the years before they met. Over shared meals, or lying in bed after sex, they spoke for hours: about best friends, most-embarrassing moments, first loves, favorite teachers, all the minutiae that define personality. She knew everything about her future in-laws long before she met them and told Travis everything about her family in return. For Jude, the need to share deeply is as much a part of love as physical attraction.

As she loads climbing gear into a box, Jude has a sudden vivid memory of Travis's accident—the way her heart seemed to stop when his body tumbled past her on the rock face, the overwhelming relief she felt when his eyes opened as the paramedics were loading him into the rescue helicopter. She dumps a snarl of ropes into the box and knows with absolute certainty that if she must choose between Travis and children, she will choose Travis. She can imagine them building a happy life together without kids. She can't imagine living without him at all.

Unhampered by previous experience of McCoy, Jude and Jason make better progress, packing boxes with things like books, clothes and sports equipment, items as uninformative as their comatose owner. A stack of pornographic magazines generates a small flurry of McCoy-bashing in Kendra and Lesley's corner, followed by much louder and more graphically expressed vilification a few minutes later, prompted by the discovery of his not-so-little black book. This ends abruptly when they leaf through the pages and see their names are the only two entries not crossed out. McCoy may be a cheater, but he appears to be, in his own way, a faithful one.

Half an hour into the packing, Fletcher suddenly scrambles to his feet and carries a comic book over to Jason, whose cheeks turn as red as his son's when he sees the cover. Intrigued, Jude goes over to see what is causing all the blushing. Lesley looks up from the album she and Kendra are studying and asks what they found. When no one answers, she gets up and crosses the room to see for herself.

"Oh, my God!" she whispers. "How could he?"

"How could he what?" Kendra asks.

Snatching the comic from Fletcher's hand, Lesley returns to where Kendra is sitting and flings it, faceup, on the floor beside Kendra's knees.

Like the cover of *Starima and the Ruby Sword*, this cover also has the masked man and the old woman in the background. The foreground shows a woman standing on a hilltop, holding a chalice above her head like an offering. Balloonlike breasts strain against the translucent fabric of a short toga, through which the pink areolas of erect nipples are clearly discernable. A ludicrously small waist cinched by an elaborate gold belt flows into curves so exaggerated the word "hips" is totally inadequate to do them justice. The hem of the tunic barely covers the woman's crotch, revealing overlong legs ending in impossibly narrow ankles. Above this parody of a body, surrounded by flowing masses of champagne hair, the face is unmistakably Lesley's.

"That's disgusting." Kendra picks up the comic and turns it over, hiding the cover. "He might as well have posted pictures of you naked on the Internet."

"It was bad enough he lied. But that?" Lesley's voice cracks on the last word. "I can't forgive that."

"I couldn't either." Kendra's expression of supportive pity warps suddenly into suspicion. On hands and knees, she crawls to the pile of comics Fletcher was packing and begins splaying them across the rug. Unlike Lesley, she responds to the image of her own face at maximum volume with some very unladylike observations about McCoy.

Crayons for Giraffes

Eric at age four

ERIC WAS HUNGRY, but not hungry enough to come out of the closet. He liked this closet better than the one at the last place. It was bigger and had a lightbulb he could turn on by pulling a string so he could draw while he waited for the man to deliver his mother's medicine.

Because he'd used up almost all his favorite red and orange crayons, Eric started drawing a rocket ship like the one in the *Space Cadet* cartoon, all silver and blue and dark, dark sky with little bits of the paper left blank for stars. He heard the door buzz like a really angry giant wasp, and his mother's footsteps crossing the living room to let the medicine man in. This man was better than the last one. His name was Hawk. Sometimes he gave Eric's mother her medicine even if she couldn't pay for it. Eric had never seen Hawk, because he came only when Eric's mother was sick and Eric was in the closet, but he recognized the deep, grumbly voice.

"You look like shit, woman."

"Everyone looks like shit without makeup. I just got up. What have you got today?"

"Depends on how much you got."

"Had a bad night last night and rent's due this week. Hundred?"

"Hundred won't get you the premium stuff, but I can give you this."

"Better than nothing."

After Hawk left, Eric finished the spaceship drawing before coming out of the closet because it always took his mother a little while to feel better. When the picture was done, he carefully collected the crayon bits and put them back in the old margarine tub before pushing open the closet door.

"Mummy? You feeling better?"

When she didn't answer, he tiptoed out of the bedroom and peered around the doorway into the living room. She'd fallen asleep really fast because she was still holding the rubber band and hadn't put the needle back in its box. This happened sometimes.

Eric went to the kitchen, where he climbed up on a chair and pulled a box of chocolate cereal out of the cupboard over the stove. He carried it back to the living room to watch TV, being careful to keep the sound low so his mother wouldn't wake up. He fell asleep watching cartoons and woke up hungry again, so he ate the rest of the cereal in the box while he watched a show about giraffes in Africa. They had funny spots and beautiful eyes, like his mother's. He got his crayons out to draw the giraffes, because they were mostly yellow and brown and he had lots of those colors left. He was still drawing, a long time later, after it got dark outside, when the phone rang.

"Hello."

"Eric. This is Sharrie. Is your mother there?"

"She's asleep."

"Well, wake her up. She's late for work again."

"Okay." Eric put down the phone receiver and tapped his mother's arm. "Mummy? Wake up, Mummy." She didn't wake up, so he pushed her arm harder. "Mummy, you're late for work." He pushed even harder, then gave up.

"She won't wake up. And she feels funny."

"What kind of funny?"

"Kind of cold."

"Eric, sweetie, how long has she been asleep?"

"All day."

"Listen to me, Eric. I think your mother is really sick. I'm going to call someone to come and take her to the hospital. You have to let them in, okay?"

"Okay."

"And tell them you're all alone, so they'll take you with her, okay?"

Eric's mother had been sick for as long as he could remember. She'd been to the hospital before. He'd stayed in a nice house with a nice lady and a nice man. He'd had a real bed with Superman sheets. They gave him macaroni and cheese, and there were toys and other kids to play with. He didn't want to go to the hospital with his mother. He wanted to go to the nice house, so that's what he said when he opened the door for the policeman a few minutes later.

The policeman told him to go to the kitchen and wait there. Eric went, because he knew his mother would be really, really mad when she woke up and saw the policeman. Lots more people came, firemen and then ambulance men, with sirens and lights that flashed through the kitchen window. Some of them looked around the door at Eric and he told them he wanted to go to the nice house, but they just went back to the living room.

Then a lady came into the kitchen and said she was Mrs. Johnston from Social Services. She had dark brown skin like Sharrie, but she was fatter and her hair was all zigzag and white, like electricity in cartoons. She asked him how long his mother had been asleep, and he told her about Hawk and the medicine. She asked him what he'd been doing, and he told her the names of all the cartoons he'd watched. She asked him if he was hungry. He asked her if she had macaroni and cheese. She said no, but she might know someone who did. She told him to wait a minute while she called to make sure and went into the living room to use the phone.

When she came back, she was carrying Eric's drawing book and the tub of crayon bits. "You must really like to draw," she said. "Will you show me your pictures?"

As he showed her his pictures, Eric explained that this was a new coloring book. He liked it better than his old one, even though all the pages had lines, because he liked to make his own pictures, not just color in someone else's. When they got to the giraffe, he told her, "This one isn't finished yet."

"Well, we have to wait a few more minutes before we can go, so why don't you finish it?"

Inspired by the lights flashing on the windowpane, Eric used the last of his red, orange and blue crayons to draw flames around the giraffe. Mrs. Johnston told him she thought it was a beautiful picture.

"You can have it," he said. "I can draw another one when I get more crayons."

Mrs. Johnston drove him to the new house. The lady who opened the door wasn't pretty like Eric's mother, but she was very nice. She squatted down until her face was level with his. She smiled and said, "Hi, Eric. My name is Beth. I hear you like macaroni and cheese."

Eric smiled back at her. He said good-bye to Mrs. Johnston and followed Beth into the kitchen. She gave him a big plate of macaroni and cheese. It was just as good as he remembered. Then she made him take a bath, which he didn't like as much. He fell asleep in a bed with teddy bears painted on the headboard and dreamed of giraffes.

Unlucky Lady

PASSING HIS HAND OVER THE TABLE, the dealer calls out, "No more bets." The white ball drops from the rim and begins its stuttering dance across the numbers on the wheel. For a few seconds, everyone around the roulette table holds their breath, then exhales in amazement as the ball drops into a slot. "Twenty-one red," the dealer says in the subdued tone of a man who has just witnessed a miracle.

"Oh, my God!" Eunice shrieks and flings her arms around Beatrice, who hugs her back enthusiastically, then turns to hug Andrew with equal warmth. Andrew lifts one arm and gingerly pats her back.

In roulette, more than any other casino game, the odds favor the house. It's also the slowest game on the floor, which is why Beatrice likes it; there's plenty of time for chatting and flirting while the dealer manages bets and spins the wheel. Usually, she places a single chip worth five dollars on a random inside bet.

Her self-imposed hundred-dollar maximum lasts about three hours. Today, perhaps inspired by her horoscope, which stated she should pay special attention to her family, she has decided to play a system based on her relatives' house numbers. Against all odds, all but one of the relatives she's played live at winning addresses. The losing number belongs to her brother-in-law, Dolph, whose legendary bad luck appears to extend to his residence. She is now twenty-five thousand and seventy-five dollars richer than when she walked into the casino an hour and twenty minutes ago.

A burly young man wearing a perfectly tailored charcoal gray suit comes over to the table. In a nasal tenor that does not match his physique, he invites Beatrice and her friends to join the owner, Big George, for a congratulatory drink before they leave. Beatrice, interested only in the social opportunities available at the casino, finds the invitation flattering and accepts it immediately. She pushes her stacks of roulette chips toward the dealer, who replaces them with hundred-dollar tokens in a tray. To his delight, she returns one to the table as a tip. Andrew, who timidly stuck to his even bets, exchanges his few remaining roulette chips for regular chips. The young man picks up the tray and leads Beatrice, Eunice and Andrew through a discreet door at the back of the casino that opens into a stairwell. At the top of the stairs, he pushes open another door into a wood-paneled office and announces, "They're here, boss."

Big George isn't very big at all. He's a wiry man whose snowy hair hangs in two tidy braids beside the lapels of his suit jacket. Taking Beatrice's hand, he raises it to his lips with an archaic gallantry that wins him a delighted giggle. "I just had to meet such a lucky lady." He presses her hand warmly before releasing it.

"Franklin here"—he nods at their guide—"can cash in your chips for you while we have our drink."

"Would you like a casino check, ma'am? Or would you prefer cash?" Franklin asks.

For the first time, it occurs to Beatrice that winning so much money may present a problem. Her second cousin's youngest is a teller at the bank where she has her account. A deposit this large will not go unnoticed, and although Beatrice and Eunice are not doing anything really wrong, they are dipping their toes in risqué waters that would create a wave of gossip back in Brockville. She looks over at Eunice, who says, quite firmly, "Cash."

Franklin nods and closes the door on his way out of the office.

After names have been exchanged, and Eunice's hand has received its own courtly salute, and drinks have been delivered by a waitress in a short and suggestively fringed dress, they move to a leather seating arrangement at one end of the office, where Andrew sits beside Eunice on one of the cowhide-covered sofas. Big George joins Beatrice on the other and asks her if she was playing a system. He grins at her explanation of how she used her relatives' house numbers, exposing long canine teeth that give him a slightly vampiric charm. "I've been in this business over twenty years, and that's the first time I've ever heard of the address system. So, do you have any plans for spending your winnings?" he asks.

"Well, I don't know. I've always wanted to go on one of those Mediterranean cruises, you know. See Greece and Italy. So romantic."

"You got seasick on the ferry to San Juan," Eunice reminds her. "I had to go whale watching by myself."

"It's different on a really big ship," Big George tells them. "You really can't tell you're not on dry land."

"You've been on a cruise?" Beatrice asks him.

"Not so lucky. I was in the marines."

Beatrice expects Andrew to ask Big George where he served, the way all her male relatives would, but Andrew just studies the two fingers of bourbon in his glass.

"I have been to Greece, though, on vacation," Big George continues, "and you're right about it being romantic. My wife loved it there. She keeps saying we should go back as soon as the grandkids start school."

Andrew perks up following this statement and contributes his own cruising experience to the conversation, a seven-day trip to Alaska. Eunice offers her cousin Flora's description of a honeymoon spent port-hopping in the Caribbean. By the time Franklin returns with a plastic bag from the Howling Wolf gift shop filled with neatly bundled bills, Beatrice's heart is all but set on a Mediterranean holiday, if she can figure out how to pay for it without revealing where the money came from.

At the end of the visit, Big George assures Beatrice she is welcome to go back to the tables and continue her winning streak, but Beatrice has run out of relatives. Instead, she offers to treat Eunice and Andrew to a meal, adding, "Cass and Lesley won't be home for dinner tonight. We have lots of time."

"There's a lovely little Italian restaurant about ten miles up the road," Andrew offers. "Delightful manicotti. We could take my car and I'll drop you back at the casino parking lot afterward."

Eunice endorses the idea with enthusiasm. "Oh, I love Italian! Just give me a minute to freshen up before we go."

Beatrice, seeing an opportunity to continue flirting with

Andrew for a few minutes, holds out her hand to Eunice. "Give me your keys first so Andrew and I can put this bag in your trunk."

Andrew foils her plan. "Actually, I should take advantage of the facilities as well." He offers his arm to Eunice. "Allow me to escort you."

Eunice passes the keys to Beatrice and says, "We'll meet you outside by the statue of the wolf," before tucking her hand into the crook of Andrew's arm and allowing him to lead her toward the restrooms.

At just after six p.m. the casino parking lot is full. Beatrice can't remember exactly where Eunice parked, and it seems as though half the cars in the lot are white sedans. As she weaves between vehicles checking license plates on likely-looking candidates, she wonders if Andrew's decision to sit beside Eunice in Big George's office was entirely innocent, and if Eunice's smile when she took Andrew's arm was just the tiniest bit smug. "I saw him first," Beatrice mutters.

Preoccupied with deciphering Andrew's intentions, she pays no attention to the thin young man in a hooded sweatshirt who appears to have misplaced his car as well. When the bag filled with money jerks in her hand, she thinks the handle has caught on a car door. She turns to free it and finds herself in a tug-of-war with the young man.

She screams, more from shock than fear.

The young man tugs harder on the bag. "Shut up and let go of the bag, lady!"

Beatrice wants very much to let go of the bag, but one of the plastic handles has stretched in the struggle and is now snagged on the projecting setting of her ring. Ignoring the instruction to be quiet, she screams again, this time with the piercing volume of real fear. Startled, her attacker gives one last desperate tug on the bag just as she tries to jerk her ring free from the handle. The thin plastic splits. Caught off balance, Beatrice topples backward as her winnings tumble out across the pavement.

The young man says a very rude word, snatches up two bundles of cash and sprints away between the cars.

Struggling to her feet, Beatrice tries to shout, "Help! Help! Thief!" But her vocal cords, strained by her last scream, can manage only a hoarse whisper.

Decisions Made in Anger

PEONY FINISHES WRITING UP THE order for table five: a cheeseburger with fries for the gray-haired woman sporting the faint greenish yellow remnants of what must have been a spectacular black eye, and a tofu stir-fry for the younger woman with an elaborate tattoo circling her bicep. As she crosses the restaurant to put in the order, she sees Sam, bushy white eyebrows high, peering out through the porthole window in the kitchen door. Sit-down customers are a rarity nowadays, but Peony is fairly certain his interest has been activated by something else.

"So?" he asks as she pushes through the door.

She hands him the order and pretends to misunderstand his question. "Cheeseburger and a number twelve."

Sam continues to peer into the restaurant. "I mean do you think they're lesbians? They came in holding hands."

Paul joins his father at the window, but loses interest when he sees the age of the customers and returns to folding take-out boxes at the long steel table that bisects the kitchen.

With emotional radar more finely tuned than her husband's, Peony is quite certain these women are lovers, a word that more accurately describes them than lesbians. Not because of the way they held hands when they came in, or even how they reach out to touch each other's wrists and forearms as they talk. These signals indicate sexual interest but do not account for the easy flow of conversation between the women and their relaxed postures of mutual trust. In Peony's opinion, this is a consummated relationship making its way toward commitment.

"I think they are hungry," she tells her husband, "and the rest is none of our business."

"A man can have his fantasies."

"Fantasize while you cook. If you keep staring at them like that, they'll leave."

While Sam prepares the orders, he and Paul discuss the house they looked at this morning with Paul's fiancée. Peony ferries stacks of folded boxes from the table to the open shelves beside the four enormous cast-iron woks. She listens to the comfortable baritone rumble of her men's voices and enjoys the temporary peace of her daughter's absence.

Over the past few days, the McAllister residence has become a war zone, with Sam firing off ingenious theories to account for his son-in-law's behavior and Kendra shooting them down with venomous logic. Paul and Peony play the role of Switzerland in these engagements, refusing to lend support to either combatant.

At first, Peony privately sided with Sam. She was very attached to her son-in-law and sure of his love for Kendra. In her opinion men were, on the whole, less inclined to resist sexual temptation. Just look at what Sam, a wonderful husband in all other respects, had done. She had no difficulty imagining her son-in-law falling into the trap of a midlife-crisis affair. That Eric actually married the schemer who seduced him seemed to Peony the act of a true romantic who believed himself in love with two women at the same time. What he did was certainly wrong, but in some ways it could be considered honorable.

After meeting Lesley this morning, Peony is now firmly, but still silently, in her daughter's camp. Beautiful as she is, Eric's other wife is far from the sexually overt temptress Peony imagined. There is no honor in the seduction of a girl as young and obviously innocent as Lesley, even if he did marry her. Equally disturbing is the way Eric successfully hid his profession for eight years. The motive behind deception of this magnitude must be a dark one, especially considering that box of money the FBI found, and Peony feels almost as betrayed by her son-in-law as her daughter does.

As Peony crosses the restaurant to deliver the orders to table five, Kendra's van parks in front of the Lucky Dragon. When the passenger door opens, one glimpse of the controlled fury on her daughter's face tells Peony it is going to be a long night. She thinks about postponing the inevitable by inviting Lesley to stay for a meal, then changes her mind when she sees the same expression on Lesley's face as she walks around the front of the van.

The tattooed woman glances out the window and says, "Shit. We might as well have eaten in Brockville."

The gray-haired woman looks out the window, then almost knocks Peony over in her haste to get to the door.

AS SOON AS SHE'S OUT THE DOOR, Cassandra calls out, "Lesley, honey, what happened? What's wrong?"

"Everything's wrong, Aunt Cass." Lesley takes the crutches from Kendra and holds out her hand to help the smaller woman out of the van. "I just feel so violated."

Kendra tucks the crutches under her arms. "You feel violated? At least you're human. He gave me a *tail*." She gives Cassandra a curt nod, then swings herself toward the restaurant door, the rubber tips of her crutches slamming the pavement like muted thunderclaps.

Reaching into the van to pull out a cardboard box, Lesley asks, "How did you know I'd be here? Are you following me?"

"I didn't know you'd be here. I'm having dinner with a friend. What happened?"

Lesley peers through the restaurant window. "Is Mom with you?"

"No, she went out with Eunice. Honey, answer me. What happened?"

"I'll tell you when the rest of them get here."

"Tell me what?" Cassandra persists as she follows her niece into the restaurant.

Lesley dumps the box down on the first table she comes to. "Later, Aunt Cass."

Satisfied that her niece, however violated, is physically unharmed, Cassandra decides she can wait to find out.

Half an hour later, after the investigator and his family have arrived and the confusion of introductions is over and Lesley and Kendra have finished venting about the travesty McCoy made of them, Cassandra sits with Robyn at the table by the window where she has been exiled by her niece, who remains adamant about making her own decisions. In one way, Cassandra is relieved. Lesley is too preoccupied with listening to Jason and Jude as they outline the process of annulling, divorcing and suing the man everyone now refers to simply as McCoy, to be curious about why her aunt is having dinner with her husband's doctor. In another way, Cassandra is worried. Decisions made in anger rarely work out well, and Lesley's bitterness is blinding her.

Lesley is now eager to have her marriage to McCoy annulled, heedless of how the inevitable scandal will affect her life and her mother's in the fishbowl of small-town society. Cassandra is sourly amused, having spent the past five years hiding her sexuality to spare her sister and niece exactly this situation. Kendra is just as eager to sue McCoy for divorce, but unwilling to file until she knows how much he can be sued for.

Across the table, Robyn looks up from the comic book she's glancing through. "You know, aside from the questionable ethics of turning your wives into sleazy cartoon characters, the psychology here is intriguing."

"Psychology of what?" Cassandra asks. "Puerile male fantasies?"

"That too. What he did to your niece is a joke, although that half-Kendra, half-cat creature is pretty sexy. But what I'm actually talking about are the story lines. Like in this one." Robyn holds up the book. "The plot is about a scientist sacrificing her career to prevent the emperor from losing his mask."

The dimensions of the scientist depicted on the cover are less dramatic than the ones McCoy gave to Lesley, but still far beyond anything a human body is capable of achieving in earth's gravitational field. There is an adoring quality in the woman's expression as she gazes at the smaller figure of the masked emperor that Cassandra finds almost repulsive. "So what?"

"It's a classic narcissist-codependent relationship. She gave him his disguise and he needs her sacrifice to maintain it."

Cassandra looks over at Lesley and Kendra, dark and light heads almost touching as they plot McCoy's downfall. She dips her last French fry into a puddle of ketchup and observes, "Looks like the scientists have stopped sacrificing."

Adoring Little Mirror

Eric at age twelve

THE MOTHERS ALL CRIED WHEN ERIC LEFT. They hugged him and told him how special he was, how they wished he didn't have to leave. Eric never cried anymore. He'd learned it made the mothers even more upset. Instead, he hugged them back and told them how much he'd miss them and how grateful he was for his time with them. He always meant it.

As the car rolled down the driveway, Eric turned in his seat and watched his most recent foster mother, Linda Halliman, wipe tears from her cheeks with one cuff of the old corduroy jacket she wore for chores. Behind her, the horses hung their heads over the half doors of the stable. His favorite horse, Calico, nodded as though saying good-bye. He watched until Mrs. Yankovic, his current social worker, turned onto the highway. His last sight of the farm was the metal sign suspended from the crossbar of the wooden posts flanking the driveway: HALLIMAN'S RIDING STABLES AND HORSE BOARDING.

"She asked if you could stay, you know," Mrs. Yankovic said. "She didn't ask about any of the other boys. Just you. But when the investigation started . . . The way they were working you . . ." She lifted a hand from the steering wheel in a gesture of helplessness. "We didn't know."

Eric tried to defend the Hallimans. "I liked the work. I liked the horses. And she was really good to us. Helped us with our homework and stuff like that."

"Still, foster children aren't free labor. You'll be asked to testify, you know."

"I don't want to. They worked as hard as we did."

"The other boys will testify."

Eric could tell Mrs. Yankovic wanted him to feel angry and abused, but he couldn't feel that way. He kept his eyes on the winter fields lining the highway and said nothing, not wanting to argue and hurt her feelings. He never hurt people's feelings. It made him feel sick inside.

Unlike most of the children he'd shared homes with, Eric was one of those who thrived in the foster care system. After eight years and ten homes, his file was filled with excellent school reports and effusive praise from foster parents. He had a knack for fitting in, finding the sweet spot in his foster parents' affections. "He's such a little angel," they wrote in their reports. "I wish all the children were like him." "He's so sweet and caring." "Sometimes I feel like he's raising me."

The file also contained a comprehensive catalog of plain bad luck. He'd lived in foster homes that broke up when the parents divorced. Twice, he'd been removed from homes when a parent fell ill. He'd been placed with families who had to move when one of the parents found work in another state. He'd come very close to being adopted when he was six, but that fell through when his foster mother became pregnant with her own child. This last home had been disbanded when it was discovered the Hallimans were using the four boys they fostered as unpaid labor.

As she drove Eric to his next home, Mrs. Yankovic told him about his new foster parents, a couple from Iran. "They've been fostering for years. All their children have done well, but they're getting older and can only take one child at a time now. Their last girl went to college in the fall and they asked for a boy this time. This is a really good home, Eric. I know you'll be happy there."

He listened carefully and thanked Mrs. Yankovic with the quiet politeness he knew worked best with social workers. He'd learned, very early on, that everything was better when people were happy. Being polite and obedient and cheerful made people happy. So did helping with household chores and getting good grades in school. By far his most successful technique was listening and emulating, sponging up interests and personality traits, reflecting them back like an adoring little mirror. He didn't think of it this way, didn't really know he was doing it. He just wanted to feel like he belonged.

The car pulled up before a small brick bungalow on a tree-lined street. Eric followed Mrs. Yankovic up the porch stairs and stood just a bit behind her as she rang the doorbell. While they waited for someone to answer, he felt his lips curve, as they had at ten other front doors, in a familiar smile. He no longer hoped for macaroni and cheese, but the smile was just as genuine.

Aftermath

FOR MOST OF THE TRIP home from Portland, Lesley drives by rote, wrapped in a spiky cocoon of outrage. Fortunately, she's behind Cassandra's car and its easy-to-follow taillights, which she sees through projected memories of her life with McCoy. All those loving caresses. All that nice-guy, strong-silent charm. All a facade.

Lesley is honest enough to admit she was easy to fool. She looks back at how she took everything he said at face value and feels incredibly stupid. Finally, she understands what her aunt meant about McCoy's oddness. It wasn't just that he rarely mentioned his past. He never talked about his work friends or what happened on his trips either. He always encouraged her to talk about her job and her family, and now she sees it had nothing to do with any real interest on his part. He was just avoiding having to talk about himself. The memory of that horrible caricature surfaces. She thumps the steering wheel and shouts in wordless rage.

Just before the Brockville exit, it starts to rain in fat, splashy drops that blur the taillights of her aunt's car. She turns on the windshield wipers and slows down for the exit. At the end of the ramp, she pulls into the left-turn lane beside Cassandra, who is waiting at the stoplight to turn right. They roll down their windows. In the sodium glow of the single streetlamp lighting the intersection, Cassandra's forehead is ridged with worry. "You sure you don't want to come stay with Trixie and me?"

A trickle of guilt seeps through Lesley's anger. She knows her aunt is worried about her, but she can't deal with someone else's feelings right now. She has enough of her own. "I need to go home, Aunt Cass. I'll call you tomorrow, okay?"

Cassandra surrenders with a nod. She tells Lesley to drive carefully. The light changes to green and they go their separate ways.

Without her aunt's taillights to guide her, Lesley forces herself to stop thinking about McCoy and concentrate on getting home. The rain gets heavier as the road climbs Saddleback Ridge. By the time she reaches the cabin driveway her rear wheels are churning up rooster tails of water behind the car. She parks as close to the porch steps as she can and makes a run for the front door.

She's not hungry, but she hasn't had anything since lunch and there's the baby to think of, so she heats a can of soup, makes herself some toast and sits at the kitchen table to eat while reading through the notes she made in the Lucky Dragon.

Annulment is a difficult process. Eventually, she will have to hire a lawyer, although she has no idea where the money for this will come from. Her salary is too small to raise a child on her own, let alone cover legal fees. Overwhelmed by her situation, Lesley wishes she had Kendra's practicality and decisiveness. It's a combination of qualities she never admired before. But now, facing life alone with the baby on the way, she recognizes the value of these attributes.

With what feels like superhuman effort, Lesley pushes away her financial worries and concentrates on what she can afford to do right now: remember everything possible about McCoy in preparation for obtaining the annulment. She gets the same notepad she used to make the *Mine* and *McCoy's* lists, flips to a blank page, and forces herself to remember. It is a painful exercise. Twice she must stop when tears blur her handwriting on the page. She counteracts them with anger, using the image of her face above that ridiculous body to punch it up. She backtracks through her notes to scrub out the tiny hearts she uses to dot *i*'s and *j*'s and tells herself Kendra's task is much more difficult because Kendra has eight years of deceit to document.

When the phone rings, Lesley glances at the clock and is surprised to see it's after midnight.

"Hello?"

"Hi, honey. It's Cass. Sorry if I woke you up."

"You didn't. What's up, Aunt Cass?"

"Have you heard from Trixie tonight?"

"No. Isn't she there?"

"Her car is. She isn't. I called Eunice, but there was no answer. I just drove by her apartment and it's dark."

"She'd never be out this late without telling you. Something must have happened. Maybe an accident?"

"If she was in an accident, someone would have called me. Everyone in town knows where we live."

Lesley isn't fooled by her aunt's attempt to sound calm. "I'm coming over."

It's still raining heavily and the short drive into town takes almost half an hour. By the time Lesley arrives, Cassandra is seriously worried. They sit on Beatrice's iris-and-lily-patterned sofa, discussing whether they should wake up her friends or even call the police.

Headlights sweep across the living room window as an unfamiliar car pulls into the driveway. A rotund man in a tweed jacket and bow tie emerges from the driver's-side door, walks around the car and helps Beatrice out of the passenger seat. Her face is starkly pale, and her hair juts up in frizzy clumps that begin to flatten as the rain soaks through them. A seam at the hip of her dress is torn and the skirt is stained, as though she's been rolling in dirt. She clutches a plastic bag to her chest with one hand and her throat with the other. The man puts an arm around her back to support her. She sags against him as they stagger toward the front door.

"Go find the brandy," Cassandra orders as she leaps up to help get Beatrice into the house.

Lesley comes back to the living room with towels, the brandy bottle, and three juice glasses, just in time to see Beatrice struggling to remain erect while Cassandra tries to push her down onto the sofa.

"Filthy," Beatrice protests in a hoarse whisper.

It is a tribute to the many years Lesley spent absorbing housekeeping skills from her mother that she actually understands the cause of Beatrice's concern. She races back to the kitchen, whips the plastic cloth off the table, and returns to the living room to spread it over the couch. Beatrice sinks down on the forget-me-nots of the tablecloth, still clutching her throat and the bag. Lesley pours her mother a glass of brandy and hands it to her along with a towel. Ignoring the towel, Beatrice lets go of the bag to take the glass, revealing the silhouette of a wolf howling at a full moon printed on the plastic.

Cassandra asks, "What happened?"

Beatrice downs half the glass, wincing as she swallows.

"Andrew," she croaks, releasing her throat to stretch a beseeching hand toward the portly man, who is standing in the hallway, dripping on the tiles and eyeing the bottle in Lesley's hand.

"I wouldn't mind one of those myself," he says.

Lesley pours another brandy, which he demolishes in a single gulp before accepting a towel.

"Since poor Beatrice can't perform the introductions, I suppose I should introduce myself. My name is Andrew Pettigrew."

Cassandra completes the introductions. "I'm Beatrice's sister, Cassandra, and this is her daughter, Lesley."

"Delighted to meet you both, although I'm sorry it must be in such unfortunate circumstances." Andrew finishes drying his head and smooths his comb-over back into place. "Poor Beatrice was attacked by a thief this evening." He holds the glass out hopefully. Lesley hands him the brandy bottle.

Beatrice pats the tablecloth beside her hip and finishes her brandy as Andrew walks around the coffee table to take a seat. He refills both their glasses before embarking on the story of the unsuccessful thief. Lesley and Cassandra sit in the wing chairs flanking the coffee table and listen while he describes the roulette win and the attack in the parking lot. He tells them about hearing Beatrice's heartrending cries and Franklin's heroic capture of the hapless thief.

Being something of a raconteur, Andrew tells this grim tale with dramatic flair. "Of course the police were called in and that horrible young man had the gall to accuse dear Beatrice, of all people"—Andrew reaches over to pat her hand—"of lying. Which no one believed once his criminal record was exposed. But it took several hours to straighten everything out, by which time poor Eunice was too exhausted to drive home. So I naturally offered my services, such as they are, to two damsels in distress. I dropped Eunice off at her apartment before bringing Beatrice home to you."

Lesley is almost as shocked by the secret gambling as she is by the attempted robbery. Once her mother's safety and health are assured, she listens with her arms folded across her chest, resisting the impulse to like this chubby man with his polka-dot bow tie and over-the-top personality. She'd liked McCoy too, and look how that turned out.

The brandy bottle is severely depleted by the time Andrew comes to the end of his story, so Cassandra offers him hospitality for the night before she takes Beatrice upstairs to help her get cleaned up. Leaving Andrew alone in the living room, Lesley follows them up to the second floor to prepare the guest room. She finds a pair of her father's pajamas in the dresser, the same red and green tartan pair McCoy wore the first night he stayed over. Remembering that night, and the way her mother seems so familiar with Andrew, she returns to the living room and asks him outright, "Are you married, Mr. Pettigrew?"

"Please call me Andrew, my dear. I'm separated."

"Does my mother know this?"

"Well, you know, I don't think it ever came up in the conversation."

"Are you going to tell her you're still married?"

"If you think it's important. But I'm sure you misunderstand my intentions toward your mother. Beatrice, Eunice and I are merely friends." Relieved by Andrew's honesty and the genuine concern on his face, Lesley allows herself to warm to his charm.

Later, as she's trying, and failing, to fall asleep, Lesley turns over and punches the pillow, seeking a comfortable position in her old bed, in her old room. It's like trying to zip up an outgrown pair of jeans. She no longer fits into this easy, safe life. The image of herself as a comic book seductress keeps floating across her mind's eye, and she can't imagine ever trusting any man again. She remembers what Dr. Strachan said just before they left the restaurant, about McCoy hiding behind the emperor's mask. Maybe everyone has a mask. Maybe no one can be trusted.

The next morning, while everyone else is still in bed, Lesley goes downstairs at eleven to make coffee. The front doorbell rings as she's measuring coffee into the filter basket. She answers it to find Alice Wilson from next door standing on the doorstep.

"Sorry to bother you, Lesley, but I was wondering if I could borrow your hand mixer. Mine just died, right in the middle of a cake."

"No problem. Come in. I'll go get it."

As she steps into the kitchen, Lesley hears Alice gasp. Turning around, she sees her neighbor, mouth and eyes round with surprise, staring through the archway separating the hall from the living room. Too late, Lesley remembers the bag of money from the Howling Wolf, still lying half-spilled across the coffee table where Beatrice left it when she went to bed. Footsteps in the upstairs hallway pull Alice's attention to the staircase just as Andrew begins to descend.

Lesley fights down a cowardly urge to flee out the back door. She tries to come up with an explanation for a casino bag containing a small fortune and a strange man in her father's pajamas, then realizes her only option is the truth. Knowing Alice, the story will be all over town in a couple of hours.

Road Trip

WHEN TRAVIS OPENS THE DOOR at nine o'clock on Sunday morning, he immediately leans to the side to look past Jason's hip.

Jason answers the question before it's asked. "She doesn't know I'm here. I just came by to see how you're doing." This is one of those true-but-not-entirely-true statements. He is also avoiding his own house, where Fletcher and his new school friends are attempting to form a band in the garage, and Jude, having run out of less intrusive house-cleaning tasks, is shampooing the carpets.

Travis grips the wheels of his manual chair and pulls back into the hall to let Jason enter. "Come in. See for yourself. I'm fine."

He looks almost fine. He's freshly shaven, and aside from the damp circles of sweat lining the armpits of his T-shirt, his clothes are clean. But his eyes are slightly bloodshot, and a reddish bump the size of a sparrow's egg is clearly visible above his ear beneath his crew cut. He seems genuinely pleased by Jason's visit.

"Not using the Extensitter?" Jason asks as he steps through the door.

"Making a few safety modifications. I'm working out. Mind if I finish up?" Without waiting for a reply, Travis swivels his chair around and rolls down the hall to the den.

Now that he no longer has the use of his legs, Travis relies on upper body strength to give himself as much independence as possible. From the waist up, he could be an advertisement for Bowflex. He credits his lack of depression to the endorphins generated by his workouts and has turned the den into a gym, adapting commercial exercise machines to meet his needs and linking them with "hand-ways" of parallel bars to move around the room.

Travis pulls a buckled strap off the bar closest to the door of the den and bends to wrap it around his ankles to keep his feet together while he works out. "So? How is she?" Grabbing the ends of two bars, he hauls himself out of the chair and swings his body toward a set of rings suspended from a crossbar in the center of the room.

Jason leans a shoulder against the doorjamb. "She's not doing as well as you seem to be."

Travis pauses and looks back over his shoulder. "Because I'm doing the right thing. You know that."

"Actually, I don't know that."

Grabbing the rings, Travis pulls his body upright until his arms are straight, then begins slowly raising and lowering himself between them. Watching his brother-in-law's pectorals flex, Jason has a sudden urge to exercise himself. When Kathy left, he went to the gym fairly regularly for about a year, then somehow let it slide after the divorce. Living with Jude is a daily reminder of how out of shape he's become. Lately, he's been pinching at his belly and thinking of renewing his membership at the gym.

Travis bares his teeth in an expression that could be a smile, or just a reflection of the effort he's putting into the exercise. "I'm almost done here. Go make us a pot of coffee and I'll explain it to you."

Twenty minutes later when Travis rolls into the kitchen, wearing a fresh T-shirt still damp from washing up, Jason pours two mugs of coffee and places them on the kitchen table. "Okay, I'm listening."

Travis blows on his coffee before taking a sip. "You knew she took the detective's exam last month, right?"

Jason nods as he sits across from Travis.

"We got the results last week. Did she tell you she scored higher than anyone else in the last ten years?"

"She didn't mention it. I'm not surprised, though."

"Before my accident, she used to talk about making detective like it was the holy grail. That's your fault in a way. She's always looked up to you, wanted to be like you."

Embarrassed by the idea his sister's successful career is inspired by his failed one, Jason says, "She's better than I was."

"I don't know about that. She says you could have made it all the way to the top if you were more of a team player."

"And she is, so she'd have a better shot at it."

"But she's not going to take it. She's talking about giving up her career so that I can be a father."

"She wants kids too," Jason protests. "Maybe, when they're very young, you wouldn't be able to help out as much as—"

Travis cuts him off. "A father who isn't a cripple?"

"That's not what I was going to say."

"But it's true. You know better than anyone how dangerous police work can be. If I was whole, and something happened to her, I'd still be there for our kids. She wouldn't have to choose between career and family." Travis leans toward Jason to emphasize his next words. "She's an incredible woman. Smart and beautiful and capable of achieving anything she puts her mind to. She's the best thing in my life. I love her like fire. And I am *not* letting my disability hold her back."

Jason puts his mug down on the table and responds carefully, "I understand that. But is that all we're talking about here? Jude's career?"

"We're talking about her happiness. Jude's ambitious. Her career is a big part of it. And can you honestly see her sitting behind a desk for eight hours? She even can't sit still for ten minutes."

Conceding the point with a nod, Jason moves on. "What about your happiness?"

"Her happiness is my happiness. It kills me, what I'm doing to her right now. But in the long run, over a lifetime, I'm doing the right thing." Travis sounds as though he means this, but his body language says otherwise. The muscles in his neck are taut and his gray eyes are challenging and defensive at the same time, as though he hopes and fears his statement will be contradicted.

Jason shakes his head. "I wish I knew, Trav. Maybe you're right."

"And maybe I'm not?"

"That too."

Travis leans back and closes his eyes.

Jason can't tell if his brother-in-law is disappointed or relieved, but the action is an obvious indication the discussion is over. He gets up to refill their mugs. "So, got any plans for today?"

"Just watching the game."

"How about taking a road trip with me instead?"

"Where?"

"Seattle. Remember McCoy?"

"Yeah. The bigamist."

"Well, his first wife wants to divorce him and the second wife is filing for an annulment. They want to know what he's worth, but the FBI isn't releasing his financial information yet. McCoy made his living as an illustrator and writing comic books, so the first wife asked me to talk to his agent, see what I can find out. The agent owns a comic book store in Seattle. I called there this morning, and I'm going up to talk to him this afternoon. Come with me. It'll be more fun than sitting around here watching Army lose again."

"They could win." Travis defends his team.

Jason says nothing.

Travis sighs. "We'll take the van."

When Travis knew he'd never walk again, he used part of the disability insurance settlement to buy a van and have it modified. The backseats have been removed and a ramp installed that allows him to wheel himself into the van through the rear doors. The driver's seat has been replaced with a frame to lock in his manual wheelchair. Levers allow him to control the gas and brake pedals with his left hand, and a knob attached to the steering wheel compensates for his inability to hand-over-hand when turning. He says it's easier to drive than a regular car.

As they head north, Jason fills Travis in on the discoveries made at the Grove Street house and the way McCoy used his wives as models for two of his characters, finishing up with the doctor's theory of the psychology behind McCoy's work. "She also thinks he identifies with the emperor, sort of a fantasy version of his inner life."

"Like how?" Travis asks.

"For example, the emperor wears this permanently attached mask. Remember how I told you McCoy was a totally different person with each of his wives, like a chameleon? The doctor thinks the mask symbolizes psychic camouflage. He never shows his real self. Jude asked if that meant he was a sociopath, but the doctor said if he was, the story lines would be about the emperor manipulating people and they're not. She said it's more like he doesn't know who he really is."

"Did you read any of them?"

"I read a few," Jason confesses. "Lots of warrior women and sex. Definitely not kid's stuff. Borderline pornography. But the doctor is right. They weren't about the emperor. He didn't do anything himself. If I put myself in a story, I'd give myself some action."

This early on Sunday morning, traffic is light. Travis pushes the speedometer over the limit and they make good time to Seattle. They have lunch in Tacoma and arrive at their destination early in the afternoon.

The comic book store is called Shazzam! and occupies a double unit in a strip mall located in a suburb a few miles inland from downtown Seattle. As well as comics, the store carries graphic novels, science fiction and fantasy novels, action figures, and role-playing games. A fair amount of display space is taken up by costumes and props. Most of the predominantly male clientele are flipping through comics stacked in bins on six waist-high wooden tables running up the center of the store. Two female customers with dead-black hair waxed into identical spikes stand over a glass case filled with arcane-looking jewelry and statuettes of dragons and fairies.

Behind the cash desk, a young woman whose heavy eye shadow and black lipstick do nothing to disguise her prettiness looks up as Travis and Jason approach. "Can I help you?"

"We're here to talk to Mr. Carerras about Eric McCoy," Jason replies.

She leans sideways to call past Jason's shoulder, "Angel! More guys are here asking about Eric."

A bald man wearing droopy jeans and a faded plaid shirt with frayed cuffs looks up from the bin of comics he is sorting to peer at them over wire-rimmed reading glasses. His face has a road-map-to-hell quality Jason normally associates with recovering drug addicts, but when the man unhooks a cane from the side of the table and limps toward them, Jason decides it's probably the result of chronic pain.

"I'm Angel Carreras, Eric's agent. You the guy who called this morning?"

"Jason Cheddick. And this is Travis Connelly. Thanks for seeing us."

After shaking hands with both men, Angel says, "We can talk in my office." He looks at the salesclerk. "You okay on your own for a while, Christy?"

"I'll call you if there's a rush," she replies with sufficient sarcasm to make it obvious there won't be one.

"We don't do that much business here," Angel explains as he limps toward the back of the store. "No one ever got rich selling comics." He holds a door open for Travis.

"But you still do it?" Travis asks as he rolls into Angel's office.

"More of a hobby. It helps me keep track of what's popular. I make most of my living, such as it is, as an agent."

The walls of Angel's office are covered in framed art, depicting everything from dragons to rocket ships. Some of the works are oil paintings, others little more than pencil sketches. A life-sized painting of Kendra in her guise as a feline alien hangs on the wall directly opposite the door. Its sinuous sexuality dominates the room.

"She's something, isn't she?" Angel says. "The highest-selling issue Eric ever produced was based on her."

Travis rolls his chair up to the painting. "Unbelievable. A dead man would wake up for a woman like this."

Jason tries to match this sleek, iridescent version of Kendra to the woman he knows. The facial features are the same, and beneath the blue-black fur the body has the same suggestion of fine, elegant bones. But the smoldering, predatory expression is one he's never seen. Is this how she looked at McCoy? Feeling the stirrings of an erection, Jason moves to sit in one of the visitor chairs in front of Angel's desk. The glittering eyes of the painting stalk him across the room.

"Eric's famous for his female characters"—Angel limps around the desk—"but Cheetara here was beyond anything he'd done before." He hooks his cane on the edge of the desk and eases himself into a high-backed leather chair. "A couple of guys from the FBI came by three weeks ago. Just about laughed my ass off when they said he was being investigated as a terrorist. They wanted to know all his previous addresses and get copies of his royalty statements and contracts. They told me he was in the hospital. How's he doing?"

"He's in a coma." Jason tells Angel about McCoy's aneurysm and the poor prognosis for recovery.

"Poor bugger. So what's your interest in him?"

"I'm working for his wife."

Angel's eyebrows climb halfway up to where his hairline would be if he still had one. "He's married? How long has he been married?"

Jason decides not to complicate matters by mentioning the second marriage. "Five years."

"Wonder why he didn't tell me? We're not close, but we've been working together for twenty-five years. Hang on a sec." Angel digs through the haphazard piles of paper on his desk to pull out a thick legal document. "This just came yesterday. Maybe his wife can sign it."

"What is it?" Jason asks.

"His contract with Paramount. I got them up to half a million for the film rights to *Kav'erse*."

True Talent

Eric at age seventeen

THE MAN HAD BEEN SITTING on the park bench for almost an hour, the horseshoe of bare skin on the top of his head turning pink in the spring sunshine. Lots of people watched street artists, but this man was different. Instead of following the way the portrait grew on the page, as most onlookers did, he studied Eric, seeming more interested in the artist than the art.

On weekends when the weather was good, Eric set up his easel just outside the stone pillars at the south entrance to Rawley Park. He had other locations, but the park was by far the most profitable. Parents on their way to the playground wanted portraits of their children, couples walking hand in hand wanted mementos of their affection, and dog owners, like the woman currently occupying the plastic lawn chair Eric provided for his clients, loved having pictures of their pets. This pet was a Scottish terrier, squirming energetically on his owner's lap, bored with the process of being immortalized.

"You can put your dog down," Eric told her. "We're almost done here."

"He's a little restless. You're just a puppy, aren't you, Snookie?" She lifted the dog and kissed his shiny black nose. Snookie tolerated the caress but did not return it. As soon as his paws hit the ground, he trotted over to the edge of the path to roll on his back in the grass, furry torso twisting from side to side ecstatically. So much happiness in such a little body. Eric wished he could draw Snookie this way instead of as a motionless lump on his owner's tweedy knees. He compromised by embellishing the dog's beard and eyebrows to make the animal's expression seem more energetic.

"Okay, I think we're done." He turned the easel toward the customer.

"Oh, my goodness! Look at that, Snookie. It looks just like you."

With an admirable lack of vanity, Snookie ignored her instruction, too busy sniffing suspiciously around the trunk of a nearby tree before marking it with his own territorial claim.

The woman opened her wallet and extracted two ten-dollar bills. "I know you only charge ten, but you are a very talented young man. You deserve more."

Eric took the money and dropped it into the coffee can at his feet. "Thank you very much." He thought about adding "ma'am" but decided she was still young enough to be offended and substituted a smile. "I'm saving for college, so every bit helps."

While the fixative dried on the paper, he chatted with the woman, then rolled the drawing into a tube and secured it with a neatly knotted red ribbon. She thanked him again before tugging

Snookie away from an intense olfactory investigation of a wire mesh trash can. Eric watched them walk away into the park, then checked the time and decided to call it a day. He still had homework to do.

The man got up from the bench and approached Eric. He looked like a Hollywood version of a 1930s mobster, with dark, hooded eyes and the kind of beard that made the skin of his heavy jaw seem blue. But in the movies mobsters usually wore nice suits. This man's suit was too big and badly wrinkled. He sat in the chair vacated by Snookie's owner and pointed to the slogan DON'T LIKE IT? DON'T BUY IT! printed on the display board leaning against Eric's easel. "I'll bet you don't have to make good on that promise very often."

"Never, so far." Eric wiped excess charcoal off his hands with an old tea towel. "You don't want a portrait, do you?"

"No. I want to talk to you about a job."

The man had suspended his study of Eric to check out a few passing women, so Eric felt sure he wasn't about to be propositioned. He nudged the coffee can with his foot. "I have a job."

"Just hear me out." The man reached into the breast pocket of his navy shirt and pulled out a business card. "My name is Angel Carreras."

Eric took the card by the edges, not wanting to smudge it with the residual charcoal on his fingers. Beneath the sailboat logo, the company name was printed in bold script: *FOUR WINDS LITERARY ART.* Smaller script along the bottom spelled out Angel's name, phone number and an address in Seattle.

"You live in Seattle?" Eric asked.

"Flew in this morning. A friend of mine was here last week. He told me I should check you out."

Eric thought back to the previous weekend, when a man, who also hadn't wanted a portrait, watched him for a while, then asked to see his sketchbook. "Ponytail? Heavy glasses? Cast on his wrist?"

"That's him. Did you really tell him you like working in crayon?"

"I told him I like the way they smell."

Angel's temples folded into deep canyons when he grinned. "Me too. Can you work in anything else besides crayons and charcoal?"

"Everything I've tried." Eric bent over to place his sketchbook in the tan leather portfolio his foster father had given him on his fifteenth birthday. "But I haven't tried much."

"Where'd you learn to draw?"

"I've always done it. For as long as I can remember. I went to a school once that had art classes, but I wasn't there for long."

"You draw anything besides people and dogs?"

Eric didn't understand the question. "You mean landscapes?"

"I mean interpretive drawing."

Still not understanding, Eric took his sketchbook back out of the portfolio and handed it to Angel, who flipped through the pages slowly. He spent a long time looking at a page of elaborately intertwined snakes, and even longer on the several pages Eric had devoted to Cindy Goldman. "Girlfriend?" he asked as he handed the sketchbook back.

"I wish. Just a girl in my chemistry class."

"You ever read comic books?"

Something in the way the question was asked made Eric realize Angel had finally come to the point, and it would be a good one. "It's about all I read. You know the Dead Roach on Main? I practically live there."

Angel seemed to like this answer. "Ever heard of Jackson Fowler?"

"Who hasn't?"

"You'd be surprised." Angel leaned forward, as though about to share a secret. "You met him last week. Jack's my client. He broke his wrist a couple of weeks ago. Problem is, he's still twenty panels short of finishing the next *Blazing Blades* issue and the deadline's only four weeks away. You're fast, and you've got real talent. He thinks you could do it if he talked you through it. No artist's credit. Onetime payment in cash." Angel lowered his voice and said an amount. It was a lot of money, about what Eric hoped to make over the summer as a Saturday street artist.

Angel stood up. "I know what you're thinking. Anyone can have a card printed. What's your name?"

Eric wasn't thinking this at all. He was thinking about studying for finals and how stupid it would be to risk throwing away his high school diploma for the chance to work with Jackson Fowler. "Eric."

"Well, Eric, you talk to Stan at the Dead Roach. He'll know who I am. If you're interested after that, give me a call."

"I KNOW YOU ARE NOT STUPID, so you must be crazy." Habibeh placed a plate stacked with freshly made pita in front of Eric.

"The boy is right, my heart." Farouk reached across the table to take a round of bread. "Education is important, worth more than a few hundred dollars."

"A man with a degree in chemistry who drives a taxi must know this," she responded, taking her seat.

Habibeh and Farouk spoke in Farsi. Five years ago, when Eric first came to live with them, he'd thought they were complimenting each other. Now that he spoke the language himself, he understood they were, extremely politely, arguing. In this argument, practical Farouk endorsed Eric's decision to stick to his studies and get his high school diploma while still in the foster care system. This infuriated romantic Habibeh, who insisted it would be foolish for Eric to throw away the chance to work with an artist he admired, especially since he hoped to get into art college.

She picked up a pita and waved it at her husband. "It is better to have one important man on your side than all the education in the world. This Angel Carreras, he is an important man according to Eric's friend at the store."

Eric dipped his bread into the dish of buttered spinach and waited for the rebuttal. When it didn't come, he looked across the table at his foster father.

Farouk looked back at him with thoughtful eyes. "In Iran," he said slowly, "my father was a wealthy man. He owned many shops. He had many relatives and friends who wanted to work for him. He gave them all jobs. Some were grateful and worked hard. My father gave them better jobs. Others did not. My father fired them." He paused to scoop up some spinach with his bread and let his meaning sink in. "Habibeh is right. A powerful man can open doors for you. But he can't carry you through them. You must walk through them yourself."

Delighted to have her point validated, Habibeh stopped arguing with her husband and concentrated on convincing her foster son. "You must take this opportunity."

"But if I can't do the job and I fail my school year . . ."

"You can do it. You have talent. Everyone says this and I see it for myself." She pointed to the framed portraits of herself and Farouk hanging on the wall over the sideboard. "I will talk with Mrs. Yankovic and write you a note for school. You will show this Mr. Carreras how good you are."

"And if he cannot see it," Farouk added, "and you fail your year, then you will live with us until you graduate. I can drive for one more year. My retirement can wait."

Habibeh stood and lifted the empty water pitcher from the table. "Good. It is settled."

On her way to the kitchen, she pressed a small brown hand on her husband's shoulder as she passed behind his chair. The ends of his gray mustache lifted as he smiled down at his plate, and Eric knew Farouk made his offer to drive another year as much to please his wife as to help his foster son. Eric understood this perfectly.

What He Never Said

CRACKER JACK SHUFFLES BACK AND forth on the headboard of Kendra's bed muttering, "Damn bird. Damn bird." It's a phrase he picked up during his brief stay with the woman who bought him. She hadn't realized how noisy a macaw could be and was more than happy to return him when Kendra called to explain she needed the bird back. "Give me the money when you can," she told Kendra. "I just want him out of my house."

Kendra reaches up behind her head. Jack sidles over to push his forehead into her palm. She spends a few minutes playing with him, then gets back to work. She's been up for an hour, making design changes to Perfectissimo's Web site and e-mailing clients. In another week she'll be able to drive again, and she intends to hit the ground, if not running, then at least walking quickly, this time in flat-heeled shoes.

When the last e-mail has been sent, she pushes her laptop off her thighs and leans back against the chipped white paint of the headboard. She pulls on a thread at the fraying edge of the bedspread and remembers her mother bringing it home from the thrift shop. Nine-year-old Kendra hated that her bedspread was secondhand, hated the very loud and very ugly orange color while her little girl's heart longed for pink. Thirty years later, she's happy her mother never replaced it.

Although the McAllisters are no longer poor, Peony has yet to embrace the concept of disposable income. As a result, the family quarters over the Lucky Dragon are still furnished the way they were when the family moved in, with an eclectic selection of secondhand furniture Sam jokingly refers to as Early Salvation Army. For most of her life, Kendra was embarrassed by her family's shabby lifestyle. Today, she inhales the morning smells of coffee, bacon and toasted bread coming from the little family kitchen at the end of the hall, and appreciates its permanence. From where she's standing, amid the shattered ruins of her marriage, she sees the stability of the life her parents created as a desirable haven.

In the kitchen, Sam and Paul are teasing Peony, their voices too deep for Kendra to make out the words. Peony's response, uttered in a higher register, carries clearly through the cheap plywood door of the bedroom. "I never said that. I said it's a lot of money to spend for two weeks."

For a month now, Sam has been cajoling his wife into celebrating their fortieth wedding anniversary by vacationing in England. At first, Peony was reluctant to leave Paul alone in the restaurant for so long. But Paul's fiancée has volunteered to take time from her job to help him out, and Peony is gradually coming around to the idea of taking a real vacation. What she doesn't know is that her husband has already bought tickets, made hotel reservations, and planned an itinerary around her current passion for British royal history, an interest she developed while watching a recent PBS series. Palaces, castles, country homes and stately mansions feature prominently in these plans. Once Peony gets over her annoyance at being tricked into a more expensive vacation than she anticipated, Kendra is sure her mother will be thrilled.

Sam planned this surprise with McCoy, the two of them huddled over McCoy's laptop in the dining room of the Parkland Avenue apartment like schoolboys plotting a prank. The trip is a modified version of McCoy's third-anniversary present to Kendra. She hadn't even known where they were going until they walked up to gate C15 in the departure lounge, and she saw PARIS on the destination board. Peony, of course, would never agree to a mystery vacation, which is why Sam and McCoy created a fake, much cheaper itinerary for her to approve.

Kendra vividly remembers her third-anniversary holiday, three weeks spent touring famous vineyards in Bordeaux with her husband, as clearly as she remembers their first kiss. This memory, along with many others revived by her attempt to document McCoy's duplicity, confuses her. She started out with more than enough anger to propel her through the task, but far from enough to survive her inability to match the spontaneous, passionate husband she remembers to the cold, secretive, calculating man he must have been.

She hears Paul's footsteps clatter downstairs to begin setting up the restaurant kitchen and the splash of running water as Peony fills the sink to wash breakfast dishes.

"Baby?" Sam pushes open the bedroom door and peers around it. "You up?"

"I'm up, Pops."

Sam enters the bedroom carrying a small metal bowl and a mug depicting a bucking bronco over the slogan SAN ANTONIO RODEO. No one in the family has ever been to San Antonio, or to a rodeo for that matter, so Kendra can only assume it's another of

Peony's "like new" charity shop finds. He hands her the mug, then places the bowl on the feeding shelf in Jack's cage, which now takes up a large portion of the bedroom. Cracker Jack flap-waddles his way to the foot of the bed and hops into his cage to check out breakfast.

"So what time is that handsome young investigator coming over?" Sam kisses the top of his daughter's head before sitting on the edge of the bed.

"Pops!"

"Don't Pops me. You think he's handsome."

"*Mister* Cheddick"—Kendra gives the title extra emphasis—"said the agent will be driving down from Seattle this afternoon and they'll be here around six."

Sam ignores her attempt to curtail his speculation. "He likes you too, you know. You were sitting beside Lesley all night and he barely glanced at her."

"He's married, Pops. He has a family. We met his son, remember?"

"He told me he's divorced."

Despite herself, Kendra finds this information intriguing. "When did he tell you that?"

"When I asked him."

"Pops! How could you embarrass me like that?"

"Because he kept looking at you."

"Well, he can look all he wants." Kendra glares at her father over the rim of her mug, willing him to change the subject.

"You still working on your statement for the police?" Sam asks.

Surprised her telepathic attempt at persuasion actually worked, Kendra replies, "No. I gave up on that last night."

"You gave up? Who are you? And what have you done with my daughter?"

She rewards this dreadful chestnut with a small smile. "It's more like what has been done to your daughter. Oh, Pops, I'm so confused."

"About what, baby?"

"Everything. I wrote down everything I could think of and there's not one thing I can remember that even hints at what a monster he is."

" 'Monster' is a little strong."

"I'm not fighting about this anymore, Pops. If you're still on his side, just don't say anything at all."

Sam holds up both hands in a gesture of peace. "I'm a hundred percent on your side. I made allowances for a guy who might have made mistakes. Hell, everyone makes mistakes. But turning you into a cartoon? That can't be a mistake."

"And that's the confusing part. He couldn't have loved me and done something like that to me. But if he didn't love me, why did he pretend he did for all those years? It just makes no sense."

"I don't get it either. But there's bound to be a reason. Let me see what you wrote. Maybe I can think of something. We spent a lot of time together before . . ." Sam gropes for a tactful euphemism.

"Before he met Lesley. It's okay, Pops. I'm over that one." Kendra reaches for her laptop to find the document she wrote yesterday. "Before we found those comics, I thought she was his midlife crisis. Now it's obvious he never loved either of us. Here." She hands him the computer.

Sam stands and moves toward the door. "My reading glasses are in the kitchen. Come have something to eat."

"Be there in a minute. I want to brush my teeth first."

Kendra picks up her crutches and hobbles to the bathroom, which is so small she has to prop the crutches in the bathtub to free her hands. As she flosses and brushes her teeth, she wonders if her father is right about Jason's interest. Until she met McCoy, Kendra had always been attracted to men like Jason: handsome, smart and steady. McCoy was different, not handsome and not really steady either, but he gave her something no other man had before, a sense of being treasured and adored. It's the loss of this feeling, the knowledge his admiration was all a lie, that hurts her more than anything else, and she has no intention of making the same mistake again. Even if her father is right about Jason's interest—and she's honest enough to admit she finds the idea exciting—it doesn't matter. She will never again fall in love with someone just because he makes her feel special.

She rinses her mouth, retrieves her crutches from the bathtub and hobbles down the hallway to the kitchen, where Sam is sitting at the table, his head tilted back as he peers at the laptop screen through his reading glasses. Peony stands behind him, drying the frying pan and reading over his shoulder. Kendra puts a slice of bread into the old pop-up toaster that no longer pops, then stands by the counter on her good leg, ready to manually eject her toast when it's done. "Have you thought of anything?" she asks them.

"Nothing new, but something did occur to me." Sam turns the laptop screen and points to a paragraph that reads: *He lied about his work. He told me he'd taken a big contract with the Pentagon and this meant he would have to spend more time traveling for his job.*

Kendra glances at it, then returns her attention to the toaster. "What about it?"

"Well, I was there when he came back from the airport, or wherever he was, and I don't remember him saying that. I remember him saying he was going to have to travel more and you saying how happy you were he'd finally decided to take the new contract."

"But that's what he meant." Kendra suddenly feels off balance. Afraid she might fall over, she pulls a chair out from under the table and collapses into it. "He never said . . ." She presses her lips together and turns her head to look out the kitchen window at the blank brick wall of the neighboring building while she searches her memory.

Sam and Peony watch their daughter closely, but say nothing. A curl of black smoke rises from the toaster. Peony pops the charred remains of Kendra's breakfast. The smell of burnt bread pricks at the back of Kendra's nose. She sneezes, and this tiny physical cataclysm brings her back to the present.

"I don't think he ever told me he worked for the Pentagon. I don't remember him saying the word. We always just talked about his contracts." Kendra pushes on the fingertips of her right hand one at a time to count off the memories. "I already knew he spoke Arabic, because he'd translated something about Iran we saw on the news. Then when I asked what he did for a living, he said he worked freelance, but couldn't tell me exactly what he did. I made a joke about him analyzing secret Middle Eastern documents at the Pentagon and"—she presses her forefinger as she makes the last point—"he asked me if that would be a problem."

Other People's Problems

WITH ANNOYANCE EXCEEDING THE SIZE OF THE TASK, Jason carries his cereal bowl to the sink to rinse it out before placing it in the dishwasher. Last week, he'd have put the bowl on the counter and left it there until he got around to doing dishes. With his sister living in the house, this kind of behavior results in a ten-minute lecture on cockroaches.

Jason feels like a visitor in his own home. He no longer leaves empty pizza boxes and beer bottles on the coffee table after watching a game. Dirty clothes are now put in the laundry hamper, old newspapers in the recycling bin. He wipes shaving residue off the bathroom sink and makes his bed every morning. While he admits his domestic standards may have reverted to college level in the three years he's been on his own, it doesn't make their enforced reacquisition any less irritating.

Fletcher enters the kitchen, his thin torso lost in another oversized T-shirt. "Dad? Can I talk to you?"

"If it's short. I've got to leave for a dentist appointment in a couple of minutes."

Fletcher takes a carton of juice from the refrigerator. "That's okay. It can wait till tonight."

"I'm going out tonight. Maybe later this week?"

Fletcher grabs a glass from the cupboard. "Okay. Maybe some other time."

"Listen, your aunt has the day off, so she's going to do the shopping this week. If there's anything you need, just tell her when she gets back from her run."

Juice splashes on the countertop. Fletcher reaches for the sponge beside the sink to wipe it up. "Yeah. Sure. Have a good day, Dad."

"You too, son."

Jason enjoys his visits to the dentist. He has never had a cavity and his regular hygienist is an attractive young woman with gentle hands and a charming habit of nibbling on her plump lower lip when engrossed in the pursuit of plaque. He leaves the dentist's office in a good mood and decides to drop in at the FBI office to see if there's any update on the McCoy investigation. There might be news to share with Kendra when he takes Angel Carerras over to visit her tonight.

After talking with Angel, Jason is no longer interested in McCoy. The guy must have spent every minute he wasn't with one of his wives fulfilling his professional obligations. He made a decent living as a freelance illustrator, popular with comic book scriptwriters, graphic novelists and children's authors. Thanks to Angel, McCoy kept the copyright on the story lines and characters he created for *Kav'erse*. The income from royalties and sales of subsidiary rights, although it hasn't made him rich yet, certainly explains how he was able to afford his high-end lifestyle with Kendra and still have enough money to contribute to a second household.

Jason's interest in McCoy has been replaced by a growing interest in Kendra. He has never met a more courageous woman, or man, for that matter. In the same situation, Kathy would have melted into a self-pitying puddle of tears. Even stoic Jude complains about how unfair she thinks Travis is being. But Kendra has shouldered her burdens without complaint. She doesn't hide her feelings, but she doesn't let them cloud her judgment either. She makes every decision only after careful consideration and, as far as Jason can tell, has benefited from none of them so far. But the quality he admires most about Kendra is the way she treats Lesley with dignity and respect. For three years, Jason has carried a grudge against Kathy's new husband. After watching Kendra cope with the fallout from McCoy's collapse, Jason thinks it's time to stop feeling sorry for himself and get on with his life.

The receptionist in the lobby of the FBI offices takes Jason's name and asks him to have a seat while she locates Agent Hauver. A few minutes later the agent steps into the reception area.

Jason rises to shake hands. "Thanks for seeing me without an appointment."

"No problem. We can talk in my office. Sandy, can you give Mr. Cheddick a visitor's badge?"

The receptionist asks Jason to sign the visitors' log, then hands him a plastic rectangle on a lanyard. He slings it around his neck and follows the FBI agent to a windowless room containing two shabby office chairs, a metal desk, four computer monitors and five large metal filing cabinets.

"Are you still working for the first wife?" Agent Hauver asks as he takes his seat behind the desk.

Jason sits in the chair on the visitor's side of the desk. "Technically. I haven't billed her yet. I hit a dead end on local information. You haven't released his financial records yet, so there hasn't been much for me to look into. I got a list of previous addresses from McCoy's agent a couple of days ago, but they're all out of state, which could get pretty expensive, so I thought I'd check in with you before running them down."

"Don't bother. We've already done it. I'll let you look through the file, but you won't find anything useful there."

"So he's been cleared?"

"Of anything we're interested in, but we still need to talk to him, so we'll keep the case open until he wakes up. There's still the bigamy, of course, but that's not in our jurisdiction."

"If all you want to do is talk to him, is it possible to unfreeze his bank account? Kendra McCoy is now his legal guardian and she's struggling to pay his hospital bills."

"That's not going to help her much. The account is almost empty. But give me a couple of days to push the paperwork through and we should be able to send her a check for the money that was in the box." Agent Hauver leans forward slightly, as though sharing a confidence. "Actually, that box of cash is what saved him. When we compared his bank accounts to his royalty statements, we saw he'd stopped depositing his royalty checks to his business account and started cashing them at those check-cashing shops instead. At first we thought he was being blackmailed, but we found every penny that was missing in the box."

Jason tests this information against what he already knows about McCoy. "The first check he didn't deposit—can you tell me when it was cashed?"

"Sure." The agent pulls up a file on his computer and swings the monitor around to show Jason the information on the screen. He points to a line of text. "It's this one."

Thinking out loud, Jason says, "So he owns a cabin in

Washington for almost four years as Eric McCoy. Then he meets Lesley Sorrenson in March. Then a month later he starts stockpiling cash and in June he gets his Washington driver's license under the name David McCoy and transfers ownership of the cabin to his new name. It's like he was hiding his assets, which would mean he was planning to leave his first wife all along."

"There's better ways to hide assets than creating a fake identity," the agent points out.

"True, but I don't think he created it to hide his assets. I think he was trying to hide himself. The only connection between Eric McCoy and David McCoy is a land transfer in a small county registry office. If he hadn't collapsed, and no one knew about David McCoy, he'd probably have got away with it."

The agent tips back his chair and studies the ceiling tiles while he thinks about this. "You could be right," he says finally. "It fits all the facts we know. But I don't see why he couldn't just get a divorce, like everyone else."

Before Jason leaves, Agent Hauver gives him a printout of the background interviews collected by the FBI. Jason takes it to Carlita's, his favorite Mexican restaurant, and flips through it while eating the taco special for lunch. Over the past twenty years, McCoy has lived in fifteen states. Everyone interviewed by the FBI knew he made his living as an artist, although most thought he illustrated children's books. All McCoy's ex-girlfriends—like Jason, the FBI found no ex-wives—remembered him fondly, although their descriptions of his character varied. Some thought he was "thoughtful and quiet"; others saw him as "a party animal" or "a romantic guy" or "a real intellectual," making Jason think McCoy's chameleon quality must be a lifelong habit.

On the drive home, Jason realizes Kendra no longer needs his services. He'll write up a final report and give it to her tonight, along with his bill. He thinks about avoiding any mention of his theory about why McCoy was stockpiling cash, which is only a hunch after all, but then decides to include it in his report. Kendra is smart enough to work it out for herself over time, and omitting it would make him seem somehow less competent as an investigator. Even though he knows he'll probably never see her again, Jason wants Kendra to respect his ability.

His cell phone rings as he's unlocking his front door. He flips the phone open, but before he can get out a greeting, he hears his son's panicked voice shouting, "Dad! I think you'd better get over here. Right now!"

"What happened? Where are you?"

The sound of shattering glass almost obscures Fletcher's response. "At the drugstore in the mall."

In the background, a man yells at someone to calm down or he'll have to call the police. Jude's voice, shrill but recognizable, shrieks back, "I am the police, you idiot! Get your hands off me!"

"Hurry, Dad! Aunt Jude's freaking out."

Wondering what Fletcher is doing at the mall on a school day, and why Jude is freaking out, Jason races back to his car.

"I STILL THINK I SHOULD REPORT THIS, even if he won't press charges," the mall security guard says twenty minutes later as he escorts Jason through a door marked EMPLOYEES ONLY into the warehouse area behind the drugstore. "I mean, she attacked a guy in a wheelchair, for chrissakes. Took two of us to pull her off him. We have witnesses."

"Is he hurt?" Jason asks.

"Naw. Guy's pretty buff. He grabbed her wrists. She didn't get anywhere near him."

Jason doubts this. Jude teaches an informal hand-to-hand combat class at the police gym. If she'd really wanted to hurt

Travis, he'd be on his way to the hospital. "Let me talk with my sister before you decide on that, okay?"

They walk through the warehouse, between floor-to-ceiling shelves stacked with cartons of paper products on one side, laundry detergent and soft drinks on the other. At the end of the aisle, Fletcher sits on the floor with his back to the wall and his knees pulled up to his chest. His arms are wrapped around his shins. His hands and wrists are stained red.

A surge of fear slams Jason's heart into his ribs. He pushes past the guard to run to his son. "Fletcher!"

"Dad!" Fletcher scrambles to his feet and staggers into his father's arms. He smells like maraschino cherries and antiseptic.

For an instant, Jason has the sensation of holding a much younger Fletcher. Then he grabs the boy's shoulders and holds him at arm's length. "Where are you hurt?"

"He's not." Travis rolls up, his shirt and pants spattered with dark red liquid. "It's just cough syrup."

Over Fletcher's shoulder, Jason nods at his brother-in-law's stained clothing. "And that's all cough syrup too? You're not hurt?"

"I'm fine," Travis says, but his jaw muscles are tight and his eyes are narrowed. "Jude is too. At least physically."

Relieved, Jason takes two deep breaths to help his heart rate return to normal. "So what happened?"

"Jude pushed me backward into a display of cough syrup bottles," Travis explains. "A few of them hit the metal bars on my chair and shattered. Fletcher picked the glass off my back."

Pulling away from his father's grip to get gesturing room, Fletcher embellishes this bald report. "She went ballistic, Dad. She yelled at him. She tried to hit him. She was really scary."

"What set her off?"

Fletcher looks over at his uncle, who looks down at the stains on his thighs. With a perfect blend of embarrassment and apology, Fletcher confesses, "Uncle Trav was helping me buy condoms. I guess Aunt Jude thought he was buying them for himself."

Jason suddenly sees, with brutal clarity, how his strategy of hoping Fletcher's problems will go away if he ignores them long enough has succeeded. Fletcher has taken his problems to Travis. Jason's chest feels cold and hollow, as though the space carved into his heart on the day his son was born has been vacated. He wants to reach out, beg forgiveness, ask for a second chance. But there's a more immediate issue to be dealt with before tackling the much tougher task of winning his son back. He pushes down his shame and says to the security guard, "I'll talk to my sister now. Where is she?"

The guard turns and points to a door farther along the wall. "In the accounting office."

Travis grimaces and grips the wheels of his chair. "Maybe I should go now."

Jason shakes his head. "No, you should stay." He jerks his thumb at the door. "Hell, you should be the one going in there. This has gone too far. I'm going to tell her who the condoms are really for; then I'm going to ask her to talk to you. Will you stay?"

Travis looks down the aisle of shelving, as though planning an escape route, then releases the wheels, puts his hands in his lap and nods.

More from an urge to touch his son again than any real worry Travis will bolt, Jason places his hand on Fletcher's shoulder. "Don't let him change his mind."

"Me?"

"Well, you have some responsibility here. They're your condoms."

The guard unlocks the door of the office and Jason enters to find Jude sitting on the floor, her back against the privacy panel of a beige metal desk, her forearms hanging over bent knees. She looks up at Jason with tragic, but dry, blue eyes. "Is Trav okay?"

"He probably won't be able to cough for a month." Jason sits beside her and pulls at one of her red-spattered sleeves. "This is all cough syrup too, right?"

She returns her gaze to her dangling hands. "Do you know what he was doing?"

"He was helping Fletcher buy condoms."

Momentarily distracted, Jude looks up. "Inez?"

"I don't know. I don't think so."

"So they weren't for Trav?" She tips her head back to rest it against the desk while she processes this. "I made a decision last night. If Travis really doesn't want kids, I can live with that. I called him this morning. Told him I was coming home tonight. Then, when I saw him holding that box of condoms, I thought he was worried I'd go off the pill without telling him. I thought he didn't trust me anymore. After all that fighting, I thought I'd lost him."

"So you attacked him?"

"I was just so mad at him for giving up on me. I wanted to hurt him back."

"If you wanted to hurt him, you would have," Jason tells her and accepts the tiny twitch at the corner of her mouth as a smile.

"I guess I owe him an apology."

He wraps an arm around her shoulders. "It's a start, but I think you owe him more than that. He loves you. He told me once that your happiness is his happiness. If you're right about his really wanting kids, then you're going to have to convince him that's what will make you happy."

While Jude considers this, Jason's thoughts drift back to regaining his son's trust. He wishes he could start the process with something easier than buying condoms, then wonders if Fletcher really is buying them for Inez, then decides condoms might be the easiest step on the road to repairing their relationship.

Jude leans sideways until her head is resting against his collarbone. "You're sure he loves me?"

"His exact words were, 'I love her like fire.'" Jason can't see Jude's face, but he feels her cheek shift against the fabric of his jacket and knows she likes the quote. "He's waiting outside. He needs to know you're okay."

"I can't go out there," Jude protests, but she lifts both hands to tidy her hair.

"Okay. I'll send him in here, then." He stands and extends his hand to help her up.

She grabs his wrist. "You're sure?"

"Positive."

Travis, Fletcher and the security guard all look up when Jason steps out of the office. "She's ready to talk to you," he tells Travis.

Travis takes one long look down the aisle to freedom, then grips the wheels of the chair and propels himself toward the office. He stops just outside the door.

Jason places a hand on his shoulder. "Just tell her what you told me on Sunday."

Setting his jaw like a man performing the bravest act of his life, Travis pushes himself into the office.

After pulling the door closed, Jason walks toward Fletcher. "Your uncle is going to be busy for a while. You'll have to make do with me for advice. After we get you cleaned up." He turns to the security guard. "Where are the washrooms?"

"Down by the food court," the guard replies. "I'll hang around out here, just in case she doesn't like what he says."

"They'll be fine," Jason assures him, hoping it's the truth.

As Fletcher and Jason walk back between the shelves, Fletcher asks, "Are you mad at me?"

"For what?"

"For asking Uncle Trav."

"No. I'm mad at myself. I wanted you to solve your own problems. I didn't want to get involved. And that was stupid because I'm your father. I am involved." Jason slings an arm across Fletcher's shoulders. "So, condoms aren't rocket science. What do you need to know?"

"Well, like, for starters . . . Don't laugh."

"I won't laugh."

"Promise?"

"I promise."

"Okay, the thing is—" Fletcher hesitates, then blurts out, "I don't know what size I am."

Starima

Eric at twenty-three

EVERY TIME ERIC STEPPED ACROSS THE THRESHOLD, he felt the same lightness, as though gravity inside his apartment had been somehow reduced. After six months here, he still had the sensation of bouncing along the hallway toward the living room.

Eric never knew privacy until he got his own apartment. In foster homes, he'd always shared rooms with other foster children. In art college, he'd shared dormitory rooms with a succession of other students. After graduation, he'd moved back in with Habibeh and Farouk, ostensibly as a boarder while he paid off his student loans, but actually to help Habibeh care for Farouk during his three-year battle with prostate cancer. It wasn't until Farouk passed away and Habibeh decided to live with her sister that Eric got his first taste of privacy. On the nineteenth floor of a generic high-rise apartment building in Newark, he finally found the solitude he'd been unconsciously craving all his life.

At first he hadn't known what to do with it. On his own, with no one whose interests he could share or social life he could piggyback on, he felt fuzzy, unable to focus. When he wasn't working, he sat for hours on the ornate red velvet sofa he'd inherited from Habibeh along with the rest of his furnishings, silently staring out the window at the empty concrete balcony. He felt safe and inexplicably happy, yet guilty at the same time, as though there was something wrong, or at least naughty, about being alone. He vaguely understood the feeling had something to do with being hidden, but never consciously remembered it as the closet feeling. Gradually, as the weeks passed, his sense of guilt faded.

In the living room, the answering machine flashed an accusatory 10 in the messages display. At least five of them would be from Trisha, determined to include him in her chaotic philanthropy. Trisha was becoming something of a problem, along with beautiful but clingy Summer and brilliant but increasingly possessive Elise, who had probably split the remaining messages between them.

He never intended to collect so many girlfriends. No one was more surprised than Eric when he found himself juggling three of them. Summer waited tables in a Lebanese restaurant where he ate fairly often. Elise did his taxes. Trisha was a veterinarian at the rescue zoo where Eric went to study raccoons for an assignment. He hadn't actively pursued them, or even asked them out. They just fell into his life and never fell out. Chatting led to coffee. Coffee led to a movie with Summer, a jazz club with Elise, and a strange but interesting evening at the public library to raise awareness about the plight of the short-nosed sturgeon, a fish Eric hadn't even known existed until Trisha dragged him to the library. Eventually, and Eric wasn't sure how it happened, all three women were dumping scrambled eggs on his breakfast plate.

Eric's agent, Angel, attributed this romantic success to the same source as Eric's professional success—empathy. "You're like a mind reader, kid," Angel told him more than once. "Deanna Troi's twin brother. I hear it from the writers you work with all the time. They send you the text and you create the perfect image, exactly what they imagined the character and setting should look like."

Eric didn't see it this way. "It's all there in the words, Angel. What the characters say, what they want, how they interact. I just draw that. It's the same with people. I just listen."

Eric pressed the PLAY button on the answering machine to hear his messages: one from Angel, three from Summer, one from Elise, and the expected five from Trisha offering menu options for the vegan meal she wanted to prepare in his kitchen. Eric had no intention of allowing anyone, even a girlfriend, into his fortress of solitude and no idea how to deflect Trisha without hurting her feelings. He postponed his dilemma by returning Angel's call first.

"Four Winds."

"Hey, Angel. It's Eric. You wanted to talk to me?"

"Yeah. I may have a job lined up for you. You ever been to Idaho?"

"Never even been farther west than Philadelphia. What's in Idaho? Besides potatoes."

"A rancher named Stella Sinkton. She wrote a book about horse training. Her publisher's looking for an illustrator. Not your usual gig, but I know you can do it. The fee's pretty good, and you'd get to spend a few months on her ranch."

In college, Eric had studied all kinds of art and techniques.

He made most of his money, such as it was, creating images of fantasy worlds for children's books and characters for comic books and graphic novels. But his first love was still his true love, and he spent most Saturdays at the park drawing children and dogs, lovers necking on blankets, old men bowling on the packed dirt of the bocce court, and the residents of the petting zoo beside it. The idea of getting close to horses again appealed to him as well. "How many months is a few?" he asked Angel.

"At least three. You'll have to pay for your own transportation, but once you're there, she covers food and lodging because the ranch is so far from the nearest town."

Three months on a horse ranch, twenty-five hundred miles from Trisha, Summer, Elise and the growing problem of preventing them from finding out about one another. Eric didn't even bother to ask about the fee. "When do I leave?"

One week later, he traded in his Honda Civic for a ten-year-old VW camper, loaded it with art supplies, and drove it up the entrance ramp to I-276 westbound. He never set foot in New Jersey again.

Idaho turned out to be nothing like the vast expanse of potato fields he'd imagined. The Double Bar Ranch occupied a small valley nestled in the western foothills of the Rockies: three thousand acres of grassland surrounded by steep forested slopes under the benevolent dictatorship of its sixty-three-year-old owner, Stella Sinkton, a woman as tough and agile as the quarter horses she bred.

Stella was a woman of few words and those she did utter were generally acerbic. She had no use for "female fripperies." Her wardrobe consisted entirely of worn denim jeans, plaid shirts, scuffed cowboy boots and a grubby Stetson of indeterminate color. She wore her white hair in two long, thick braids, the ends of which still showed a rusty hint of their original flame. She liked horses better than people and had little patience with fools, a category to which she assigned the bulk of the human race. When the mood struck her, she rode out alone into the foothills, sometimes for two or three days at a time.

While she was gone, the ranch was run by her foreman, Jake Harrison. Old Jake was much more talkative than his boss. From him, Eric learned the valley legends that had grown up around Stella. There was the grizzly she'd faced down with nothing more than a burning branch snatched from the campfire, and the time she shot the hat off an especially persistent suitor who eventually settled for her sister. Eric's favorite story was the one about the starving cougar cub she found and raised to adulthood, teaching it how to stalk and kill small prey by example.

Eric found Stella fascinating. He admired her independence, her take-no-prisoners approach to getting what she wanted. He developed a spiritual crush on her and filled two sketchbooks with drawings of her as she worked with her beloved horses.

At the end of his four months on the Double Bar Ranch, Eric drove down to Seattle to help Angel move out of his small shop in the downtown core to larger premises in a new strip mall on the eastern edge of the city. As they assembled shelves one morning, Eric told Angel about an idea he had for a story built around a redheaded adventuress based on Stella and asked if Angel thought one of the writers he represented would be interested in doing the script.

"Done any sketches?" Angel asked.

"Got some out in the van."

"Let's take a break. My back is killing me. You go get your drawings and I'll get us a couple of beers out of the fridge."

The office furniture hadn't been delivered yet, so they sat on packing crates while Angel looked through Eric's sketchbook.

"I'm impressed," Angel said as he leafed through the pages. "Got a name for her?"

"I think of her as Starima. But that's really up to the writer."

"Maybe you should try writing it yourself."

"I can't write."

Angel closed the sketchbook and picked up his can of beer. "You've got the story line. You've got the art. The writing is mostly dialogue, and you're a good listener. I think you should give it a try. If it doesn't work, I'll look around for a writer."

Eric rented an apartment in Seattle and gave it a try.

Gossip Hits the Fan

GIVEN A CHOICE, LESLEY PREFERS to work with the toddlers at Wee Tots. She loves the energy of the older children, the honesty of their emotions, and their often hilarious explanations of the world as they understand it. Today, however, she is working in the crèche room to avoid the sidelong glances and sudden silences of her coworkers.

Brockville is abuzz with gossip surrounding Andrew's sleepover and speculation regarding Beatrice's big win at the casino, which the grapevine rapidly converted into a gambling addiction. Lesley has been guilty of a more than a few sidelong glances herself, so she knows there is no real malice behind the rumors. They are just something exciting to talk about in a town where strawberry suppers and church bingo dominate the social calendar. Eventually new topics will push aside Beatrice's transgressions, but this thought is less than comforting, since one of those topics will be the annulment of Lesley's bigamous marriage.

At the Foodville market, she drops a bomb of silence over the two checkout desks when she stops in for milk after work. Her mood darkens a bit more when she's forced to park on the street outside her aunt's house to avoid blocking the police cruiser in the driveway, which she assumes is the result of another one of Beatrice's false alarms.

For the past three days, Beatrice has been a twitching wreck, jumping at every sound, insisting on having her bed moved into Cassandra's room, obsessively peering out windows looking for lurking robbers. She refuses to be left alone in the house and protests vehemently whenever Lesley tries to return to the solitary cabin up on Saddleback Ridge. Last night she called the police when a possum knocked over a flowerpot on the back deck. Cassandra is at the end of her patience. Lesley isn't far behind.

Inside the house, Chief of Police Floyd Wilcox sips iced tea and samples Beatrice's famous oatmeal raisin cookies from a plate on the kitchen table while Beatrice and Cassandra argue.

"This is ridiculous. You're just drawing more attention to yourself." Cassandra pulls a blister pack of nicotine gum out of her sweater pocket and removes a piece.

Beatrice is still unable to talk without discomfort, but this doesn't stop her from responding, "I don't care if I look silly. Everyone in town knows about the money, thanks to Alice. I'm not going to the bank without protection."

"I offered to take you. You didn't have to bother Floyd about it."

Floyd brushes crumbs from the front of his uniform. "It's okay, Cass. If it makes Trixie feel better, I'm happy to drive her to the bank."

"She's all yours, Floyd," Cassandra calls over her shoulder as she stomps out the back door.

Beatrice's ingenuity in calling her brother to drive her to the bank amuses Lesley, who hopes things will calm down once the money has been safely consigned to the Wells Fargo vault. She watches from the porch as her uncle escorts Beatrice and her bag of cash to his green and white cruiser with solemn and official courtesy, which he destroys by winking at Lesley just before squeezing his belly in behind the steering wheel. Lesley waves them good-bye, then walks around to the back of the house, where Cassandra sits smoking on the steps of the deck. The discarded gum lies on the grass a few feet away.

"She's driving me crazy." Cassandra takes a deep drag.

"I know, and I'm sorry about tonight, but Kendra says it's important. I should be home before nine. Maybe you could drive to Portland when I get back and spend the night with Robyn."

For an instant, Cassandra's gray eyes gleam with hope; then she shakes her head. "I wouldn't be back before you have to leave for work."

"Maybe she'll settle down when the money's in the bank. And if she doesn't, I'll take her to work with me."

"She's not ready to face them."

This is true. Beatrice, never having been on the receiving end of the kind of gossip she's so good at dishing out, has no desire to face the wagging tongues of Brockville. It's also true Cassandra's annoyance has as much to do with losing her planned date with Robyn as it does with Beatrice's behavior.

Ignoring the smoke curling up from the cigarette, Lesley sits down beside her aunt on the step. "Why do you protect her? She doesn't appreciate it. I'm not even sure she knows you're doing it."

Cassandra steps on the cigarette to extinguish it, then flings the butt out to join the gum in the grass. "Habit? Pity? I don't know. She's just so helpless. Like a kitten."

"I was thinking about that the other day. How easy her life is.

How easy everyone makes it for her. Like it's her job to be helpless."

"Are you saying it's my fault?"

"More like you inherited her from Dad and Grandpa."

"I can't just abandon her. She wouldn't last a week on her own."

"I think if you did, she'd just latch on to someone else."

Cassandra snorts. "Poor Andrew."

"Well, someone like Andrew, anyway. But that's not what I mean." Lesley searches for the best way to explain her thoughts without offending her aunt. "I know you think I'm being stubborn about making decisions by myself. And right now, you're probably right. It's not like I've got any good choices."

Cassandra takes Lesley's hand, stroking the smooth knuckles with a gentle thumb. "Sometimes there aren't any, honey. But there's always a least worst. It gets easier to see with practice."

"So maybe that's what Mom needs. Some practice. If you're not here tomorrow morning, she'll get some."

"It's not that simple."

Having tried to make her point, and had it rejected, Lesley gives up. So she's surprised when Cassandra continues. "But it won't kill her. And I might, if I'm stuck with her much longer. Okay. I'll text Robyn, see what she's doing later tonight." She gives her niece a grateful hug. "And thank you. I really appreciate this."

Watching her aunt carefully peck out a message to Robyn, Lesley has an epiphany. Problems aren't as big when they're shared. She waits until Cassandra sends the message, then asks, "You know my boss?"

"Ruth? Sure. Not really well. She was a couple of years behind me in school."

"She's talking about selling Wee Tots. She says she's getting too slow to keep up with the kids."

"You think you might lose your job? The next owner would be foolish not to keep you on. The kids love you and the parents trust you."

"Actually, I was thinking maybe I could be the next owner."

Instantly, Cassandra switches to pessimist mode. "Oh, honey, running a business is much harder than working for one. There's so much paperwork, so many rules."

"And I'm not very good at that. I know. But you ran a business with Norah. You could teach me." Lesley sees her aunt preparing another objection and holds up her hand to forestall it. "Just listen for a minute. I know it's going to be hard. But not as hard as raising my baby on minimum wage. I'm good at my job and it's all I know. It's like you said, the least worst choice. I know I can't do it myself. I need a business plan and a bank loan and all kinds of stuff I don't even know about yet. That's why I'm asking for help."

Cassandra reaches for Lesley's upraised hand, cradling it in both of hers. She studies her niece's face intently, as though meeting her for the first time, then nods. "Okay, then."

Lies of Omission

IN THE CRAMPED BATHROOM OF the McAllister apartment, Kendra is putting the finishing touches on her makeup when her brother calls up the stairs, "Kens? Lesley's here."

She detaches a few sheets of bathroom tissue from the roll hanging by the toilet to blot her lips before hobbling into the hall and leaning over the railing. "Can you send her up here?" Dropping her voice to just above a whisper, she adds, "And keep Pops busy downstairs."

"Sure. How come?"

"I want to ask her something and I don't want Pops to hear us until I know what she says."

Paul pulls an imaginary zipper across his lips and disappears into the restaurant. A minute later he returns with Lesley. He waves her toward the stairway, then stands at the bottom of the steps, mesmerized by the elaborately stitched orange swirls on the back pockets of her jeans. Kendra can't blame her brother for this interest. Lesley, predictably, is one of those women who blos-

of her right elbow. "They'll know soon enough when I start the annulment."

"Small-town gossip?"

"You can't imagine." Lesley tells Kendra the tale of Beatrice's lost reputation. "It'll be worse for me. Gambling and lovers are nothing compared to bigamy. I'll be the bigamist's wife for the rest of my life." She quickly adds, "But don't worry. I said I'd do it and I will. I'm not backing out."

Impressed by Lesley's courage at being willing to stick to her word regardless of the cost, Kendra is pleased to tell her the sacrifice can at least be postponed. "Maybe you should hold off on that for a while. I got a call from Agent Hauver at the FBI today. They haven't found anything on McCoy. They've decided to put everything on hold until he wakes up."

Lesley closes her eyes and sighs. "He's been cleared."

"You sound relieved. You were always so sure he was innocent."

"I was. But he *seemed* guilty to them. Especially after they found all that money."

"Well, apparently they don't think that way anymore. My brother is taking me to their offices to pick up the stuff they took from the house on Grove Street, and Agent Hauver said he'll send me the results of the financial investigation, along with a check to cover the cash in the box, in a few days. He also said there wasn't a lot of money in the bank, so before we start anything, I think we should find out how much money there is. And there's no guarantee McCoy will ever wake up."

"Don't say that. He's going to wake up."

Kendra defends herself. "Don't look at me like that. I don't want him to die. All I'm saying is there's no guarantee he'll ever wake up, and it would be less of a legal hassle for us if he didn't."

The tenuous bond forming between the two women comes

perilously close to snapping. Then Lesley surprises Kendra with a grin. "You sound just like Aunt Cass."

"Kens!" Paul calls up the stairs. "You've got another visitor."

"Be down in a sec," Kendra calls back.

Before they leave the kitchen, Lesley reaches into her pocket for her wedding ring and puts it back on.

Downstairs in the restaurant, Angel Carreras leans on his cane by the cash desk, talking to Peony and Sam. As she crosses the restaurant, Kendra wonders if she misunderstood Jason's explanation of who this man is. He looks more like an escapee from a soup kitchen than an agent who negotiates contracts with major studios. A battered canvas satchel hangs at his hip. The strap, slung crosswise over his chest, has rucked up his plaid shirt on one side, exposing a band of pale pink underwear, a color she assumes is the result of inept laundry technique rather than actual preference, given the state of the rest of his clothing. He tips his head forward to look at Kendra and Lesley over the top of his glasses. His jaw sags open.

From behind the cash desk, Peony asks, "Is something wrong?"

He blinks, as though trying to clear his vision.

"Mr. Carreras?" Kendra holds out her hand as she approaches. "I'm Kendra, and this is my friend Lesley. Is Jason coming later?"

Instead of taking her hand, he just stands there, his gaze shifting between Kendra and Lesley.

"Is something wrong, Mr. Carreras?" Lesley echoes Peony's question.

"Sorry. Call me Angel." Belatedly, he shakes their hands. "Something came up and Jason can't make it tonight. He said he'll call. You know, this is the first time I've met any of Eric's models. I'd have recognized either of you on the street."

Cheetara

Eric at thirty-four

BEFORE ERIC REALLY KNEW KENDRA, when he thought their affair was nothing more than her rebellion against a dull marriage, he built an entire alien race for Kav'erse around her personality. The Talin were feline, luxuriously sensual and ruthlessly pragmatic. She was Cheetara, ambassador and spy, sent to seduce the Exiled Emperor and reveal his true identity. The publisher loved the story and gave Eric the highest advance he'd ever received.

Half a year into their relationship, Eric realized Kendra was different from other women he'd dated. She didn't have the biological clock that had complicated his previous relationships, never dropping hints about marriage or cooking him dinner in her studio apartment when he came to visit her in Portland. She chased her dreams with ferocity and brutal practicality, but

Disappointment at Jason's absence makes Kendra's reply come out more waspish than she intends. "Well, if we'd known he was going to use us like that, you wouldn't be meeting any now."

Sam, deducing the cause of her annoyance, winks at her. She glares back at him to discourage immediate comment, although she knows she's merely postponing the inevitable teasing until later.

"You mean you didn't know? He never told either of you?" Angel asks.

Both Kendra and Lesley shake their heads.

"Well, I guess it's up to me, then."

never tried to weave him into her plans. To these attractions she added an uninhibited approach to sex and a need for solitude that almost matched his own.

Eric felt he had found the one woman he could be happy with for the rest of his life. Their relationship met all his needs and made no uncomfortable demands of him, a perfect balance of separation and togetherness. He relaxed into Kendra like a drowning sailor washed up on a warm tropical beach.

There was only one problem. Early on in his career, Eric had discovered he was uncomfortable with fame, even in the limited arena of adult-comic fans. As a result, he avoided telling new acquaintances his exact profession by saying he was a contractor. When pressed, he fell back on his Farsi and claimed to be a translator, a job he'd actually held for a while when he worked for an immigration assistance firm in South Carolina. Kendra had added a glamorous twist to this explanation by assuming his reluctance to talk about his job meant he worked for the government. Complicating the situation even more, he felt certain she would not be amused to see her face topping the body of a sexually aggressive alien seductress. Which was why he flew to Seattle immediately after the first vacation he and Kendra took together.

When Eric walked into Shazzam! Angel was unpacking action figures on the sales counter, looking, as always, as though he'd obtained his clothing from a Goodwill store. This ability to make anything he wore, even a tuxedo, appear slept in was what made him such a good agent. People always underestimated Angel.

"Hey, kid!" Angel greeted Eric. "What are you doing here?"

"I came to ask you about something."

Angel called his assistant to mind the store, then limped ahead of Eric into his office.

"Did you hurt your leg?" Eric asked.

"Doctor thinks it's sciatica. Going in for tests next week."

They took seats on either side of Angel's desk. Eric held up the four-foot-long cardboard tube he'd brought with him. "Present for you."

Angel popped the top off the tube and tipped it to slide out a rolled painting. "Big one," he said as he spread the canvas across the mounds of contracts, comics and drawings on his desk. He reached the edge of the desk after exposing only half the painting. "This is incredible!"

"It's the original Cheetara image. I can't sell it, so I thought you'd like to have it."

Angel looked up from studying the canvas. "Are you nuts? This could be worth a fortune in a couple of years."

"That's what I came to talk to you about. I want to pull the issue with the Talin."

"Break the contract?" Angel fell back into his chair. "That's crazy."

"I really don't want that issue to get out."

"I can talk to the publisher, but unless you won the lottery, I don't think we can afford it, kid. This close to release, they'll want us to reimburse production costs."

"Can't you at least try?"

"If you're sure about this. But why?"

Eric had no intention of telling Angel about Kendra yet. If they met, Angel would never be able to resist telling her about Cheetara. Until the Talin issues had been pulled and Eric was sure Kendra wouldn't leave him, he wasn't going to tell Angel anything. "Because it could get me in trouble. One of the

Talin"—he avoided specifying which one—"is based on a real person."

"Libelously? Are we talking lawsuit?"

"It's not libel."

"Who is it?"

"No one you know. And it might not be important, but I'd rather not test it if I can avoid it, so will you talk to the publishers?"

Angel talked, but the publishers refused to listen. They thought the Talin were the best characters Eric had ever produced. They loved Cheetara and had invested heavily in the marketing campaign. They also rejected his attempt to return the advance for the second issue. The Talin went on to become a permanent feature of Kav'erse, although much to readers' dismay, Cheetara died at the beginning of the second issue, which never showed her face.

Eric intended to tell Kendra about his real profession. He moved to Portland to show her he was serious about their relationship, but she resisted his suggestion they move in together, making him uncertain of her affection and unwilling to risk revealing himself. Because he couldn't work in his apartment until she knew, he bought a run-down cabin across the river in Washington for practically nothing and set up his studio there. She accepted his absences and even welcomed them, since they gave her more time to work on setting up her new event planning business. Their relationship deepened, becoming exactly the affectionate, uncluttered bond Eric wanted.

Then one day he realized it was too late. The lie had worked too well. Eric's fake profession had melded into the fabric of their life together. Kendra liked dating a guy who did important work for the government and enjoyed deflecting the curiosity of her friends with offhand references to the "sensitive nature" of his assignments and "security clearance." He considered getting a real job, one he could admit to, but his only other marketable skill, translating Farsi, would never support the lifestyle she loved.

Gradually he accepted the permanence of the lie. It wasn't difficult to maintain. Kendra, independent and driven, lived primarily in her own world. She rarely asked about his.

Hot Coals

IT'S EASY TO DESPISE A charismatic and unscrupulous man who uses his women as models for male fantasy objects, but impossible to maintain this opinion after Angel tells the tale of McCoy's attempts to prevent publication of the comics based on his wives. Although McCoy failed with Cheetara, he succeeded with Lesley's character, the Holly Virgin, by nearly bankrupting himself to buy the entire print run before it hit the shelves. Angel thinks the issue they found among McCoy's possessions is likely the only copy in existence and offers an astonishing amount of money for it. Kendra tells him she'll get back to him.

After Angel leaves, Sam comes over to the table where Lesley and Kendra are sitting in slightly stunned silence and takes another run at convincing his daughter to cut McCoy a break. "You got to admit, he tried to do the right thing."

"Okay," Kendra concedes, "but it's only half the right thing. He regretted what he did, but that doesn't explain why he did it in the first place."

Lesley backs her up. "And it's still a lie, another secret he kept. Regret doesn't make things right. Apologies do."

From her place behind the cash desk, Peony says, "To understand everything is to forgive everything."

Kendra responds to these words as though they are slaps. "Well, if I ever understand, you'll be the first to know. Lesley has to leave soon, and I need to talk to her before she goes. We're going up to my room."

Lesley gives Sam and Peony a confused half smile before picking up the Paramount contract Angel left for them to look at and following Kendra to the staircase. As they climb, she asks, "What did your mother mean?"

On the landing at the top of the stairs, Kendra stops to wipe tears from both eyes with the heel of her palm. "It's a Buddhist saying. I don't know what it means. I don't even know why she said it. She never takes sides."

Lesley considers abandoning the topic, not wanting to make Kendra more upset than she already is. But somehow it seems important, so she rephrases her question. "If he'd told you about what he did, would you have left him?"

"If he'd told me at the beginning, when it was still just an affair? Probably." Kendra pushes open the door to her room.

Cracker Jack turns away from watching traffic on the street outside the window to greet her. "Hey, babe!" He cocks his head to focus a pale and avaricious eye on the waistband button of Lesley's jeans.

Lesley has never heard the bird's startlingly realistic imitation of McCoy's voice. It's like hearing a ghost. She shudders with a spasm of longing for her lost husband.

Kendra closes her eyes and mutters, "Oh, shut up, Jack."

"Shut up, Jack," he repeats with the same distinct diction,

then hops to his swing, flops himself upside down and rocks back and forth.

Over the creaking of the swing, Kendra continues answering Lesley's question. "After we got married, I really felt committed. I probably would have forgiven him. What about you?"

The bedroom is small. The narrow bed and tallboy dresser have been pushed against one wall to accommodate Jack's oversized cage. Lesley sits on the foot of the bed. "I don't know. I keep thinking about what your mother said about understanding and forgiveness."

"It's just a Buddhist saying."

"The thing is, if she's right, we may never understand everything. So I don't see how to forgive him."

Kendra sits at the other end of the bed and leans against the headboard. "Does it matter? It's not like it will change anything."

"Except how we feel. I don't want to go through the rest of my life mad at him. That's just stupid."

Kendra laughs out loud, a bright peal of pure amusement that startles Cracker Jack into squawking, "Blimey!"

"What's so funny?" Lesley asks.

"You could be a Buddhist."

"I don't get it."

"It's another one of my mother's sayings: *Holding on to anger is like grasping a hot coal to throw at someone else; you're the one who gets burned.* And you're both right. If there's any revenge, the aneurysm has already taken it. I guess we just have to hope there's some other way to forgive him." She reaches out to take the contract from Lesley's hand. "So do you think I should sign this?"

"It's your decision. You're his guardian."

"It's your decision too. Part of the money would be yours."

Unaccustomed to having her opinion solicited, Lesley considers her answer carefully. While she thinks, she watches Cracker Jack, who has returned to an upright position and is busy grooming the feathers on his chest. The parrot reminds her of Patches, McCoy's horse, still being boarded at the stable, another dangling end to be dealt with. She feels suddenly relieved McCoy never divorced Kendra. She doesn't like this about herself, but accepts its truth.

"If part of the money would be mine," she says finally, "then so would part of the responsibility. Robyn says when he wakes up, he'll probably be brain damaged." This is the first time she has said these last two words out loud. It gives them a heavy reality. "He'll need special care, maybe for his whole life. I have to put the baby first. I don't want any money. I'll help out where I can, but I can't be responsible. I'm sorry."

Kendra takes equally as long to think before replying. "You're right. I can't afford the responsibility either. We should take this movie deal, invest the capital and use the interest to pay for his care. Angel said there is royalty income as well."

Lesley offers the assets on her side of the river. "There's the cabin too. And the horse."

"Well, the horse is worth considering, if you don't want it."

"Definitely not."

"But I think we should save the cabin as a last resort. It can't lose value and we don't know how long the money has to last. Besides"—Kendra smiles—"I don't want to evict a pregnant woman."

They talk about how best to invest the money. Kendra feels the integrity of the capital is more important than high interest, given the unspecified duration of McCoy's illness. "Like you said, if he wakes up, he'll need special care and we'll want the best there is available. Who knows how much that could cost?

And if he doesn't wake up, if he needs to go on life support . . ." She presses her lips together, as though unwilling to voice her thoughts.

Lesley reaches over to lay a hand over Kendra's. "You're worried about him, aren't you? You're worried he won't wake up."

"If you'd asked me that before we talked to Angel, I'd probably have denied it. But now that I know he was trying to protect me—and you—I think what he did was wrong, but he did it with good intentions. And I just know he'd hate living on life support like a vegetable."

"My dad used to say there's no point in fixing something that isn't broken yet. We can think about that if it happens."

Kendra nods. "Your dad was right. But maybe, while we're talking about it, we should consider what to do with the money if McCoy dies. I think we should put it in a trust for his child."

Lesley remembers this generosity as she drives home to relieve Cassandra of Beatrice-sitting duty. While the trust fund would be nice, what Lesley really likes is the way Kendra said "we" and respected her opinion and gave her an equal vote in McCoy's future. Being treated like an adult makes Lesley feel powerful in a way that is much more satisfying than the way McCoy made her feel. The circumstances that initiated her into adulthood are difficult, but she suspects that someday, in a future she can almost imagine now, she will be grateful for them.

Last Will and Testament

KENDRA AND PEONY SIT IN the living room of the apartment over the Lucky Dragon, going through the contents of the boxes containing McCoy's papers. As Peony reads out details from the documents, Kendra adds to the list of McCoy's possible assets and enters information into a bookkeeping program she's using to help her keep track of his income and expenses.

Peony places a document in the discards box at her feet. "Rental agreement for his apartment in Lahaina."

"Why did he keep all this stuff?" Kendra wonders. "Some of it is years old."

"Maybe he didn't like paperwork." Peony reaches for the last document in the current box. "What do you make of this?"

Kendra takes the paper, a warranty card for something called a Whizzy, made by Zolan Mobility, Ltd. She Googles the name. "You're never going to believe this. It's a walking support, like a fancy Zimmer frame on wheels." Clicking on the assets spreadsheet, she pages down the list of bizarre things McCoy may or may not still own and enters "Whizzy walker" in the next available space. What embarrasses her most about this list is how well McCoy understood her and how little she knew about him. "Ma? What do you think?" she asks her mother, then instantly regrets the question. Peony is not famous for sugarcoating.

Peony unfolds the top of the next box. "Ah, the contracts. About what?"

"About McCoy. About our marriage."

"I think he loved you. I think he fell in love with Lesley. We're all vulnerable to falling in love. You were. I was."

"You had an affair? Was it when Pops had his?"

Peony takes her glasses off to polish them on the hem of her blouse. Without them, her eyes seem naked. "No. I never had an affair. But I wanted to."

"With who?"

"Someone you never met." Peony places her glasses back on the bridge of her tiny nose, and her eyes regain their sharpness. "In a way, it was a good thing. *The foot feels the foot when it feels the ground.*" She reaches into the box and hands her daughter the top folder, then picks up another for herself.

"I never did understand that one. What does it mean?"

"When you touch something, you can only experience the sensation of touching it. You cannot experience the thing itself. It was easier for me to forgive your father, because I had similar feelings."

Kendra flips her folder open, but her eyes don't focus on the document it contains. She understands her mother is telling her the key to forgiving McCoy can be found in her own affair. But who would she be forgiving? She never knew McCoy, just her illusion of him, and that would be like forgiving herself. The idea confuses her. She pushes it aside and returns to the task at hand.

"Kendra?"

"What?" Kendra looks up from the contract she is reading.

Peony holds out an envelope. Scrawled across the front in McCoy's handwriting are the words *For Kendra, in the event of my death.*

Reluctantly, Kendra reaches out and takes the envelope. She turns it over in her hands. "He's not dead."

"This is important. He meant for you to find this."

"But I didn't know anything about Grove Street. How would I have found it?"

"I don't know, but he wanted to tell you something."

Kendra puts her laptop on the floor and gets up from the battered Naugahyde La-Z-Boy to sit beside her mother on the equally battered futon that serves as the McAllisters' couch. She slides her thumbnail under the flap of the envelope and extracts a legal document and a handwritten letter on thick, creamy sketchbook paper. Ignoring the legal document, she leans against her mother for support while they read the letter together.

Dearest Kendra,

I hope you never read this. If you are, it means I never found the courage to tell you the truth while I was alive.

By now you probably know I never worked for the government. I drew comic books for a living. When we first met, I created a character, Cheetara, for one of my stories. I gave her your lovely face. At the time, you were married. I thought our affair was your way of testing yourself and your feelings for your husband. That's not an excuse for what I did. I just want you to know I thought we weren't going to last.

When I realized how much I loved you, I tried to take back the issues with Cheetara but it was too late. I always meant to tell you but I was afraid you'd leave me if you found out what I'd done and how much I lied. I waited for the right time, for the right words, but I guess they never came.

If there were any way I could have spared you this pain and still arranged for you to collect your inheritance, I would have taken it. But there wasn't, so I am enclosing this letter with my will.

I am so sorry. I hope you can forgive me, but if you can't, I understand.

Good-bye, my love,
Eric

The letter tells Kendra nothing she doesn't know already. She unfolds the will and sees it was drawn up just over a year ago, when he was dating Lesley. It is short and generic, leaving everything to "my lovely wife, Kendra" with no details of what "everything" might include. She returns to the letter and studies the way he signed his name at the bottom. *Good-bye, my love.* The irony is, if he'd really died, if she'd never found out about Lesley, Kendra would have treasured this letter.

She turns her attention back to the problem of the will. Its terms leave Lesley and her baby with nothing. McCoy was an orphan. If he had known about Lesley's pregnancy, wouldn't he have wanted his child to inherit his estate? And the will was in the same envelope as the letter. Perhaps he never intended it to be executed. Perhaps it was written to make the letter more believable. But why did he write the letter in the first place? Was it just another lie, like hiding his profession, to protect her feelings?

Confusion overwhelms Kendra. She's tired of trying to understand McCoy, exhausted by the effort of searching for explanations she's never going to find. Picking up the will and the letter, she limps to the kitchen, where she takes a metal mixing bowl out of the cupboard, rips the papers in half and drops them in the bowl.

"What are you doing?" Peony asks from the doorway.

Kendra places the bowl in the sink and reaches for the safety matches used to light the old gas stove. "I'm burning the will."

"You can't do that. It's a legal document. Those are Eric's last wishes."

"Written before he knew he had a child. And even if these are still his last wishes, he doesn't get what he wants anymore." Kendra strikes a match and drops it into the bowl. "Lesley and I decide now."

The paper burns quickly. At first Kendra thinks it's the smoke making her eyes sting. She waits until the flames die down, until no legible scrap of the will or letter remains. But the tears don't stop. They splash down on the ashes in the bowl, extinguishing the last spark of illusion. "It's over," she whispers, and finds peace in the acceptance of what is and cannot be changed.

Perfect Little World

JUDE'S RETURN TO TRAVIS LEAVES Jason and Fletcher living in a house with a sparkly clean interior, but a sadly shabby yard. Determined not to backslide, Jason picks up a few bags of cedar chips to fill the bald spots in the inaccurately named maintenance-free landscaping and coerces Fletcher into helping with the yard work by offering to bankroll pizza at the next band practice. As they work, Jason asks his son how it's going with Inez, hoping to gain some insight into the boy's plans for his newly acquired condoms.

"Pretty good. I think she's almost finished making me pay for all the times I was mean to her when we were kids." Fletcher deposits a shovelful of chips under the Japanese maple and destroys his father's delusions of subtlety by continuing. "That's not why I got the condoms."

Jason responds with an encouraging grunt as he rakes dead foliage out from under the azaleas flanking the front walk.

"They're for the groupies," Fletcher continues. "As soon as

the band gets gigs, we're going to have groupies. And drummers always get the most. I need to be prepared."

Jason finds this confidence both touching and overly optimistic. He's heard the band practice. In his opinion, the condoms won't see daylight anytime soon. "Well, that explains why I never had any groupies. I played bass."

"You were in a band?"

"For a while, long ago."

"What did you call yourself?"

"Flaming Moronics."

"That's a dumb name."

"Probably one of the reasons we never got famous." Jason reverses the rake and wiggles the head. "Can you get me a flathead screwdriver from the garage?"

When Fletcher returns, he asks, "How come you never said anything about your band?"

"Thanks." Jason takes the tool and starts tightening the screw holding the rake head to the handle. "Your mother and I had our first big fight about it when you were six months old. She thought I spent too much time with the guys." He slides the screwdriver into a back pocket and tests the rake head. "Back then I was still in uniform, working double shifts, studying for the detective's exam. I didn't have time to be in a band and be a father as well. So I quit. I never mentioned the band because I thought your mother felt guilty about complaining, and I didn't want her to think it was a big deal for me."

Fletcher hefts another shovelful of cedar chips from the wheelbarrow and flings them under the maple. "Yeah. Let's not mess up her perfect little world."

"It wasn't about her perfect little world, Fletch. It was about your perfect little world. She never complained about the band until it took me away from you." Satisfied he's planted a seed, Jason points out a bald patch of ground by the foundation of the house.

Across the street, a screen door slaps shut. Jason watches Inez cross the road and has the unusual sensation of wanting to see a beautiful girl in a longer skirt. A quick glance at his son confirms Fletcher does not share this wish.

"Hi, Mr. Cheddick," Inez calls out as she walks up the driveway. "Hey, Fletch. Look what I just got!" She holds out a thin red plastic case.

Fletcher wipes his hands down the sides of his jeans before reaching out for the case. He flips it open and exclaims, "No way! This isn't out till next month. Is it from your cousin?"

"Yeah. Want to come over and check it out?" Inez may be dressed maturely, but her grin is the same one Jason remembers seeing under a tilted pink plastic helmet on her tenth birthday as she wobbled along the sidewalk on new Rollerblades.

"What is it?" Jason asks.

Her response does nothing to improve his understanding. "It's the new Diamond Warp."

Fletcher comes to his father's rescue. "It's a video game. Her cousin reviews them, so he gets advance copies. Are we almost done, Dad?"

Jason looks across the street and sees Mrs. Lopez nodding at him from her living room window, so he volunteers to finish the yard work himself. Fletcher disappears into the house to get cleaned up. Inez remains standing at the edge of the driveway.

"Mr. Cheddick? Is it okay if I let Fletch drive when I take him to school?"

"Has he asked you to?"

"No, but he really needs more practice. I just thought since he's in the car anyway, why can't he drive it? I'm a very good driver. He'd be safe with me."

"Why do you think Fletch needs more practice? He's a fine driver, just a bit too defensive."

"A bit? He's like having a talking driver's manual in the car. And he doesn't trust other drivers. He thinks they're going to swerve in front of us or try to run a red light. He really needs to get used to traffic."

Before the condom incident, the word "trust" would not have caught Jason's attention. Now it bounces around in his head like a mountain echo, obliterating Inez's next words. "What was that, Inez?"

"I said, is it okay?"

"You know, it'll be good for Fletch to get lessons from someone else. I think you'll be a good teacher."

"Thanks. It's what I want to be when I grow up, you know. A teacher. Mom says they don't make much money, but I don't think that's as important as liking my job."

Half in love with this child-woman himself, Jason reflects Fletcher could do much worse than convince Inez to be his girlfriend. "Can you teach him about smaller shirts while you're at it?"

Inez smiles with Mona Lisa confidence. "No problem."

After the shortest shower in history, Fletcher reappears in clean clothes. Jason allows himself a minute to appreciate Inez's outfit from behind as the kids cross the street, then gets back to work.

While he shovels cedar chips, he thinks about what he didn't tell Fletcher: how much it cost him to leave the guys in the band. They were his last bachelor friendships. Without them, he found himself locked into a milky, baby-oriented monoculture of other young families, pretending he was happy for his increasingly dissatisfied wife. Things got better when Fletcher went to school and Kathy found a job. More money let them buy this house and led to a brief resurgence of happiness while she decorated it. But Jason never stopped missing the band and the fun of hanging out with the guys. It became a symbol for everything else he gave up to be a husband and father. Eventually, his attempts to hide resentment evolved into avoidance. Ultimately, they became the wedge that split his marriage apart.

When Jason and Kathy first went to marriage counseling, the therapist talked a lot about emotional availability. At the time, Jason thought these comments were directed at Kathy, who sat through every session with her arms and legs crossed, glaring at Jason as though the demise of their marriage was entirely his fault. In hindsight, the least useful form of vision, Jason now knows the therapist was also talking to him, but he doesn't see how he could have achieved emotional honesty with Kathy.

Jude was right when she said he had a white knight complex. It was Kathy's aura of pliant helplessness that originally attracted Jason, although in practice he soon realized he was the only adult in their relationship. Perhaps, if he'd married a woman like Kendra, one who faced problems head-on, who never shirked responsibility . . .

His thoughts are interrupted by the ringing of his cell phone. He answers it and flashes on the painting in Angel's office when he hears Kendra's low-pitched, perfect diction on the other end of the line. If Cheetara had a voice, this is exactly what she would sound like.

"Hi, Jason. It's Kendra. I was wondering if I could ask you for some advice?"

"What about?"

"It would be easier to explain if I could show you something. Are you busy?"

"Just doing some yard work."

"Is it okay if I come over now?"

"No problem."

"Great. See you soon."

She hangs up without asking for his address. He thinks about calling her back, then remembers his address was printed on the invoice he sent her. He rubs his jaw, wondering if he has time to shower and shave before she arrives, then realizes he's imagining something Kendra can't possibly be ready for. "You're as bad as Fletcher," he mutters as he goes back to shoveling cedar chips.

Loose Ends

KENDRA IS DELIGHTED TO BE driving again. She sees her recovered mobility as an escape from the nightmare of the past four weeks, the real beginning of her new life.

The mess McCoy left her with still has to be cleaned up, but that won't be as difficult now that she has accepted her marriage is over. The layers of confusion that complicated the task of being McCoy's legal guardian are gone. All that's left is the responsibility. At the moment, that's mostly paperwork, which she is very good at.

One loose end remains to be tidied up. She could ask Agent Hauver at the FBI about it, but he wasn't very helpful during the investigation. Jason has a way of looking at all sides of all the facts before forming an opinion, and he doesn't let his own prejudices, if he has any, cloud his judgment. She also feels the need to say good-bye to him in person. That last phone call was an entirely unsatisfactory ending to their relationship, even if it was just a business one.

"Turn left on Potter's Trail in one hundred yards. Turn left in one hundred yards," her GPS navigation system instructs. She eases into the turn lane, braking with her left foot to spare her weak ankle. After turning, she drives less than a block before the GPS announces arrival at her destination.

Jason's house, a two-story Old Portland–style home with a double garage and neatly landscaped lot, is more ostentatious than she expected. It doesn't really match his off-the-rack suits and self-effacing humor. She checks her makeup in the visor mirror before retrieving her laptop from the passenger seat and stepping out of the van. The front door opens as she approaches it.

"I could have come to the restaurant." Jason stands aside to let her enter the house. "You didn't have to drive over here."

"I needed to get out. This is the first time I've been able to drive for weeks. Thanks for seeing me on such short notice."

"My other plan for tonight was cleaning out the fridge. It wasn't really a contest. Can I get you something to drink?"

"Coffee?"

"You take it black, right?"

"I'm surprised you remember. You're very observant, aren't you?"

"About some things. Not so much about others." The corners of his mouth flex when he says this, as though he's sharing a private joke with himself.

Kendra follows him through the living room to the kitchen, noting how out of place he seems in his faded sweatshirt, with a screwdriver in the back pocket of his jeans. The house is extremely clean and tidy, the decor slightly formal, like a reproduction of an English country manor.

"Your home is lovely. Did you do the decorating?"

"If I had, it wouldn't be so impressive. My wife hired an interior decorator just after we bought it. It's comfortable—that's what I like about it."

The phone rings as they enter the kitchen. Jason waves Kendra to the table as he picks it up.

"Hello . . . I'm busy right now. But thank Mrs. Lopez for me. Tell her maybe some other time. What about homework? . . . All right, but be home by ten. . . . Okay, bye." After hanging up, he tells Kendra, "You're lucky. Normally, Fletcher would be practicing his drums in the garage around this time, but he's having dinner at a friend's house tonight."

"Your son's a drummer?"

"He might be, eventually. Right now he's got more determination than talent. He's trying to put together a band. What did you want to talk about?"

"Something I found in one of McCoy's bank accounts." While the coffee is brewing, Kendra opens the computer to show Jason the statement she downloaded from the bank's Web site. "This is his business account. Most of the withdrawals are transfers to the joint accounts he had with me. But this one"—she points to a thousand-dollar entry—"is to an account that isn't his. It's deducted on the fifteenth of every month."

Jason leans over her shoulder to get a better look at the screen. His sweatshirt smells faintly of cedar. She has an impulse to turn her head and sniff the fabric, which she counters by shifting the position of her finger on the screen. "See the bank transit code? I looked it up. It's a credit union in California. According to the list of previous addresses in your report, he never lived in California. I called them and explained about the coma, but they wouldn't tell me who the account belongs to."

"You don't have any idea who it could be? Do you even know if it belongs to an individual? It could be a business."

"That's why I'm here. I want your input on how to find out."

The coffeemaker gurgles and hisses, signaling the end of the brew cycle. Jason pours coffee into two porcelain mugs decorated with cornflowers that are the same saturated shade of blue as his eyes. "You could stop the payments. See what happens."

"I don't want to do that."

"Why not? You think he's being blackmailed? The FBI must have checked those payments out. Although if I were a blackmailer, I probably wouldn't volunteer that information to a federal agent."

"I never thought of that." Kendra sips her coffee while she considers the possibility. Being married to a bigamist is one thing. Being married to a serial killer or a child molester is quite another, and not something she wants to find out by seeing McCoy's picture on the evening news. She explains this to Jason, then adds, "Remember why I hired you? To find out where he was when he wasn't with me or Lesley? If this money is going to another woman, I don't want to cut it off and leave her wondering what happened to him."

"I see your point. Give me a minute to think about this." Jason closes his eyes. He stays this way for so long Kendra stops envying his eyelashes and begins to wonder if he's fallen asleep. "Jason?"

"Sorry. I was working out how to do it. But before I tell you, I need to know what you're going to do when you find out who's getting the money."

"If it's another wife, or even a girlfriend, I'm going to tell her. I know you said he wasn't married in the States, but if he was married in another country, she could be his first wife, his real legal guardian. Or maybe he's paying child support. Even if I am his legal guardian, I can't sign away his children's inheritance."

"And if it's not a wife or a girlfriend?" Jason leans forward until his eyes are level with hers. "If it's blackmail, will you promise to take it to the police?"

Many years ago, on holiday in Egypt, Kendra watched a cobra sway up from the mouth of a clay pot, hypnotized by the weaving end of a snake charmer's flute. She feels like that snake now, unable to break eye contact. Uncertain if she's promising or just bobbing like a hypnotized snake, she nods.

"Okay, then," Jason says. "The easiest way to find out who owns the account is to write them a letter asking them to contact you and get the bank to forward it for you. Until you find out who you're dealing with, I think it's best if you hire a lawyer to make the first approach."

"Of course. I should have thought of that myself. And the lawyer's a good idea. I really appreciate your help with this."

"No problem. I admire the way you're doing the right thing. A lot of people would be tempted to overlook the possibility of another wife."

"It's not nobility. It's pity. I remember how I felt about him, or at least who I thought he was. I'd have been frantic if he just disappeared, if I never knew what happened to him."

Jason picks up the empty mugs and carries them over to the countertop. "Still sounds noble to me."

Kendra takes this as the signal for her to leave. She closes the laptop. "Well, guess I should be going. Thank you again."

"How about another coffee before you go? I don't have to cook tonight, since Fletcher isn't coming home for dinner, and I'd like to hear how your meeting with Angel went."

His invitation ignites a tiny flicker of happiness, like a distant candle. She doesn't know if it's residue from the snake moment, or that Jason's interest, if her father is correct, is reciprocated. Either way, she'd have to be an idiot to get involved with someone else so soon.

Something of her confusion must show on her face, because Jason quickly qualifies his invitation. "I'm not hitting on you." Then he qualifies it again. "I mean, under the circumstances . . ." His eyes widen into a deer-in-the-headlights look. "Not that you're not very attractive . . ." He gives up, looks at the floor and runs a hand through his hair. "I really screwed that up, didn't I?"

Kendra laughs. "Actually, I thought it was pretty good. You're right about the circumstances, but I think another coffee would be okay."

The Baby Whisperer

BABIES JUST LOVE BEATRICE. THEY are fascinated by her flaming hair and Delft blue eyes, enthralled by the flutelike quality of her lilting baby talk and delighted with her uncanny ability to deduce from the first hesitant whimper of infantile dissatisfaction the exact nature of the complaint that prompts it.

And Beatrice just loves babies. This is her third day of accompanying Lesley to work, and what began as avoidance has become a delight. She is impatient to leave for Wee Tots in the morning and refuses to return home at night until her last freshly diapered charge has been picked up.

While Beatrice tends to her highly satisfied clientele in the crèche room, Lesley has time to study the copy of *Bookkeeping for Dummies* that she bought on Cassandra's recommendation. Math was her worst subject in school and she expected to dislike bookkeeping. But it's not really about adding and subtracting. It's about organizing money in a way that makes it easier to keep track of income and expenses. As she studies the examples and does the exercises at the end of each chapter, she feels increasingly confident about her ability to run a business and thinks she might even enjoy being a businesswoman like her aunt and Kendra.

From the rocking chair where she is cuddling six-month-old James Foster Barkley, Beatrice says softly, "Lesley, honey, I've been thinking."

Lesley looks up from the trial balance example she is studying. "About what, Mom?"

"I want to give you the money I won at the casino to help you buy the day-care center."

"I thought you were going to take a cruise."

"There's no one to go with. Cass doesn't like that kind of thing, and you have to work."

"What about Eunice? She'd love cruising."

"Eunice isn't the friend I thought she was."

Concerned by her mother's rejection of a lifelong friendship, Lesley asks, "What happened?"

Beatrice's lower lip pushes out into a pout. "Apparently, she's invited Andrew to the church fund-raising breakfast next week."

Lesley suppresses an urge to laugh and tactfully returns to the original topic of conversation. "Well, I'd love to borrow the money from you, Mom, but I couldn't pay you back for at least two years."

"I don't want the money back. I want to be a partner. I could work here with the babies. I like being here. I feel useful here."

Debbie, one of Lesley's coworkers, peers around the crèche room door. "You have a visitor, Lesley."

Lesley tells her mother they'll talk more later and enters the playroom, where she finds Kendra standing just inside the main entrance of Wee Tots, staring in horrified fascination at a table surrounded by liberally spattered toddlers enthusiastically creating finger-paint masterpieces. Interpreting Kendra's expression as fear for her pristine cream wool slacks, Lesley suggests they go to the Silver Mug coffee bar across the street to talk.

"Did you drive all the way up here?" Lesley asks as she leads Kendra to the Silver Mug. "Is your ankle healed?"

"Had my last physio session yesterday. The therapist says I'm good as new. It's such a relief to be mobile again."

The Silver Mug is a coffee-and-dessert emporium owned and run by Lesley's second cousin Frank and his wife, Jenny, both of whom amply demonstrate the superior quality of their wares. Lesley introduces Kendra as a friend from Portland. They order lattes and take their drinks to an arrangement of upholstered chairs situated far enough from the service counter to ensure their conversation cannot be overheard.

All the furnishings in the Silver Mug are donations from Wilcox family attics and basements. Lesley sits in a brown corduroy tub chair she recognizes from her uncle Ted's family room when she was a child. Kendra opts for a faded avocado tweed armchair that stood beside a matching sofa in Frank's parents' living room forty years ago. They put their mugs down on the stained surface of a slatted knotty pine coffee table brought back from Seattle by Cassandra.

Kendra looks around the room with amusement. "This is rural."

Resisting an urge to defend her cousins' decor, which she finds comfortable and nostalgic, Lesley asks Kendra why she came.

"Because I didn't want you to hear this over the phone."

The ominous nature of this opening disturbs Lesley. She tenses and wraps her arms around her stomach, preparing for bad news.

Kendra continues. "You remember I said we should go through McCoy's assets before making any decisions?"

Lesley relaxes, relieved that Kendra's news is not about McCoy's death. "Sure." She picks up her mug and licks cinnamon-dusted foam off the top.

"Well, I found something interesting in his bank statements." Kendra goes on to explain about McCoy's business account and the regular monthly payments to an unknown account. "So I had a lawyer write the letter, like Jason suggested." She reaches into the pocket of her blazer and pulls out a folded paper, which she hands to Lesley. "This is the woman who owns that account."

Lesley unfolds the paper and reads: *Ayla Champlain, 1372 Pinecove Crescent, Eureka, CA.* "He sends her a thousand dollars every month?"

"For at least four years. That's how far back I can get statements for. Does it remind you of anything?"

Some of the children Lesley cares for at Wee Tots come from broken homes. She talks to their mothers all the time and recognizes one possibility instantly. "Alimony?"

"If he married her. If he bothered with a divorce. It could just be child support."

"No!" The volume of Lesley's denial causes Frank to look up from behind the service counter with raised eyebrows. She flaps her fingers to show him nothing is wrong before leaning forward to continue in lowered tones. "Not possible. If he had children, he'd never live so far away from them."

"He lied to you about me; why not about children?"

"Maybe he lied about everything else, but he wasn't lying about wanting children. He really loves children. He used to come to pick me up at work two hours ahead of time so he could play with the day-care kids. He never stopped talking about how wonderful it would be when we had our own children. The only room in the cabin that's completely decorated is the nursery."

In the face of this vehement, detailed denial and her own inability to measure the level of McCoy's lying, Kendra is willing to concede the point. "Okay. You could be right. But he's still supporting a woman in California, and we still don't know for sure where he was when he wasn't with us."

"We have to go see her. I'm sure he isn't sending the money for child support. But I'm pregnant, and he doesn't know about it. She could be too."

"I've already decided to go see her, but you don't have to come. It's a whole day's drive and another day back."

"I want to go with you. I want to hear what he was like for her."

"What about your job?"

"I'll ask my mom to fill in for me. She's been doing my job for three days now anyway."

They return to Wee Tots. Kendra skirts the edge of the toddler-strewn playroom as she follows Lesley into the crèche room, where Beatrice, having finally managed to soothe all her charges to sleep, is reading a magazine. She touches her finger to her lips and whispers to Kendra, "Hello, dear. Nice to see you again."

While Lesley explains to her mother about the woman in California, Kendra moves around the room, studying the babies in the cribs. She stops and leans over to get a better look at little Sarah Olivera, reaching out as though to touch the child's minuscule fingers, then quickly drawing back her hand when the infant opens eyes as dark and glistening as blueberries in the rain. "How old is this one?" Kendra asks. "It seems so frail and tiny."

Lesley replies, "Sarah's three months old. She's small for her age because she was born prematurely."

Sarah begins to grizzle. Beatrice crosses to the crib. Tucking the baby into the crook of one plump arm, she says, "But she's a real fighter. Aren't you, sweetheart?" She looks at Kendra. "Would you like to hold her?"

Kendra takes a step back. Her reluctance amuses Lesley. "They don't bite."

"Well, they do," Beatrice says, "but they don't have teeth yet, so really they just gum. Have you never held a baby?"

Kendra, eyes fixed on the infant's face, shakes her head.

"Well, it's high time you did. Sit in the rocker," Beatrice insists.

For an instant, Kendra seems to be on the verge of running from the room. Then, walking stiffly, like a sleepwalker, she crosses to the rocking chair. Beatrice leans down to gently place the baby in her arms. Little Sarah immediately begins to cry.

Kendra stiffens. "She doesn't like me. Take her back."

Beatrice refuses. "You're tense. Babies can tell. Just relax. She will too."

Leaning back in the rocker, Kendra makes an effort to relax.

Gradually, Sarah calms down. Her cries become whimpers, then dissipate entirely. She waves a vague hand at Kendra's face. Her tiny mouth stretches open in an expression that could be a smile, but is just as likely to be gas.

Kendra places a hesitant finger in the baby's hand and smiles back. "She's quite beautiful, isn't she?"

Sarah's little body convulses. A dribble of regurgitated milk slides from the side of her mouth, landing in a slimy blob on the front of Kendra's burgundy silk shirt.

Holly Virgin

Eric at forty

ERIC LAY IN BED, DRINKING coffee, and pretending to surf the Internet while watching Kendra dress for work. The outfit for today's event, a wedding, took longer than usual.

Kendra approached her toilette the way NASA launched rockets, in carefully planned stages, selecting a dress or suit appropriate to the event, matching it to the perfect shoes and proper undergarments, choosing cosmetics in complementary shades and lining them up in the order they would be applied. The last and most important detail—the "flair," as she called it—often took longer to decide on than the outfit it embellished. Today, after trying on and discarding a dozen items from her extensive "flair" collection, she finally settled on diamond stud earrings and a peacock blue Liberty of London scarf tied asymmetrically.

She twisted in front of the mirror one last time, checking the effect from all angles. "I should have worn the rose chiffon. This is too drab. I look like a potato sack." She made a face at herself.

"An amazingly sexy potato sack," Eric assured her. To forestall the complete makeover required to switch to the rose dress, he asked, "What time do you have to be at the church?"

She glanced at the bedside clock. "Oh, God! I have to run. How long will you be gone?"

"A week at most. I'll call you when I know for sure."

She leaned over the bed and air-kissed his cheek to avoid smudging her lipstick. "Great. You'll be here for Pops's birthday. I hate having to go alone."

"Wouldn't miss it," he said, and meant it. He liked Kendra's family almost as much as he liked her, and the father-daughter fireworks were guaranteed to be amusing.

"Travel safe." She was gone in a whisper of café-au-lait silk and a swirl of perfume.

He heard her on her cell phone, telling the florist she'd be there in twenty minutes as her heels clicked on the hardwood floor. The apartment door closed, cutting her voice off in midsentence. Thirty minutes later, Eric was on his way to the cabin, looking forward to five days of work and solitude.

The cabin had proved an excellent investment. He liked the isolated location, which reminded him of Stella's ranch in Idaho. When he wasn't working, he spent his time fixing up the place, enjoying the physical labor and the sense of accomplishment he got from completing tasks. He'd bought a horse to indulge his love of riding and stabled it at a nearby farm. As an experiment, he'd planted a garden one year and discovered his green thumb, an appendage he'd never known he owned.

These pleasures were all the more enjoyable because they were his and his alone. Every minute he spent at the cabin was a minute spent on himself, without considering anyone else's wants, needs or tastes. He still enjoyed pleasing people. Now he knew the joy of pleasing himself.

As he drove, he mulled over the problem of the Exiled Emperor's heir, or, more precisely, the heir's mother. When he'd developed the plotline, he'd intended to pull the heir's mother from the emperor's harem, one of the many wives taken to cement alliances with powerful families. But none of the beauties he'd created to populate the harem had been chosen for their maternal qualities, and a child born to one of them would create a shift in the balance of power in Kav'erse, which would complicate future episodes. Eric decided to create a new character, one with strong maternal instincts and no political ties.

When he arrived in Brockville, he stopped in at the Silver Mug coffee bar. From the plump woman behind the counter, he ordered an Americano and a cinnamon bun and carried them to a comfortable-looking armchair tucked into a nook by the front window.

The town of Brockville was originally settled by Swedish immigrants in the late nineteenth century. Their genetic legacy showed in the predominantly blond heads of the children running around the yard of the Wee Tots day-care center across the street. One boy in particular—a sturdy, energetic toddler with an angelic, imperious face—seemed like a perfect model for the emperor's son.

A woman came out of the day-care building. She could have been the boy's mother with hair so pale it was almost white and the same rounded jaw and wide, full mouth. A narrow waist between lavish curves of breasts and hips made her body voluptuous, but her face was ethereally innocent, as though it had never been touched by pain or disappointment. She had incredibly long legs. Eric realized he was looking at the next Mrs. Exiled Emperor.

She crossed the street and entered the Silver Mug. "Hey, Jenny," she called out. Eric had a brief flashback image of his mother's face and remembered she had also spoken in that breathy, Marilyn Monroe voice.

"Hey, Lesley. You're late today," the barista replied.

"Yeah. We got another call from Sherri Jensen. I mean, I understand why parents want apple slices and carrot sticks, but I don't see how adding a chocolate chip cookie is harmful."

While Eric listened to the two women discuss juvenile nutrition, his mind was busy creating the Holly Virgin: a woman mature in body, but with an innocent trust that made her capable of deep and unconditional love. Over the following month, she hijacked the next *Kav'erse* story entirely. He developed her background as a novice nun at the Temple of Orphans, dedicated to salvaging abandoned children. She became the archetype of motherhood, a nurturing fountain of uncritical affection, as fiercely protective of her charges as a lioness with cubs. She lured the emperor into love with the naive sensuality of a virgin. Eric thought she was the best character he'd ever created.

A few months later, he was out riding Patches late one afternoon when he heard a woman calling for help in an abandoned orchard. Her voice was unmistakable, and he was not surprised to find the model for the Holly Virgin standing beside a palomino horse. She was lost, injured and wisely distrustful of meeting a strange man in what she seemed to think was the middle of nowhere, although the orchard was less than a mile from the main highway. He offered her a lift and watched her expression change from skepticism to resignation as she considered her options. She accepted his offer, introducing herself as Lesley Sorrenson. In Washington, to avoid any accidental connection to his much more social life in Oregon, Eric introduced himself as Dave, and this was the name he gave to Lesley.

To put her at ease, he encouraged her to talk about herself as he led her horse down the hill. But she didn't talk about herself. She talked about the children she cared for at work: shy Tabitha, whose mother had to be talked out of enrolling the girl in a toddler beauty pageant; thoughtful Arnie, whom she suspected might need glasses; tomboy Petra, who feared nothing and needed to learn caution. She clearly loved her charges, but more than that, she understood them. She knew what they needed and how to give it to them. He was surprised by how much she resembled the character her appearance had inspired.

Eric knew the exact moment he fell in love. They'd just arrived at the stable. She told him she wanted a really big family. He asked her how big as he reached up to help her off her horse and knew he was lost when she replied, "Really big. Six kids, maybe more," as she placed her hands on his shoulders and slid off the animal with total trust in his ability to support her. The spectacular body sliding by, just inches from his face, didn't detract from the moment either.

The almost forgotten longing he'd felt as a child while waiting to meet a new foster family surged through Eric. With every fiber of his being yearning to close the gap between their bodies, he forced himself to step away from her and shoved his shaking hands into his pockets. Taking a deep breath to be sure his voice was under control before replying, he said, "And they'll all be very lucky to have you as their mother."

Her eyes sparkled with pleasure at the compliment. "Oh, I hope so. Now all I have to do is find the right father." She rubbed the small of her back and looked down at her ruined sweater. "It's not going to be Jimmy Brock, that's for sure. I don't care how rich he is."

When he drove Lesley home, her mother invited him to stay for dinner. He knew perfectly well he should have made some excuse and gone back to Portland, but the words refused to pass his lips and he found himself sitting across from Lesley at the kitchen table, listening to her describe the disastrous date, while her mother pressed him to take "just one more slice" of pot roast, and her aunt advised him to leave room for dessert because Beatrice had baked an apple pie that afternoon. Later that night, lying in the guest room, intensely aware his bed was separated from Lesley's by nothing but a thin wall, he tried to analyze what made this woman so different from all the others he had known.

Eric had a long history of wanting to please women, starting with his foster mothers. But this feeling was not just about wanting to please Lesley. It was about what she could give him in return: a true family, the bond of belonging he'd yearned for and never found as a child in the foster care system. In Portland, Eric's world revolved around Kendra's tastes and ambitions: a half-life of gallery openings and charity dinners, events chosen to find or impress potential clients. In Brockville, he'd learned to live his own life, filled only with things he wanted. Lesley and her longing for motherhood could give him the best of both his worlds, and the true family he'd given up hoping for. He desperately wanted to be the father of her six—or maybe more—children.

Eric returned to Portland and tried hard to fit back into the life he no longer wanted. He forced himself to stay away from the cabin on Saddleback Ridge and pretended to enjoy himself as he escorted Kendra through her frantic social life, hoping time would turn pretense into reality. If anything, it had the opposite effect.

On Kendra's birthday, he took her to dinner at Le Poisson Rouge, an expensive French seafood restaurant Kendra liked primarily for the clientele, although the food was certainly excellent. As they walked to the restaurant, Kendra tucked her hand around Eric's bicep and talked about her new clients.

"They're fabulously wealthy, but you'd never know it from their apartment. I mean, it's nice, but not even as nice as our place." She pulled him toward a store window displaying housewares. "What do you think of that china pattern? Simple, but so elegant."

Eric looked at the dishes and thought about the busy blue-and-white-patterned plates he'd eaten pot roast from two weeks before. "I think you're right," he said out of habit.

"So, anyway," Kendra said, continuing the story of meeting her clients, "the daughter doesn't want a big wedding, just family and a few friends. Her fiancé has two children from his first marriage, and she wants them in the bridal party, but she had to take out a restraining order on the first wife, so that's going to be awkward."

"A restraining order?" Eric asked.

"I don't know the whole story, but apparently his first wife went a bit crazy when he told her he wanted a divorce and started harassing my client where she works. Mind you, I can't really blame her. Imagine how humiliated she must have felt, being ditched for a woman half her age. Oh, look!" Kendra disengaged her hand from his elbow and pointed to a bookstore window. "That's the book everyone was talking about at the party last night. I've got to get it."

After the book, and the little dress Kendra just had to try on because "it would be perfect for the gallery opening on Friday," they arrived at the restaurant half an hour late and discovered they'd lost their reservation. They sat at the bar to wait for a table. Kendra took a call from a panicked client—something about the napkins being the wrong shade of lilac—while Eric thought about the man who'd left his wife and children for love and suddenly realized how foolish it was to even attempt to stay in the wrong life with the wrong woman any longer. He had this one chance to be truly happy. He had to take it.

Eric never even considered asking Kendra for a divorce, not after hearing that restraining order story. Her anger and jealousy would destroy any chance he had with Lesley, who was too idealistic to steal another woman's husband. There was really only one thing he could do to end his marriage without jeopardizing his future.

Eric stared at himself in the mirror over the bar and began planning to fake his own death.

The Wall

EUREKA IS A SMALL CITY in northern California, tucked between Humboldt Bay and what remains of the lush redwood forests that made its nineteenth-century citizens wealthy enough to build the Victorian mansions for which it is famous. Lesley, who has no interest in architecture, is driving so Kendra can take pictures of the more spectacular buildings they pass. The GPS system in the van is turned off, since they stopped listening to it after Kendra spotted her first Painted Lady mansion.

"It's almost six," Lesley says as she pulls to the curb in front of a turreted pink and white edifice that looks more like a gargantuan wedding cake than a house. "If we're going to talk to her tonight, we should go soon. You can take more pictures tomorrow on the way out."

"Sorry. I didn't realize how late it is. I love this city." Kendra takes two pictures before tucking her camera back into its case.

"It's pretty nice."

Kendra reaches out to turn the GPS back on. "But not as impressive as big trees, right?" she teases, referring to their trip through the Rogue River–Siskiyou National Forest, where Kendra drove while Lesley gawked at the tops of the giant redwoods towering above the road.

"I guess I like the trees better," Lesley agrees, as she obeys the navigation system's instructions to turn right.

Ayla Champlain does not live in a Victorian mansion. She lives in a plain, Mission-style bungalow, well inland from the more spectacular streets in the old part of the city. A shaggy, lop-eared dog rises to its feet on the doorstep as they get out of the van and starts to bark when they step on the front walk, preventing them from approaching the house.

"Quiet down, Chutney." A woman, as round as she is tall, appears behind the screen protecting the front door. Unbound masses of electrified salt-and-pepper curls hang to her shoulders, giving her the geometry of a triangle topping a balloon. It is difficult to tell the age of a face so plump and smooth, but she has to be in her mid-sixties at least. Kendra turns to Lesley, who shrugs. It seems unlikely this woman could be McCoy's wife or girlfriend.

"Can I help you?" the woman asks through the mesh of the screen.

"We're looking for Ayla Champlain," Lesley says. "We might have written down the wrong address."

"No, you found her. What can I do for you?"

Kendra says, "My lawyer contacted you about Eric McCoy. Are you a friend or a relative?"

"Eric is my sister's foster son. The lawyer's letter said he's ill. Are you the executor?"

"I'm his wife. My name is Kendra. This is my friend Lesley."

Ayla's heavy eyebrows rise in surprise, or possibly shock. She recovers quickly and pushes open the screen door. "Well, I suppose you'd best come in and talk to my sister. Don't be afraid of Chutney. He likes to bark, but he's a coward."

As though to prove this statement true, Chutney slinks through the door and between his owner's legs, disappearing into the house like a shadow.

The interior of the bungalow is cool and dim. Ayla leads them into a sitting room furnished with faded and tarnished rococo elegance. She tugs at a tasseled cord to turn on a Tiffany-shaded standing lamp and gestures toward a gold plush settee. "Have a seat. I'll see if Habibeh is awake yet. Can I get you something to drink? I just made lemonade."

Lesley agrees to lemonade. Kendra asks for water. When Ayla returns with their drinks, she is followed by a woman pushing what must be the Whizzy walker Kendra found the warranty card for.

Habibeh is as thin as her sister is fat, dressed entirely in black, with sticklike arms and a gaunt, wizened face that bears a strong resemblance to the old woman on the cover of McCoy's comics. Her hair, more salt than pepper, is pulled into a taut bun at the back of her head. She studies Lesley and Kendra with dark, vivid eyes as she lowers herself with difficulty onto a brocade settee on the opposite side of the gateleg coffee table.

"I am Habibeh, Eric's foster mother. My sister says you are Eric's wife. What happened to him?"

Kendra edits the story she tells Habibeh, leaving out the bigamy. She stops talking when tears begin to slide down the withered skin of Habibeh's cheeks.

"He was such a good boy." Habibeh pulls a tissue from the box her sister holds out and dabs at her face. "So talented. He was the only one who stood by me when my husband became ill. This seems so unfair."

"And he still stands by you." Ayla places a comforting hand on her sister's shoulder.

"He pays for my medication," Habibeh explains. "Although I suppose now . . ."

Kendra looks a question at Lesley, who nods. "Don't worry about that," Kendra assures the sisters. "I'll make sure the payments continue."

Lesley takes an engraved pewter coaster off the stack in the center of the coffee table and sets her empty glass on it. "Can I ask you something?" When Habibeh nods, she continues. "What was he like when he stayed with you?"

"He loved to draw. He liked to help me around the house. He played chess with my husband and let him win. He made people happy, but distantly, like sunshine. He could warm you, but you couldn't warm him. He'd lived in so many other foster homes before he came to us. I remember his social worker telling us that if anyone could reach him, we could. But I don't think we did."

"But he stayed in touch," Kendra pointed out. "He must have felt something for you."

"Oh, yes. He calls every year on my birthday. But he never told me where he was unless I asked. He never told me he married. He always kept his secrets." Habibeh looks down at her hands. "He had a wall inside. I didn't want to push him. Maybe I was wrong."

"You did your best, Habby," Ayla consoles her sister.

Lesley leans forward, a gesture that adds sincerity to her words. "He was a very happy man. And he made everyone around him happy. If he had a wall, it didn't hurt him."

The statement surprises Kendra, although she can't imagine why, since she never thought of McCoy as an unhappy man.

Habibeh looks at Lesley with gratitude. "This is good to

know. I have something of his. Would you take it and give it to him when he wakes up?"

"Of course," Kendra agrees.

"It is in my room. Come with me, please."

Habibeh's bedroom is large, furnished in the same ornate style as the rest of the house. Kendra recognizes the two framed portraits hanging over the bed as McCoy's work. She moves closer to examine them.

The woman is recognizably a younger, slightly plumper Habibeh. Her mouth is serious, but her eyes are wide and bright, as though McCoy had captured her in the instant before she burst out laughing. The man is thin-faced and intense, with passionate eyes and a spectacular long-tailed mustache obscuring the corners of his mouth.

"My husband, Farouk," Habibeh says simply, then asks Lesley to open the closet. She points to a box on the shelf above the clothes rail. "That big box on the end. Would you take it down for me, please?" Lesley places the box on the bed. Habibeh opens it and shuffles through its contents. "When the social worker brought Eric to us, she gave us a copy of his file. My husband put it away. I found it last year, when I was cleaning up old papers. It has all the names and addresses of his foster parents. Ah, here it is." She hands Kendra a blue three-ring binder. "I meant to tell him about it the next time he called."

Kendra opens the binder and flips through the pages. Lesley comes to look over her shoulder. The book contains photocopies of forms and reports, interspersed with pictures of McCoy as he grew, all posed against clinical white backgrounds. Kendra is struck by the dryness of the documentation and the number of different people who produced it, who pushed the boy they documented through the system as though it were a factory assembly line. She pages through to the end of the book and is about to shut it, when Lesley reaches around her to slide a folded page out of a pocket on the inside back cover.

Lesley unfolds the paper to reveal a Picasso-style drawing of a brown-spotted yellow tube topped by enormous, lopsided eyes and surrounded by zigzag spikes of red, blue and orange. It is drawn in crayon on the kind of ruled paper Kendra used to take notes on in school, and has a raw power she never saw in any of the work McCoy did when she knew him, or in the drawings and paintings they found in the house on Grove Street.

"If he had a wall," Lesley says, "this looks like something from behind it."

Perfect Solution

Eric at forty-two

FAKING HIS OWN DEATH TURNED out to be more complicated than Eric expected. He explored many possibilities, but they all had the same flaw. There would be no body, no proof he was dead. At best, he'd be a missing person. In the end, he gave up on more elaborate plans and decided simply to disappear, become one of those people who goes to the store for milk and is never seen again. Kendra wasn't the kind of woman to jump to conclusions. She'd search for him, but when no body turned up, she might assume he was still alive, perhaps with amnesia. On the whole, Eric thought that might be easier for her to bear than his death.

Even the relatively simple solution of disappearing proved difficult to engineer. It wasn't just a matter of leaving his marriage; he had to leave everything behind, including his profession, since the most cursory missing-person investigation would link Eric McCoy to *Kav'erse*. He decided it would be best to give up art entirely—a great sacrifice, since it had always been a big part of his life, but one he felt was worth making.

To support his new life, he decided to expand his garden and grow organic vegetables. It would take time to bring in his first crops, so he started cashing his royalty checks and putting the money aside to see him through the first year. He needed identification for David McCoy, so he obtained a Washington driver's license by using his real documentation as a model to forge papers that were good enough to pass the cursory inspection they got from the harried clerk at the busy Department of Motor Vehicles in Tacoma. Then he transferred ownership of the cabin to David McCoy. As Eric McCoy, he sold his old truck in Portland, then took the bus to Seattle and bought a nearly identical replacement as David McCoy.

Everything connected to his professional life had to be organized and kept somewhere not connected to the cabin. He couldn't just put it all in storage. He needed to work until he was ready to disappear or Angel would become suspicious. After buying back the print run of the issue featuring the Holly Virgin, he couldn't afford to maintain another residence. He scanned newspapers and Internet advertisements for weeks, finally finding Rita Gardener's ad for a house sitter. When she offered him the position, he took it in spite of the problem of the parrot, which he solved by giving Cracker Jack to Kendra. It was the kind of present she loved, exotic and unique. He sent Rita Gardener an e-mail telling her the bird had some kind of flu and he was taking it to the vet. Two weeks later, he wrote to tell her the bird had died. She thanked him for his efforts to save her pet and hoped he'd stay on in the house until she got back. He felt guilty when he assured her he would.

He couldn't do anything to shield Kendra from the pain of

never knowing what happened to him, but he could do something to ease her sense of betrayal when she discovered how he had deceived her. He wrote her a letter, explaining he'd never worked for the government and why the deception was necessary. He put it in an envelope labeled *For Kendra, in the event of my death*, along with a will naming her his sole beneficiary, which he slid into the box containing his contracts. The will wasn't executable, since a person cannot be presumed dead unless there is evidence that makes death a reasonable possibility. He did it as a gesture. Money was important to Kendra; she might be comforted by the knowledge he wanted her to have his.

As soon as his professional life was safely transferred to Grove Street, Eric took Lesley out to see his place on Saddleback Ridge and find out if she liked it. Her clumsy seduction caught him off guard. Her virginity terrified him. Afraid she would mistake his intentions if he waited too long to declare them, he bought a ring the next day. He made the mistake of buying it at Thorssen's Fine Jewelry in Brockville and became the last person in town to know he was engaged when he asked Lesley to marry him three weeks later and she said yes.

Lesley wanted to get married right away, but Beatrice's heart was set on a summer wedding for her only daughter. Eric, who needed more time to save enough money to get him through his first year as a farmer, backed his future mother-in-law. Then, a month before the wedding, Angel found him a job that paid too well to pass up. Eric didn't want to postpone the wedding—Lesley hadn't wanted to wait six months in the first place and might interpret his reluctance as cold feet—so he went through with it. He'd been married to Lesley for two months when the final payment for his last job came through.

There remained only one problem without a solution: how to connect Kendra to the contents of the house on Grove Street in a way that wouldn't make his disappearance seem planned. Ideally, he wanted an intermediary, someone who didn't know either him or Kendra, someone who could innocently appear in her life with information that would lead her to the house. After two weeks of searching for this hypothetical person, he reluctantly gave up and decided Kendra would have to wait until Rita Gardener came home and found his possessions still in her house.

On the last Friday before he planned to disappear, Eric drove back to Portland from Seattle after a meeting with Angel. When he arrived, he parked behind the mall, where he kept both his vehicles to prevent his Grove Street neighbors from seeing them and possibly remembering the license plate numbers. He'd skipped dinner, so he decided to pick up a snack at the new coffee place. Transferring the comics he'd bought in Seattle to his backpack for reading material while he ate, he locked the car and climbed the stairs to Seventeenth Street.

The coffee shop was busy. While he paused on the sidewalk just outside the glass door, estimating his chances of getting a table, he noticed a man standing in line waiting to order. Unlike the other customers, who isolated themselves by looking at the pastry display case or the shelves of coffee accessories lining the back wall, this man studied the people around him. He seemed interested in bodies and hands as well as faces, as though searching for clues.

Eric wondered if he was a cop, then suddenly realized a cop would be exactly the right kind of person to contact Kendra. Eric could strike up a conversation, casually mention he lived on Grove Street, ask the cop to watch his backpack while he went to the washroom, then slip out the back door. The plan wasn't perfect, but it was better than nothing, and Eric didn't want to hurt Kendra more than he had to.

He ran back down the steps to the parking lot, tossing his Portland wallet, cell phone, and the keys to the Lexus into his backpack as he ran. When he got to the truck, he took his Washington wallet from the glove compartment and tucked it into his back pocket. As he raced back up to the street, he remembered his computer was still in the house on Grove, and on it were documents that would lead Kendra to David McCoy. He'd have to run over and remove his computer after he abandoned the backpack.

He entered the coffee shop just as the man dropped his newspaper onto a small pedestal table in the middle of the room. Eric took his place in line behind a thick-bodied woman with skin the texture and color of cocoa powder. He looked around and caught the man looking back at him, bright blue eyes sharp with curiosity. It made Eric nervous until he realized he could use that interest to his advantage. To calm himself, he studied the people around him as he waited, imagining how he would draw them.

When her turn came, the stocky woman stepped up to the counter, ordered a grande mochachino in a precise, lilting accent, then pointed to a plate of pastries in the display case. "Is that an apple Danish?"

"No, it's cheese," the barista told her.

"I am lactose intolerant. What about the carrot cake? Does it have walnuts?"

The barista studied the cake. "I think so."

"I am allergic to walnuts. What kinds of muffins are those?"

None of the five varieties of muffins proved acceptable, especially the banana muffins, which contained walnuts. The brownies also contained walnuts. All three varieties of cheesecake were ruled out on the basis of lactose intolerance. The cinnamon buns looked like a winner, until it was discovered raisins lurked beneath the frosting. Raisins had no medical side effects—the woman just didn't like them. With every rejection, the barista's pinned-on smile flattened a bit more. Finally, the choices narrowed down to marble pound cake or chocolate almond biscotti. The biscotti won.

As the woman took her cookie and moved along the counter to collect her drink, Eric took her place. Spreading his hands on the countertop and leaning slightly forward, he made solid eye contact with the barista as he smiled at her, hoping she would remember him. "I'm not allergic to anything," he said.

She laughed and took his order for a small Americano. While he waited to pick it up at the far end of the counter, he looked down the hallway leading to the washrooms and was grateful to see the fire door propped open, giving him a clear view of the alleyway beyond. Picking up his coffee, he walked over to the policeman's table and pulled out the unoccupied chair.

"So, what did you decide?" he asked.

Awakening

SEVENTY-THREE DAYS AFTER HIS HEAD landed on Jason's soggy newspaper in the Well Roasted Bean, the man who was once Eric and David McCoy wakes up.

Kendra receives Robyn's call while she is with a client in Callum's kitchen, testing hors d'oeuvres for the party that will launch a local designer's spring collection. She immediately turns the tasting over to Callum and drives across town to the hospital. But when she arrives, she is reluctant to go in.

While McCoy was unconscious, her responsibilities as his legal guardian included nothing more challenging than administering his legal and financial affairs. With McCoy awake, this will change. Now there will be much more difficult choices to make, choices that can't be reduced to numbers or plotted on a spreadsheet, choices that will affect the quality of his life. She no longer loves him. She knows now the man she loved existed only in her imagination, as much a product of her own desires as his deception. But she remembers the way he made her feel and wants to do the best she can for him.

She is still sitting in her van in the parking garage when Lesley arrives. At the beginning of her second trimester, Lesley already walks with the exaggerated posture of a pregnant woman, the base of her spine curved slightly inward and her shoulders angled back to compensate for her shifting center of gravity. Her tiny baby bump pushes against the fabric of her sweater in a shallow, graceful arc.

Kendra gets out of the van and meets Lesley as she approaches the garage exit.

"Have you seen him?" Lesley asks as they meet.

"Not yet. Robyn said she wanted to talk to us first. Did she say anything to you?"

"Basically the same."

Kendra sees this as a bad sign. "It can't be good news, or she'd have told us on the phone."

Lesley is more optimistic. "He's awake. That's good news."

They take the elevator to the fourth floor in nervous silence. Robyn rises from behind her desk when they enter her office. "Good. You came together. I'd like to prepare you before you see him. Have a seat."

"How is he?" Lesley asks as she takes the visitor's chair farthest from the door.

The doctor resumes her seat and folds her hands on the desktop. "He is conscious, but disoriented, which is to be expected. His speech is severely impaired and his movements are uncoordinated. What I'm most concerned about is his memory."

"You mean like amnesia? He doesn't know who he is?" Lesley asks.

"He doesn't know his name or where he lives. When I asked him if he'd like me to contact his relatives, he didn't know if he had any. That's why I wanted to talk to you before you see him. He may not recognize you."

At first, Kendra thinks the sensation rising up from her stomach is a hiccup, then realizes she's going to laugh. She covers her mouth with both hands, trying to stop it from coming out, but can only muffle the sound. "He won't know me?" she gasps between explosions of laughter. She feels Lesley's hand cup her shoulder. The warm pressure helps her regain control. "Sorry. I'm sorry," she apologizes when it's over. "It just seemed so funny. He doesn't remember me, and I never knew him."

"He could remember," the doctor says. "But for now, he is extremely distressed by his inability to remember anything. It would be a very bad idea to confront him with two wives while he's in such an emotionally unstable state. All I've told him is that two people who know him are coming to visit."

"Maybe he'll remember something when he sees us." Lesley stands. "We should find out."

Lesley and Kendra wait in the hall outside room 417, listening to the doctor prepare McCoy for his visitors. If he replies, they cannot hear it. A moment later, Robyn appears in the doorway and nods. They follow her into the room.

The bed is raised. McCoy lies back against the pillow as though his head is too heavy to lift. He is terribly thin and almost as pale as the sheet covering his torso and legs. His arms lie flaccid at his sides. There is dull hope in his mild brown eyes as he looks at Lesley and Kendra, but it soon changes to confusion, then disappointment. His mouth twists open. He moans. His body shakes violently. Tears spill down his hollow cheeks. He tries to turn his head away and the movement causes his body to slump sideways. He tries to push himself upright, but his hand slides off the edge of the bed, leaving his arm dangling over the side.

Kendra's knees tremble, forcing her to grab the metal bar at the foot of the bed for support. A wash of pity extinguishes a last ember of anger and resentment, one she hadn't even known she was carrying.

Lesley moves to McCoy's side and lifts him gently, settling his body back against the pillows. She places his arm on the bed and keeps hold of his hand. "Don't worry," she assures him the way a mother comforts a child. "You'll get better soon."

Second Chances

Sam and Peony wheel their suitcases along the sidewalk outside the departure level at the airport. Side by side, they look like a bat and a ball, the living manifestation of Jack Sprat, who could eat no fat, and his wife, who could eat no lean. As the entrance doors slide open in front of them, Peony stops suddenly, grabs Sam's arm, and says something urgently. Sam bends down to whisper in his wife's ear as he places his palm on her back to propel her gently through the door. Peony covers her mouth with her hand to hide her giggles as they enter the terminal.

Kendra watches her parents disappear through the doorway and tries to imagine what last-minute objection her mother could possibly have come up with and what her father said to deflect it. Probably nothing profound. Against any other opponent, Peony would have stood outside that door arguing her point until she won it or was convinced by logic. Sam has no logic. He never argues with his wife and is the only person Kendra knows who always gets his way with Peony.

Until recently, Kendra never gave her parents' interactions much thought, too familiar with their relationship to even notice it. She pays attention now, though, looking for seams of dissent, crevices of disagreement. She sees only a kind of polarized unity, as though it is their exact oppositeness that holds Peony and Sam together, an emotional centripetal force that Kendra can't help comparing to her own marriage of total, but false, compatibility.

In the months since McCoy's collapse, Kendra has come to accept responsibility for how little she actually knew about the man she married. Certainly he'd hidden his true self from her, but instead of searching for the real man, she'd treated him like a blank canvas, painting a perfect husband over his evasions and lies. It's a mistake she will never make again. She no longer wants to find a perfect man. She hopes someday she will find an honest one.

Checking her watch, Kendra decides she still has enough time to get in a workout before going home to get ready for her interview. She's excited about this opportunity to organize the very exclusive party at the art gallery that will unveil the Dutch Masters exhibition on loan from the Rijksmuseum for the summer. It's a dream job, the kind that will guarantee work for years to come. Three satisfied former clients sit on the selection committee, so she feels fairly confident about her chances of getting it.

Just as she buckles her seat belt, a car double-parks beside the van, blocking her exit. The passenger door opens and a teenage boy, all knees and elbows and a mop of curly black hair, unfolds himself onto the sidewalk. Her heart gives a double beat as she transfers her gaze to the driver's side to watch Jason get out. She powers down the window. "Jason!" He looks around but doesn't see her. She sticks her arm out the window and waves. "Jason! Over here."

He shuts his car door and approaches her window. "Kendra! How are you?"

"Good. How have you been?"

"Pretty good. You dropping someone off?"

"My parents. They're flying to England this morning for their fortieth anniversary. How about you?"

"My son's going to San Francisco to spend a week with his mother for her birthday." Fletcher comes to stand beside his father. "Fletch, you remember Mrs. McCoy."

"Hi, Mrs. McCoy." If Fletcher recalls the circumstances of their last meeting, he is too polite to give any indication of it. "Dad, can I have the keys? We're blocking traffic here."

While Fletcher unloads his suitcase from the trunk, Jason asks Kendra about McCoy.

"Oh! He's awake now. And doing really well, all things considered." Tossing her workout plans, Kendra continues. "I've got a couple of hours to kill. If you're not busy, we could have a coffee and I'll tell you about it."

"Sounds good. Just let me get Fletcher sorted out."

She eavesdrops as Jason places his hand on his son's shoulder and says, "Keep your opinions about Norris to yourself, okay? It's only a week. You can do this."

"I'll try."

"He's not a bad guy, you know. He wants you to like him."

"I know." Fletcher leans over his suitcase to give Jason a hug. "Love you, Dad."

Jason wraps an arm loosely around Fletcher's shoulders. "Love you too, son." He closes his eyes for a moment, then drops his arm. "Call me when you get in."

Fletcher steps back, pulls the handle out on his suitcase, calls out, "Bye, Mrs. McCoy," and walks toward the terminal. He hesitates as he reaches the door and looks back at his father.

"You'll be fine," Jason calls out.

Fletcher nods and disappears into the airport.

Kendra follows Jason's car to a small strip mall about a mile from the airport. They park side by side.

"Fletcher seems like a good kid," she says as they walk to the coffee shop.

"He's a great kid. Much more together than I was at his age."

"It must be difficult for you, sharing your son like that."

"Easier now that he lives with me and just visits his mother." Jason pulls open the door for Kendra. "Looks crowded. See if you can find us a table, and I'll get the coffees. What would you like?"

"Small nonfat latte. Thanks." She scans the room for a table, sees two women stand up and hurries over to stake a claim. As the busboy cleans the table, she looks at Jason standing in line at the counter. He is somehow different from the last time she saw him. His clothes are still ordinary and his features look the same, but he seems more open and relaxed. She finally decides it must be because she is no longer his client.

Jason returns with their drinks. Taking the seat across from her, he asks, "So, how is McCoy?"

"He woke up with total amnesia," she replies. "At first we didn't know if he'd ever recover. He could barely move. He had a hard time talking. He moaned and cried all the time. I was worried he'd be permanently disabled, but Lesley's pretty much decided that's not going to happen." She tells him about McCoy's therapy, how he has completely recovered his ability to speak and can now walk on his own. "He still can't remember anything. Not me. Not Lesley. Not being married."

"How did he take it when you told him he's a bigamist?"

"We haven't. He's so fragile, so upset all the time. Can you imagine what it's like not knowing who you are? Telling him would be like kicking a puppy. Lesley goes to see him every day, so we told him she's his wife and I'm their friend and financial advisor. Which is true enough. The bigamy question is still up in the air. We're waiting to see how far his recovery goes."

His next words, delivered as a statement, surprise her. "You've forgiven him."

"There's no one to forgive, really. Eric is gone. I felt sad for a long time, but it's not like he died. More like he never existed."

Jason's face remains serious, but his eyes brighten. Kendra feels another hypnotized snake moment coming on and picks up her cup to ward it off.

"How about Lesley?" he asks. "Has she forgiven him?"

Kendra puts down her cup, disappointed now the moment has passed, but pleased Jason is kind enough to ask about Lesley's response as well. "Oh, she's way beyond forgiveness. Remember we went to see his foster mother? Well, she gave us his file, the social services one about his childhood. Lesley read it; then she gave it to Robyn to read, and Robyn says she thinks his behavior was an adaptation from his childhood, so now Lesley thinks we shouldn't tell him about what he did." She spreads her fingers, palms out, as though surrendering. "And honestly—I don't really see the point either. So unless he remembers on his own, we'll probably never tell him."

"Who's Robyn?"

"Dr. Strachan. Did you know she's dating Lesley's aunt? It's the cutest story. Apparently they met years ago, but Cassandra was in a relationship. Robyn never got over her, and now they're like long-lost loves." Realizing she's on the verge of gushing, Kendra stops talking.

"It's good to know there's a silver lining for someone. I'll have to tell Jude about them. She wondered about the doctor's behavior that night. So what happens now?"

"Robyn says he's almost ready to be released from the hospital. I'm researching long-term-care facilities. Lesley and I are getting together next weekend to figure out where he can go." She finishes the last of her coffee, but feels reluctant to end the conversation. "Have you got time for another one? My treat this time."

He holds out his cup. "Double-shot espresso."

When she returns, she shifts the conversation over to Jason. "So what's been happening with you? Did Fletcher ever form his band?"

"He did. And they don't sound half bad. We even have a gig lined up when Fletcher gets back."

"We?"

"The bassist got grounded for the summer. They asked me to fill in on the condition I don't steal any of their groupies."

Kendra chuckles. "Guess you'll have to bring your own."

Jason smiles. "Position's open. Maybe you know someone who'd like to apply?"

This time Kendra gives in and allows herself to be hypnotized by the warmth in those incredibly blue eyes.

Making a Home

AS THE END OF HER pregnancy approaches, Lesley's energy level rises. She has an irresistible urge to set the cabin to rights before the baby is born. Over the winter and spring, her uncles and nephews pitched in to finish the repairs and give the walls a fresh coat of paint. Furniture donations from various family members have made the house comfortable. Now only the finishing touches are needed to make the cabin a home.

She slides the kitchen curtains she just finished making onto curtain rods. Holding the last one up, she admires the way the light from the window filters through the pleated yellow gingham, brightening the room even though it's an overcast day. She hears a car approach and places the curtains on the countertop before going out to the front porch to greet her mother and aunt, who have arrived bearing gifts.

"How's my grandson?" Beatrice asks as she climbs the porch stairs.

"Kicking like a horse." Lesley is carrying high and forward.

The sweater straining over the mound of her pregnancy pulses outward in the clear shape of a tiny foot. She takes her mother's hand and places it on the side of her belly. "Feel this."

"Oh, you're such a strong boy!" Beatrice firmly believes all babies need positive reinforcement, even the ones whose ears aren't exposed to hear it yet. The hand that is not cradling her grandson's foot offers Lesley a plastic bag. "Look what I found. I couldn't believe it was still around."

Lesley reaches into the bag to pull out a threadbare teddy bear with a homemade pirate patch covering one missing eye. "Oh! It's Captain Cuddles! Where did you find him?"

"In Floyd's attic. You know how my cousin Essie is researching family history? She asked about the family Bible, so Floyd and I were going through his attic looking for it and we found Captain Cuddles in your grandmother's trunk. Heaven knows how he got there. He's too frail to be a toy, but I thought he'd make a nice decoration for the baby's room."

Lesley sniffs the bear's head. "He's a bit mothball-y."

Cassandra places the box she's carrying on the porch swing. "Hang him on the clothesline. He'll be fine after a couple of days. How are you feeling, honey?"

"Okay, I suppose. Definitely ready for this to be over. What's in the box, Aunt Cass?"

Cassandra reaches into her pocket for a pack of nicotine gum. "Eunice's swag lamps. She remembered you liked them and thought you might want them."

Beatrice snatches the bear from Lesley's hand. "That woman has more money than sense. I'm going to hang this on the line out back." She stomps down the steps and around the corner of the cabin.

Relations between Beatrice and Eunice have deteriorated steadily over the past few months as the competition for Andrew's affections has heated up. He does not show a preference for either woman, cheerfully accepting invitations to church suppers and bingo evenings from both of them. Running out of ways to throw themselves at him—short of actually throwing themselves at him—Eunice and Beatrice are forced to fabricate increasingly elaborate plans to snare him. Eunice's latest ploy, refurnishing her apartment with antiques from Andrew's shop, infuriates Beatrice, primarily because she did not think of it first.

Lesley pulls open the box to look at the lamps. "Is she going to be crabby all day?"

"She'll get over it. Just hide the box where she can't see it." Cassandra pops a lozenge of gum into her mouth. "I'm a little surprised you're including us in this meeting."

"My go-it-alone days are over. I want to know what you think. Come into the kitchen. I need your help hanging the curtains."

Kendra arrives while the curtains are being hung, followed a few minutes later by Robyn. Lesley gives them a tour of the house while Cassandra makes coffee and Beatrice arranges the macaroons she made earlier in the day on a plate. Then they all sit around the ancient oak kitchen table. Beatrice takes out the baby sweater she's knitting, an elaborate eyelet lace pattern in powder blue.

Kendra opens her briefcase, extracts four brochures and splays them across the center of the table. "These four places all have openings and are within our budget."

Robyn pulls a brochure out of the group. "I've heard a lot of good things about this facility. They're well established and the staff is first-rate."

Lesley opens the brochure and turns it on the table so her aunt can read through it with her. "It's too far away," she says finally. "I'd only be able to see him on weekends."

"This one's in Astoria." Kendra slides a brochure toward Lesley. "It's only thirty minutes away. That's less than you're traveling now."

Lesley doesn't bother to pick it up, basing her objection on the picture. "It's too big. It's like a jail. How much therapy will he get there?"

Everyone looks at Robyn, who says, "Actually, she's right. It's really a long-term-care hospital for critically disabled patients. They focus more on comfort than cure."

Lesley rejects the third brochure on the basis of location again. She reads through the fourth one carefully, then shakes her head.

"What's wrong with that one, honey?" Cassandra asks.

"Nothing, really. I just don't see how he could ever feel at home surrounded by strangers."

"Everyone's a stranger to him," Kendra points out.

"But we know him," Lesley insists.

"That's why I picked these. They're all in Washington and Oregon."

"That's not what I mean. Putting him in a place like this is like keeping a dog in a kennel. It's not a good life."

Cassandra puts down her macaroon and says, with the faintest tinge of frustration in her voice, "He needs care. It's not like locking him up. It's like taking your dog to the vet when it's sick."

"But he's not sick," Lesley objects. "He's was in a coma. It's not like he's going to get worse. He's getting better."

Cassandra looks as though she's about to argue the point. Robyn shakes her head slightly. Cassandra subsides against the back of her chair and digs into her pocket for more gum.

"There are two issues to be considered here," Robyn says in her doctor's voice. "One is that he's not ready to take care of himself yet. He can't be left unsupervised for extended periods of time. The other is that he still needs therapy to improve. His mental functions are disorganized. In many ways he's like a child. He needs structured activities and constant encouragement to perform them."

At the end of the table, Beatrice looks up from her knitting and says, "He has to come here. He has to come home."

Lesley feels the wisdom of this sink into her body. It's the same physical sensation she had when she realized Dave was the man she would marry, as though the world has righted itself around her, settled into its true form.

Cassandra folds her arms across her chest. "No one's going to be here, Trixie. Lesley's coming to live with us in a few weeks."

"She's only coming to live with us because we don't want her to be alone when the baby arrives." Beatrice pokes the needles through her knitting and places it on the table. "If I move up here, she won't be alone."

Cassandra tries again. "Even if you did move up here for a month or two, after you leave, Lesley still can't run the day-care center and tend to a baby and McCoy at the same time."

"Yes, but I'm sure we can do it together. I'll stay for as long as it takes."

"He still needs therapy," Robyn says.

Sudden anger straightens Lesley's spine. She places both hands on the tabletop, fingers spread wide. "It's here." She slaps the table for emphasis, feeling the ridges in the grain of the old wood beneath her palms. "His therapy is here. This is his home. He made this place his home. He planted a garden. He fixed up the barn for his horse. He made a nursery for his child." She feels tears spilling down her cheeks. She ignores them. "This is where his therapy is. Here. In his home. Not making paper chains in some horrible institution."

Kendra, Cassandra and Robyn rock back in their seats, shocked by Lesley's outburst.

Beatrice rises calmly from her chair and walks around the table to wrap her arms around her daughter's shoulders. "Of course it's his home, honey."

For long moments the only sound in the room is Lesley's ragged breathing as she struggles to control her emotions. Then Kendra sweeps the brochures up from the table and puts them back in her briefcase. "We could get a therapist to come out here and work with him."

"I could come by every week to evaluate him," Robyn offers.

"Are you sure about this, Trixie?" Cassandra asks. "You can't back out of it, you know."

"Cass, I've spent half my life helping my family through times like this. I think I can take care of my grandson while my daughter takes care of her husband. And, you know, if you came to live here with me, no one would notice how often Robyn stays over for the night."

It's Time

Two years later

KENDRA SHIFTS HER BODY IN the passenger seat to face Jason. "Has Fletcher decided where he's going yet?"

"I wanted Portland University, but he decided on California State. He's going down to Chico at the end of August to look for a place to live." The old Jason would have left it at that, waiting for Kendra to make the first move. The new Jason knows he has a better chance of getting what he wants by asking for it outright. "I think it's time we talked about moving in together after Fletcher leaves." He takes his eyes off the road for a moment to check her reaction.

She looks back at him calmly, a good sign. "And if I'm not ready to move in?"

Her response doesn't worry him. He's familiar with these little tests now. Kendra is skittish about commitment after her experience with McCoy. Jason doesn't blame her. "Then we stay the way we are. I'll probably sell the house. I only kept it for Fletcher. I know you like the place, so I didn't want to do anything without talking to you first. You know, in case it's an incentive."

He can hear the smile in her voice. "Well, it is a fabulous house. Why don't you come over and cook me dinner next week? We'll talk about it." She sniffs twice. "Oh, my God, she's done it again." She twists around to look at Jason's infant niece in the backseat. "And she's still asleep! It's amazing."

"We're almost there. I'll change her as soon as we get there."

Kendra reaches over to the console between them to power down her window. Warm, pine-scented summer air blows away the less appealing odor emanating from the backseat. "Better you than me. When are her parents getting back?"

"Jude called from the clinic last night. They're flying back tomorrow night."

"Did she tell you how the testing went?"

"Too soon to tell, but the doctors say Travis is a good candidate based on the location of the original injury and his physical condition."

Jason turns off the highway onto the steep driveway leading up to the McCoy farm. As he rounds the last curve, he sees Beatrice already standing on the edge of the porch, shading her eyes against the late-afternoon sun as she watches them approach. He parks beside the truck and switches off the engine. "She couldn't have heard us coming."

"Lesley says she has some kind of baby radar." Kendra pushes her door open. "Hi, Beatrice. You changed your hair. It's stunning."

Jason is sure she means this in the literal sense, but Beatrice takes it as a compliment. "Thank you, dear. I decided I'm getting too old to be a redhead." She pats curls that are now very close to the color of the tape he once used to cordon off crime scenes.

In the backseat, ten-month-old Samantha Connelly notices the cessation of movement and wakes up. "Dah-bah," she calls out.

Beatrice trots down the porch steps. "Is that my little angel? How is she?"

"Little angel needs changing," Jason says as he gets out of the car, hoping Beatrice will take the bait.

She does. "Oh, let me do that. You two go round back and say hello to Lesley."

"It's a bad one," Kendra warns.

"All the more reason to give it to a professional." Beatrice slides open the side door of the van. "Hello, little Sammy," she coos. "Does someone's diaper need changing?"

"Beh," Samantha agrees.

While Beatrice extricates Samantha from the baby seat, Jason gets the diaper bag from the trunk, passing it over with sincere gratitude. He loves his niece, but he isn't averse to handing her off to an expert when the offer is made.

After Beatrice carries Samantha into the house, Kendra retrieves her briefcase from the front seat. In it are the papers terminating her guardianship of Eric McCoy, issued by the Oregon State probate court following his successful competency hearing held the previous month in Salem. Kendra has told Jason she is relieved her responsibilities are at an end, but her expression as she shuts the door makes him wonder if she's having second thoughts.

"You look worried," he tells her.

"I just don't know if this is the right thing to do. It's a lot of money now."

He puts his arm around her shoulders. "Thanks to his financially brilliant guardian."

She accepts the compliment by putting her arm around his

waist, then returns to her concerns as they walk around the cabin. "It's just that he's always been so disorganized and impulsive, even before the coma. You didn't see the mess everything was in when I took it over. If he hadn't been offered the movie deal, he'd have been bankrupt in a year."

"Lesley isn't going to let that happen. She's a levelheaded girl. And you can always give them advice. You know they're going to ask for it."

Kendra stops walking just before they reach the corner of the cabin. She leans against Jason's chest. He bends his head to kiss the top of hers. "You have to let go, sweetheart," he murmurs into her lemon-scented hair.

Her voice is muffled by his shirt. "I don't love him anymore."

"Well, that's good to know," he teases.

"But I still worry about him. It's like a habit now."

There had been many times over the past two years when it seemed McCoy would never come back to his mind. After the first six months of steady progress, his recovery became a series of creeping advances punctuated by short regressions and long plateaus of no change at all. Then, just as everyone except Lesley was ready to give up hope, he would creep forward again. Kendra believes Lesley pulled him back to normalcy by sheer willpower.

Kendra flattens one palm against Jason's chest and pushes herself back a few inches. "Habits can be broken," she says with determination and stands on tiptoe to kiss him.

The ability to make a decision and stick to it is one of the many things Jason finds appealing about Kendra. Once she puts her mind to a goal, always after carefully weighing the pros and cons, nothing can prevent her from achieving it. She's like her mother in that way, not given to the moodiness and emotional blackmail that destroyed his marriage. When they first started dating, he'd worried about keeping up with her, but Sam's advice to "just stand back, son, and watch her whirl" turned out to be sound.

As they round the corner of the cabin, they see Lesley setting flatware on the picnic table under the canopy of an old silver maple. She is still beautiful, but not in the way she was when Jason first saw her. She has hardened, become more competent and opinionated. It shows in her face, which now promises to age more like her aunt's than her mother's.

"Hey, Lesley," Kendra calls out.

Lesley drops the cutlery and crosses the lawn to greet them. "Hi! Where's the baby?" She reaches out to hug Kendra.

Kendra hugs her back. "Like anyone gets to hold a baby when your mother's around."

"Or change them, thank God," Jason adds as he gets his own hug. "Where's Dave?" He uses the name McCoy goes by now, since only a handful of people in Brockville know about his former existence as Eric.

"Picking vegetables with Lars." Lesley gestures toward the immense garden on the other side of the barn just as a man carrying a bushel basket steps out from between tall green rows of corn. A sturdy toddler with hair bleached almost white by the summer sun follows behind him hugging three ears of corn to his little chest.

Dave McCoy is not the man Eric McCoy was. His left arm is stiff and awkward. The hearing in his right ear is permanently impaired. He has mild difficulty with short-term memory and writes himself notes to remember important things. Amnesia has reconfigured his facial features, replacing the brash confidence Jason remembers from their first meeting with hesitance and caution.

But the dimple is still there when Dave greets them. "Just in time. Thought I was going to have to tackle the barbecue myself."

He drops the basket to shake Jason's hand, then gives Kendra a loose, one-armed hug, which she returns equally lightly.

Whatever sexual tension they once had is gone. Kendra says she can see no trace of the sophisticated man she married in this quiet, slow-speaking farmer. Interestingly, it's McCoy's old Brockville persona that most closely matches the man he has become. Lesley and Cassandra can tell the difference, but the rest of their extended family believes he is just like the old Dave, minus his memories.

"Uncle Jason! Aunty Kendra! Look!" Lars McCoy, named after the grandfather whom everyone says he is the spitting image of, holds up his harvest with pride.

"You picked those yourself?" Jason ruffles the boy's hair.

"I pulled. Daddy helped. Grammy loves corn." Eager to display his achievement to his beloved grandmother, Lars races toward the house with the controlled-fall stagger that passes for running in a two-year-old.

Jason fires up the barbecue and grills steaks from one of the steers raised by Dave the previous year. They are eaten with potato salad, baby carrots, green beans and corn on the cob, all harvested from the garden. Jason and Dave try out Dave's new brew. Kendra shares a bottle of Chardonnay with Beatrice. Lesley and her son stick to lemonade. Normally, Lesley would have a beer. As he holds out his plate for a second helping of Beatrice's pecan pie, Jason wonders if Lesley is pregnant, but no one says anything.

After dinner, they walk down to the back field to feed carrot tops to Patches and the gangly foal she gave birth to in the spring. When they return to the front porch of the cabin, they talk while darkness falls: about Fletcher's new girlfriend, whom Kendra thinks may be "the one" and Jason sincerely hopes is not; about Beatrice and Lesley's plan to expand the Wee Tots playground by buying the vacant lot that just came up for sale behind the day-care center; about the new field Dave is clearing to grow his own hops next year.

Later, when the children are asleep, and Beatrice has gone home to Brockville, and Lesley and Kendra are talking in the kitchen, Dave comes out to the front porch and places another mug of beer down on the table by Jason's elbow. "I need your help," he says.

Jason nods as he picks up the mug. "Sure. With what?"

"A couple of weeks ago I started having these weird dreams where I'm telling people I'm sorry."

"About what?"

"I don't know." Dave sits on the porch swing. "I didn't know who any of the people were either, until last night. Last night I was apologizing to you. We were sitting at a little table in a restaurant and I was trying to tell you how sorry I was." His face is in shadow, but his voice blends fear and hope as he asks, "Did I know you before? Did I do something to you?"

Not sure how to answer the first question, Jason compromises by answering the last one. "You never did anything to me."

Dave's body deflates with disappointment. He props his elbows on his knees and slumps forward. "I feel like I'm going crazy."

"If dreams made us crazy, we'd all be in big trouble," Jason assures him.

They sit in silence for a while, watching fireflies flirting above the lawn; then Dave stretches and yawns. "I'm falling asleep. You okay out here on your own?"

Jason resists the urge to wish him pleasant dreams. "I'm just going to finish my beer, and I'll be right behind you. See you tomorrow morning."

After Dave goes inside, Jason picks up his beer, walks around to the back of the cabin and sits at the picnic table. He sees the light in Dave and Lesley's bedroom come on, then the bathroom light. The lights go out in reverse order. He waits a little longer, then walks toward the back door of the cabin. As he passes the open kitchen window, he hears Kendra's voice.

". . . just don't know if I can. I told him we'd talk about it next week."

"Moving in together isn't like getting married," Lesley says.

Jason stops beneath the window.

"I used to think that way," Kendra responds. "But now I think we either commit to a relationship or we don't. The paper doesn't matter."

"Do you love him?" Lesley asks.

Jason's breath catches in his throat. He stands perfectly still.

Kendra sighs. "Define love. I want him to be happy. I feel like a better person when I'm with him. I want to really be the person he thinks I am. He thinks I'm brave and strong."

"You are brave and strong," Lesley insists.

"Not like you. I couldn't have stood by Dave the way you have."

"There's all kinds of bravery. And what you said about wanting Jason to be happy? That's not everything I feel for Dave, but it's a lot of it."

After a long silence, Kendra replies, "Ma says the Buddhist definition of love is wanting others to be happy. Maybe you're both right. It's a better definition than the one I had."

Jason's shoulders relax as a warm, peaceful feeling settles over him. There is hope, and that's enough for now. He takes the last few steps to the kitchen door.

Lesley and Kendra look up when he appears in the doorway. He presses a forefinger to his lips, then beckons them to come outside and leads them to the picnic table.

"Why all the secrecy?" Kendra whispers as she and Lesley sit across from Jason.

Jason doesn't whisper, but he keeps his voice low. "We have to talk, and I don't think Dave should hear this until we agree on what to do. He told me about a dream he had last night. I think he's starting to remember."

"What was it about?" Lesley asks.

"About me. He was trying to apologize to me in the coffee shop where we met. I think we have to tell him."

In the darkness, Kendra's hair and eyes blend into the night, turning her face into a mask of concern. "Tell him what? We don't know what he's going to remember."

"I know he seems okay, but he's not ready." Lesley's pale hair sways as she shakes her head.

Jason says, very gently, "Wouldn't it be harder on him to remember on his own and know we lied to him?"

Kendra and Lesley turn their heads to look at each other. They don't say anything, but Jason has the impression of a silent conversation.

Finally, Kendra reaches over to take Lesley's hand. "I guess it's like you said. There's all kinds of bravery."

Acknowledgments

About twenty thousand words into the first draft of this book, I realized (with considerable concern, since I'd already committed to producing an eighty-thousand-word novel) that I had a serious case of writer's block. In desperation, I turned to three fellow writers for assistance: Claire Sullivan, Lloyd Graham, and J. R. MacLean (if J.R. has a real name, he never shares it). They volunteered to read through the manuscript, and while Claire and Lloyd made excellent suggestions, many of which have been incorporated into the work, it was J.R. who put his finger on my real problem when he said, "I lost interest after the first chapter." I was devastated. No writer wants to produce a boring book. I asked him why. "Well, for me," he replied, "McCoy is the most interesting character, and you killed him off in the first chapter." Obvious, once someone else points it out, right? I put McCoy into a coma and the first draft practically wrote itself.

By definition, works of fiction are a pack of lies. I count on my beta readers to tell me if my lies are believable. For this book,

Donna Gorgas, Rita Pogue, Christopher Miller, and Wendy Djuric provided their usual outstanding fake-reality check.

Things that seem obvious to the writer frequently turn out to be obscure to the reader, which is why editors are so important, and why I am extremely grateful for the expert guidance of Danielle Perez, executive editor at NAL.

After thirty-five years working as a computer programmer in Canada, the U.S. and the Netherlands, **Brenda L. Baker** moved to India, where she rediscovered her high school ambition of becoming a writer. Her first book, *Sisters of the Sari*, was published by NAL Accent in 2011. She now lives in Ontario, Canada. When not indulging her passion for writing, she volunteers at the local public library and is learning to ring English handbells with a beginners' choir.

CONNECT ONLINE

www.brendalbaker.com.
facebook.com/brendalbaker.author

CONVERSATION GUIDE

The ELUSIVE MR. McCOY

Brenda L. Baker

This Conversation Guide is intended to enrich the individual reading experience, as well as encourage us to explore these topics together—because books, and life, are meant for sharing.

Author's Note

When I was in my forties, a divorce epidemic broke out in my circle of friends. It was a traumatic time. We autopsied our failed relationships over long, drunken dinners, during which skeletons of unpalatable truth about both ourselves and our soon-to-be exes came tumbling out from the marital closets: infidelities, addictions, secret longings, hidden agendas. Every one of us, husbands and wives, looked at the person we had once shared a bed with and wondered who the hell we'd married.

We all survived the ordeal with no greater damage than badly bruised egos—because let's face it, rejection by the person you live with, who should know you better than anyone else on the planet, can be seen as a fairly convincing argument that there may be something wrong with you. In retrospect, though, I'm inclined to believe our faults, if there were any, grew from seeds of good intention.

CONVERSATION GUIDE

Deceit is a necessary part of bonding, at least in the early stages.

When we fall in love, we want the object of our affection to see our best side. Topics like binge-eating and Internet porn never seem to come up while we're holding hands over a red-and-white-checkered tablecloth and gazing soulfully into each other's eyes by the flattering light of a candle stuck in a Chianti bottle. These are lies of omission, justifiable because now that we've found our true love, we don't need those things anymore, right?

When we fall in love, we don't want to hurt our beloved's feelings, so we avoid painful truths. "No, honey, those jeans don't make your ass look fat." "But, darling, I never fake orgasms." These are lies of compassion, justifiable because they make the other person feel good and that makes us feel good.

Those tiny, kindly lies define the initial boundaries of a Bermuda Triangle where we hide inconvenient and embarrassing truths for the greater good of the relationship. Over time, in the interest of reducing emotional friction, the boundaries expand to hold unvoiced opinions about things like annoying habits and in-laws. Then we start tossing in unfulfilled dreams, because there's no point in mentioning how we'd love to buy that forty-foot boat and sail around the world to a partner who gets seasick in the bathtub. Eventually, what we don't say exceeds what we do, and the bond of affection becomes more of a dotted line of tolerance, skipping over longer and longer segments of secrecy.

During the divorce decade, none of us was really in a position to be casting stones. We'd all contributed to the demise of our relationships, either by action or inaction. The death blow was really just a matter of which spouse cracked first.

They say what doesn't kill you makes you stronger. It takes courage to discard our illusions, to forgive others and ourselves for past transgressions. But on the whole, I think it makes us happier, wiser people—and much better partners.

QUESTIONS FOR DISCUSSION

Creating discussion questions for a book about infidelity can be something of a minefield.

A long time ago, I belonged to a book club. We didn't talk much about books. Mostly we drank wine and griped about our partners. If you happen to belong to that kind of book club, then you don't need any discussion questions; you've already covered this ground. On the other hand, if you belong to a book club that actually talks about the books, you don't want your meeting hijacked by personal trauma. Therefore, the following questions are intended to be completely innocuous. If, by chance, a question hits one of those big red psychic buttons we all carry around, I sincerely apologize.

1. We writers like to play a little fantasy game called Cast the Characters. (Okay, maybe it's more than a game. It's not like I can write about real people. Besides, if Spielberg

calls, I want to be ready for him.) So here's your chance to play along. Pretend you're a Hollywood casting agent. What actors would you choose to play your favorite characters in this novel?

2. There is a difference between facts and opinions. When it comes to romance, those of us who aren't mind readers must make do with opinions. In the first half of the book, Kendra's and Lesley's versions of McCoy were based on their own preferences and experiences. Did you feel one of the women had a better understanding of her husband than the other? Was your opinion of McCoy, given your own preferences, different from theirs?

3. Although I am not a Buddhist, I appreciate the philosophy of taking responsibility for one's own actions and emotions. One of Peony's roles in the story is to help her daughter accept this responsibility by confessing to her own long-ago temptation. Do you think she was right? Does it help us to forgive another person when we have had a similar experience? Does forgiving someone else help us forgive ourselves?

4. And while we're on the topic of forgiveness, how did you feel about McCoy by the end of the book? Did you feel sympathy toward him? Would you have forgiven him if you were Kendra or Lesley?

5. I got mixed feedback on Cheetara and the Holly Virgin. Some people felt McCoy's artistic tribute to Kendra's and Lesley's sexual attributes was a form of flattery. Others thought it was demeaning. I'm mostly in the second camp, which is why I had McCoy regret

his actions when he fell in love. Which camp are you in, and why?

6. Fletcher's adolescent fantasies are included as a foil for Jason's more mature problems with relationships. What do you think of the way Jason deals with his son's sexuality? Is he being progressive and realistic or foolishly permissive? If you are a parent, which is more in line with your parenting style?

7. If this were a romance novel, McCoy's total focus on pleasing his wives would have made him the ideal partner—other than the bigamy thing, of course. In real life, no one is that self-sacrificing, or at least I don't believe they should be. What do you think? Can such a lopsided relationship be successful?

8. Lesley is a stereotypical old-fashioned girl, while Kendra is the epitome of an ambitious modern woman. Do you think Lesley's protected upbringing played a role in her naive inability to initially recognize the extent of McCoy's betrayal? And was Kendra's first response, to cut McCoy out of her life, justified in light of her materialism and social aspirations?

9. The way characters in a story react to the setting and props in a scene can tell the reader a great deal about personality and motivation. In this book I particularly enjoyed using the big city/small town contrast to highlight the differences between Kendra and Lesley. I grew up in a small town and have lived in big cities for most of my adult life, which gave me the ability to sympathize with both characters. Were there any scenes in the book where the physical setting helped you understand one of the characters better?